Jack of all Trades

Lauren Trickey

BALBOA.
PRESS

A DIVISION OF HAY HOUSE

Balboa Press books may be ordered through booksellers or by contacting:

Balboa Press
A Division of Hay House
1663 Liberty Drive
Bloomington, IN 47403
www.balboapress.com.au
1 (877) 407-4847

Print information available on the last page.

ISBN: 978-1-5043-1928-7 (sc)
ISBN: 978-1-5043-1929-4 (e)

Balboa Press rev. date: 09/02/2019

This book is dedicated to
Casey, Joyce, Julie, Kiarra, and Sharney

Because without them, these characters, and their world, wouldn't exist

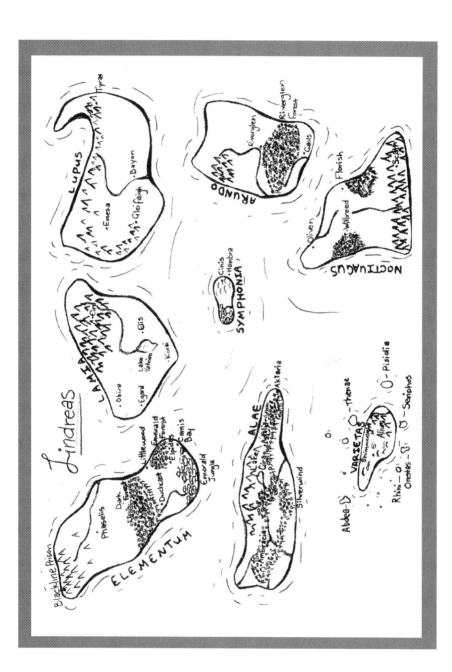

1

Aelana walked out of the shop, pushing her sunglasses onto her nose from on top of her head, blocking the ever-present sunshine. She took a moment to decide where to go next, wandering down the endless line of shops until one snagged her interest. It was one of those stores that she would never buy anything in simply because she didn't have the money, though if Rachel or Amanda had been with her, she could have convinced them to buy her something.

She weaved her way around the racks of clothing. As she found her way to the back of the store, an alarm sounded above her head, and she threw her hands over ears. The alarm wailed, its insanely annoying sound seeming to seep out of the ceiling. Aelana immediately started navigating her way back to the store entrance. But when she reached the doors, they were closed; the safety doors had rolled down, shutting off any exit. Or escape. If this wasn't happening for a good reason, if someone had just mucked up, Aelana was going to be pissed.

She decided that instead of standing there, she would probably be better off looking for someone, a staff member, to tell her what was happening and to get herself out of this. Her shirt snagged on a rack as she passed, and when she turned to release it, she heard a scream.

The alarm was definitely going off for a reason.

As it continued to blare, Aelana sank to the ground after freeing her sleeve. She wondered what she could do. Her heart beat faster than she had ever felt it before. And she couldn't think of anything helpful; her brain just wouldn't supply the thoughts.

Out of all the shops, I had to come into this one, she thought. *Why couldn't I have chosen somewhere else? I'd never come in here before in my life, so why now? Anywhere else would have been better than here.* If she'd chosen a different store, Aelana could be completely unaware of what was going on right now. But no. She *was* here, and she really wished she wasn't.

Loud footsteps echoing on the tile floor snapped her out of her thoughts. She quickly climbed under the circular clothing rack beside her, hoping she was hidden well enough. The footsteps came closer and then stopped.

For a moment, Aelana thought she was safe since she couldn't hear them anymore and could see no shadows around her. But then a hand grabbed the back of her shirt. She heard a tear as she was pulled out from underneath the rack through a curtain of assorted fabrics.

"Thought you could hide, huh?" a rough, husky voice said next to her ear, too close for comfort.

She didn't say anything. She just stood up straight and stayed completely still. Whoever had hold of her fixed his grip on the back of her shirt and dragged her around racks and over to the register at the side of the shop. A group of people variously sat or crouched in what vaguely resembled a circle in front of the register. One of them was clearly the cashier, and she looked more scared than anyone else.

Aelana was pushed down with them. She stumbled over somebody's bag before crashing to the floor in a heap. Her phone slipped out of her pocket, cracking the screen. She shoved the phone back in her pocket before anyone could think she was trying to text for help.

"Now where is the safe?" the man yelled, pulling a gun from within the huge coat he wore and pointing it at Miss Cashier. His eyes were bloodshot, and his hair clearly hadn't been brushed in a while. Or washed. Aelana didn't know a lot about this kind of thing, but she was pretty sure someone must have thought he looked suspicious. *There are security guards at this mall, right?*

"I don't know," the cashier whimpered. "I only just started working here. They didn't tell me that."

With an explosive sound, his gun fired, and the bullet hit the wall just above her head. Aelana got up and scrambled backwards, hands over her ears. It was by far the loudest thing she ever heard, even louder than the stupid alarm. She could feel tears starting to run down her cheeks and took a deep breath, trying to stop them.

"Trying to run now, are we?" he asked, pointing the gun at her. She stopped in her tracks and looked up at him, shaking her head quickly. "Get back over here," he ordered.

But Aelana couldn't will herself to move, no matter how much she wanted to. She seemed to be frozen in a block of ice and couldn't break her way out of it, like her mind couldn't communicate with the rest of her body. The tears started again as quickly as they had stopped. And this time, she didn't realise it. Even if she had, she wouldn't have been able to stop them.

The sound of his gun firing again broke the tension in the air, and Aelana jumped back. Her hand hit a basket sitting on the counter she had backed up against. Rings and bracelets rained down on her head, and she felt a startling pain in her calf as the contents clattered to floor around her and stuck in her hair and clothes and bounced in her lap. Her hands sprung to grab her leg, but she ended up falling into a heap on the ground.

The silver jewellery continued to fall around her. It stung everywhere it touched her skin, feeling like it was burning her. She had always been allergic to silver and had never been able to wear it, but her previous reactions to it were never as bad as this.

Her vision grew hazy. She tried to focus on the strands of her hair fanning out from her, stark black against the floor's immaculate white tiles. But they blended into each other, and then everything she could see became black, shifting around in her view.

She could hear people rushing around her, but the world felt very far away now, and she couldn't move. She felt hands on her, trying to get her to sit up. Heads close to her own, voices in her ears. But the world was fading, along with her consciousness, and she couldn't.

<hr>

When the lights finally went out in the movie theatre, Jade and her friends cheered along with everyone else. After sitting through twenty minutes of mind-numbingly boring ads, the thing they actually came for was finally beginning. The whole theatre went silent in suspense as the curtains revealed the full size of the screen.

Seated between her two closest friends, Nick and Willow, Jade could feel her phone vibrating in her pocket, but she ignored it. No, she had been waiting too long for this movie.

As she relaxed back in her seat while the opening credits played, she felt her phone ring again, and she continued to ignore it. But it went off again. And again. Then nothing. And then again, a few minutes later. Jade ripped the dumb device out of her pocket. She used her hand to shield the theatre from the light of the screen as she checked who was calling.

Her mother.

Jade groaned inwardly as she stood up, shuffled her way to the end of the aisle, and rushed out of the theatre to take the call. "Hello," she said, waiting for an answer.

"Hi, darling. How are you?" the beautiful voice on the other end asked.

"I'm fine, Mum. The movie only just started."

"Oh, okay. I'll let you go then. Don't want to interrupt."

"Thanks, Mum," Jade replied, looking around the movie theatre's lobby. It was completely empty except for her and the employees, which wasn't surprising, considering how late it was. Jade was just glad her mother let her go out this late. She never let Ivy or Zalisha out when they were her age.

"I love you, Jade," her mum said.

"I love y—"

That was all she could get out before a hand clamped down over her mouth, and the phone dropped from her grip in surprise. Almost too shocked to react, she tried to pry the hand away. But whoever had a hold of her was strong. She was held back against the person's body. She kicked her legs out, and one of her heels connected with the person's shin. The hand instantly released her, accompanied by a male shout from behind her.

The first thought was that maybe it was Nick just trying to catch her by surprise, so she spun around. No. The tall, blond man was definitely not Nick.

Without thinking, Jade started running as fast as she could towards the exit. For a second, she considered running back to her friends in the dark theatre. But it was too late to change her mind now. If she went back, she would run into that strange man, though the street probably wasn't the best place to go, either.

Then she wondered, *What about the staff inside? Why didn't they do anything? Maybe they called the police.* But she realized now that she hadn't seen any of them.

Jade dashed out onto the street and immediately ran into a woman. She was about to say, "Excuse me, sorry," and then push past, but the woman grabbed her, and a hand was again cupped over Jade's mouth. She screamed anyway. The woman was surprisingly strong for her size. Though Jade tried to struggle out of her grasp, she couldn't.

"Stop squirming," the woman growled in her ear, then pulled a knife from her jacket. Jade froze. "Good."

The man then appeared from the entrance to the theatre and walked over calmly, hands in his pocket, as if he didn't have a care in the world. He strode over to the nondescript van, where the woman was holding Jade. He opened the back doors, and the woman shoved Jade into the back. The two then jumped in after her, and the van started to pull away.

"Where are you taking me?" Jade willed her voice to sound confident and not like she was about to burst into tears. This was absolutely insane. Why could they possibly want her? Or had they just picked her randomly because she walked out of the damn movie?

The inside of the van was pristine, new. It looked and smelt new but was dark and cold; the light on the ceiling was off, and there were no windows, save for on the back doors, which were blacked out.

"Nowhere," the man said, in reply to her question. "Just going for a drive."

When he spoke, she realised that he had a thick accent, but not one she recognised. He then turned to the woman, and they started talking in another language. Jade had time to really look at them before they turned back to her.

The man was quite handsome. Tall, with ruffled blond hair. He couldn't have been older than twenty, but he had an evil gleam in his eye that normal twenty-year-olds didn't possess. So did the woman. She had long blonde hair that flowed down her back and beautiful, bright blue eyes. So did the man. They were both of a strong build. And the woman couldn't have been older than twenty, either. Probably even younger.

They turned back to her, the evil gleam in their eyes, and the man pulled out a knife and held it tightly, like someone who knew what to do with it. They both started walking towards her, and she backed up against the side of the moving van.

"What do you want with me?" This time, she didn't sound confident; she sounded utterly terrified. She was. But she refused to give them the satisfaction of crying. She kept her face neutral as they cornered her.

"Just to mortally wound you so you never want anything to do with us ever again," the woman answered cheerfully.

"I don't want anything to do with you anyway," Jade whispered, because it was the only way to not sound totally and completely terrified.

"But you would eventually," the man said, approaching her. "Now you won't."

She felt a slicing pain down her arm and jerked away, banging her elbow against the van. Then she was cut across her stomach. She tried to pull away, to escape, but there was nowhere to go; she was trapped in the corner. She slid to the floor, and the man and woman started attacking her face with their blades. She tried to shield her face with her hands, but that just ended in cuts across her knuckles and palms, which hurt more than her face.

She slumped down in the corner and curled into a ball as best she could, but then she felt hands grab her arms, and she was pulled to her feet. The back door of the van swung open, and Jade was pushed out of the moving vehicle. She did her best to tuck her head in as she hit the road, but her body fell limply to the road.

Now battered, bruised, and bleeding, and stinging all over, Jade lay on the deserted road, looking up at the moon. A thought passed through her mind that this was probably the last thing she was ever going to see. She guessed she was okay with that. The moon looked pretty.

<hr />

Ash dove into the water after Sakura. Under the waves, she could see Sakura's long pink hair floating around in the hazy salt water. Ash surfaced next to them, splashing water over them.

"Hey, Ash, watch it!" Sakura yelled playfully.

Chris splashed water back at her.

They weren't too far from the shore, and Riko, Chloe, and Tiger Rose stood on the sand, just out of reach of the waves, watching them and laughing.

"What are you looking at?" Chris yelled, splashing water as hard as he could at them. Ash and Sakura watched the exchange, amused.

Riko ran into the water and kicked water out at them. "We were staring at your stupid face," he replied to Chris.

"Why don't you come closer and say that, Riko!" Chris yelled back, his smile growing.

"Fine. I will!" Riko replied.

He waded into the water and then swam out to them; water was everywhere, and Ash turned her head away to stop it from getting into her eyes. Sakura and Ash, instead of swimming away, made the bad decision of joining their stupid war, splashing water back at them.

"Come join us, TR!" Ash called to Tiger Rose on the beach.

"Yeah, you too, Chloe!" Sakura added.

"Maybe in a minute," Chloe called back, answering for the both of them.

When Chris and Riko heard this, they headed back to the shore. They walked onto the sand, and Riko grabbed Chloe. Chris grabbed Tiger Rose, and they carried them into the water and dragged them to where Ash and Sakura were waiting.

"Riko!" Chloe shouted, obviously trying to sound angry, but laughing while she said it.

"If we don't want to come into the water, don't force us," Tiger Rose said, doing a better job of sounding angry, but it was still pretty obvious that she didn't mind. Though, if there was one thing that could be said, it was that she looked strange with her fringe plastered against her scalp with water. In fact, they all did.

Ash flicked her hair out and splashed more water at all her friends with it, starting the fight again. She swam away, trying to avoid what she had started, but felt something tugging at her ankle. Seaweed? Probably.

She brushed her hands all the way down her leg but didn't feel anything, but a moment later, she felt it again. She dipped her head under the water but saw nothing; no seaweed floating around her, and nothing on her leg. She brushed her hands over her leg again, with more force this time, but still found nothing attached to her ankle.

Her head broke the surface of the water but only long enough for her to take another breath, and she was pulled down, by whatever had grabbed her ankle. It yanked her down and down; the water surrounding her grew murky, and it was hard to see. Something flashed around her, and she barely saw it long enough for it to register in her mind. A face?

There was no sand beneath her feet. Ash tried to swim back to the surface, but whatever had ahold of her was holding fast, and she couldn't break free. She started to panic. What the hell was happening? She looked around and couldn't see anything around her but murky water.

She needed air now. She needed to get back to the surface. Holy crap, she was going to drown, wasn't she? Held down by some invisible force. She struggled to get away, but it was like she was frozen under the water. Now it really was getting dark around her, not just murky. She was passing out, wasn't she? She was going to drown. Oh God, she was going to drown.

Ash saw a shape flit in the water around her, then something grabbed her wrists and started pulling her to the surface. But it was already too late; she needed to breathe and couldn't wait any longer. Unintentionally, she opened her mouth and took a breath in; the water flooded into her lungs.

<hr />

Aelana's eyes flew open; she looked around her and realised she was lying on her back in the park, the moon and stars shining down on her. She stood up, trying to get her bearings, and started walking, not remembering when she had lay down or how long she had been there.

As she walked, the trees started feeling closer and closer together, and she started losing sight of the path; the moonlight grew dim. At first, she had been sure she was in the park near her house, but now it was different and unfamiliar, and she was sure wherever she was, she had never been there before. But where was she?

Something didn't feel right about this place, but she couldn't quite put her finger on it. Everything was just wrong.

She wandered slowly through the trees, and when she turned back, it was like they had closed up behind her, blocking the path she had just taken. It almost felt like she was walking in circles. Somehow, she couldn't see anything but the trees that were inches from her face.

She carried on, hoping to find a way out and get herself home, wherever she had ended up, and it wasn't long until she could see a faint light glowing through the tightly knit trees.

Something rustled in the bushes beside her, and she saw a figure moving. Aelana stopped in her tracks and checked all around her, trying to see in the near blackness. More rustling. Then someone emerged from the bushes.

It was a man with very pale skin, ragged torn clothing, and black hair. Almost like a zombie, minus the rotting flesh. Though he couldn't have been far from it. Like a new zombie, maybe.

Aelana screamed, louder than she had ever screamed before, and turned around to start running, but another zombie-person jumped out in front of her. She quickly changed direction, bursting away through a small opening between the stupid trees that were everywhere.

She could barely see where she was going; she could barely see anything. She tripped on a tree root, slipped, and fell to the ground, hitting her head on a low branch as she fell. For a second, she just lay there, stunned, then she pushed herself up, rubbing her head, and tried to see into the bushes around her. The ground was damp beneath her, but she couldn't even think of what she could be sitting in and how it would be ruining her clothes because the zombie-people pushed their way from the trees like wraiths and circled her.

Her eyes locked on that of the black-haired one, who now held a long, wicked-looking spear in his hand. Aelana froze where she sat, looking into his amber eyes as he smiled and threw it.

Skylar was returning to class down the empty corridors, looking at her feet and following the patterns in the dark carpet, when something pushed her, and she stumbled into the lockers. She had seen someone walking towards her but hadn't looked up. She did look up now, to see Rachel and her stupid friends, Amanda and Kristy.

"What are you doing out here?" Rachel asked, trying to sound nice, but failing to hide the nasty look on her face.

Skylar pushed herself away from the block of metal lockers, not rubbing her shoulder despite the pain, and glared at her but didn't answer.

"Well?"

Skylar still didn't answer and started to walk away. She just couldn't be bothered to deal with them. Especially Rachel.

"Oh, come on, Sky, wait just a moment. Let's talk." Rachel grabbed her shoulder and pulled her back, then pushed her at the lockers again.

Skylar took a deep breath and tried to keep her gaze even. "Don't ever call me Sky." Her voice came out more venomous than she had intended, but nevertheless, it perfectly conveyed her dislike of both Rachel and nicknames.

"Sorry," Rachel said, with a failed attempt at sarcasm that Skylar almost laughed at.

Skylar was silent for a long moment, and when Rachel, Amanda, and Kristy said nothing, she asked, "Can I go now?" They all remained silent nearly as long as her.

"You think you're so amazing because you and your sister are actresses on that stupid TV show," Rachel said, finally dropping the "I just want to be nice to you" act. "But you're really not."

Amanda and Kristy nodded in unison, Kristy's black hair flying around her head, both of them making sounds of agreement. Rachel's eyes flashed with anger, and then she kicked out.

At first, Skylar didn't feel anything, then pain shot up her leg from her knee, and she sank to the ground. Rachel stood over her. Skylar's lips pulled back in a growl that was surprisingly animalistic. She was just as surprised—and almost as scared—as the trio looked when they all jumped away from her.

"Quick, Kristy! Hand me the gun!" Rachel said in a panic.

Gun? Skylar thought, rising to her feet. *How is nobody hearing this?*

Kristy pulled a tiny handgun from her stupid little shoulder bag that was apparently supposed to be a school bag. The gun she retrieved looked more like a water pistol than anything, and she handed it to Rachel, who held it in her hands, just staring at it, looking like a million thoughts were racing through her head. Or maybe her head was completely blank. Skylar really wouldn't be surprised. But then Rachel raised her arms and fired the tiny little thing. Instead of water, a real bullet shot out of it and hit Skylar in the shoulder, faster than she could even comprehend. Someone had to have heard that, right? Or was everyone just giving up on school and listening to music instead, while the teachers simultaneously gave up on them?

Skylar stumbled back and fell against the lockers, sliding down and leaving a small smear of blood. She stared at it, but everything about this scene just felt so wrong, and the sight of her own blood leaking out of her like that, along with the pain, made her feel kind of sick. And she was pretty sure she was passing out.

Jade woke up in a forest. That much she was sure of.

Sunlight was shining down through the trees, making the ground, wet with recent rain, glitter.

She was sitting beside a pool of water in a bright clearing, the water clearer than she had ever seen. She was reflected perfectly on the surface, her long hair tied up in a ponytail, the vivid colour faded in the water. Her hair reached down to her waist, where a black belt was tied, pulling the purple dress she wore in, but it flowed out again, ending just below her knees. Her boots were high. She could feel their black mass underneath the dress, even though she couldn't see it the reflection. And she had a cap. She had no idea where this outfit had come from, but she liked it. It felt right to be wearing.

There was a sound in the bushes beside her; she picked up the bow and arrows sitting beside her, without really knowing how she knew they were there. A rabbit hopped out of the bushes, and Jade was overwhelmed with relief. Something was out there looking for her, and she was looking for it, but she wasn't sure what.

Jade turned back to the water and cupped her hands to drink some. It was by far the best water she had ever tasted, even though water didn't have a taste. It was different and better somehow.

After a last sip of water, she picked up her bow and quiver of arrows once again and stood up, heading into the forest, down a small dirt track. Eventually, if she kept following the path, she would be back in the city, she knew. How she knew this, again, she wasn't sure.

She hadn't been walking long when a shadow fell across her path from the trees above her. She looked up to see a massive shape that dropped down in front of her. A giant tiger opened its mouth and emitted the angriest sound Jade had ever heard. She took a step back, drew an arrow, and raised her bow.

The tiger started to circle, and Jade let the arrow fly, its tip glinting in the sunshine as it flew and struck the animal. Before she could reach for a second arrow, though, she felt a sharp pain in her ribs and turned her head to see a zombie-like man holding the hilt of a knife that was wedged into her side. He pulled it back, and Jade fell. For the second time in her life, she looked up at the sky and couldn't believe what was happening to her.

<hr />

Phoenix had the feeling that her sister was in trouble. She just knew it. She had a sixth sense for knowing when Skylar was in need of her help.

She stood from her seat, walked to the front of the classroom, and asked her teacher if she could go to the bathroom, then walked out into the corridor, with its bright walls and dark carpeting.

She started running as soon as she knew she was out of her teacher's line of sight. A loud bang echoed down the corridor, and she stopped for a second but then raced off even faster. She reached the corner and peered around, seeing Rachel and her idiot friends, except for Aelana. But really, Aelana was never at school, always skipping.

The first thing Phoenix noticed was the tiny gun that Rachel was holding, her hands shaking violently. Amanda and Kristy stood behind her, eyes wide. Skylar was slumped on the ground, leaning up against the lockers. It took Phoenix a second to realise she was unconscious. And there was blood.

"What the hell did you do?" Phoenix yelled, running over to her sister and sliding onto her knees beside her. "Skylar, you're going to be okay; you're okay. I won't let anything happen to you." She grabbed Skylar's neck and felt for her pulse, sighing in relief when she found it.

"I-I-I- …" Rachel stuttered. The gun slipped from her hands and hit the ground with a thud.

"How do you even get a gun?" Phoenix asked without looking up. Her voice was cold, and she could feel the anger rising in her. Rachel didn't say anything, but Phoenix hadn't expected an answer, anyway. Honestly, she looked like she was about to faint.

She took her phone out of her pocket and was about to dial when she saw Amanda dart forward and pick up the gun from where it had fallen.

"Put the phone down," she said with a shaking voice. Phoenix looked up at her and didn't move. "If you try and call the police, I'll shoot. I swear." Her terribly terrified voice said otherwise. Whether she was terrified of getting in trouble or of what was unfolding before her was the question, though.

Phoenix still didn't move. She didn't put her phone down, but she also didn't dial. She was watching the way Amanda's red hair was going all frizzy and beginning to fall out of its stupid bun on top of her head.

Her finger moved across her phone screen, and she pressed zero. She smiled at Amanda as she pressed it again.

"Triple zero is quite easy to dial, you know. I just have to press it once more." She expected Amanda to freak out and drop the gun, and maybe pass out from shock, like Rachel was about to. At least that's what it looked like she wanted to do. Her face was pale, and her hands were shaking.

But she didn't.

Instead, there was another deafening bang, and Phoenix dropped her phone, gasping at the sudden explosion of pain in her side. Acting had definitely not prepared her for the actual pain of being shot.

"Oh, my God! What did I do?" Now Amanda dropped the gun and started backing away.

Rachel and Kristy followed her, and they ran down the corridor, footsteps thundering in Phoenix's ears as she fell to her side, ear pressed to the scratchy carpet.

She reached out for her dropped phone with one hand and held her side with the other, her palm feeling like it would never be enough to hold her together. She could feel the tears running down her face and cried out when she pressed her hand against the ridiculous wound.

Never mind how Rachel had gotten her hands on that dumb gun; if Phoenix didn't do something right now, she felt like she might just die from the pain, rather than blood loss or anything else. She had to get someone to come out, to find her and Skylar.

She banged her hand against the metal lockers behind her, shouting for help, again and again. The pain from hitting the hard metal was nothing compared to what she felt in her side.

The door to a classroom down the corridor opened, and a student peered out. His face turned pale when he saw her, no doubt the bottom of her shirt drenched in blood, and he disappeared back inside.

For some reason, none of them had heard the gunshots, but apparently, banging on a locker was just loud enough for one person to hear it. Yeah, that made sense. Whatever; Phoenix didn't care what made sense, as long as someone was actually coming to help her.

A teacher stepped out of the classroom and instantly saw her. His face, too, went pale, but he started running and leaned down beside her when he reached her. Without a word, he crouched down beside her and picked up her phone, dialling triple zero.

"Hello," he said into the phone. "Yes, it's an emergency. Two girls have been injured, but I'm not entirely sure how. Yes. The address is 213 Belgrove Street. Redlakes High School." He kept the phone to his ear but was silent, then he looked down at her, clear worry on his face. "You're going to be okay," he told her. "An ambulance is on its way. How do you feel?"

"Like I've been shot," she said, whispering without meaning to.

Everything was starting to turn fuzzy, black spots springing over her vision, and the teacher's face was coming in and out of focus.

"Michael," the teacher yelled down the hallway, and she could just make out the boy from before standing in the corridor. "Please inform the Principal that there's been a incident and an ambulance is coming." He rushed off, and then the black spots filled her sight.

⟶ ✦ ◆ ✦ ⟵

Ash opened her eyes and was taken aback by the castle she saw standing before her. It was a rather flat castle, small, with a single tower reaching towards the sky. And from that tower, Ash could see a light, shining even brighter than the sun, hanging in the sky over the castle and its sandy surroundings.

There was something drawing her to whatever was up in that tower, creating that light, so she crossed the drawbridge that lay open before her.

The castle seemed completely empty at first, the extravagant rooms, with their high, painted ceilings, deserted. Room after room was empty of the people you would expect to see in a place like this. The rooms contained only furniture, no servants, or royalty, just the fanciest furniture Ash had ever seen. That was, until she reached the room in the tower the sparkling light had come from.

A spiral staircase led up the tower, dizzyingly high. The door, thick wood painted a light pink and blue with gold accents, was open, and the room itself was absolutely beautiful. Small and round, the walls matched the door, only darker, and the only object was a pedestal directly in the centre, a golden ring sitting on top of it. Though it wasn't glowing now, Ash was sure it was the source of the light she had seen.

She stepped into the room and noticed the maid, the first person she had seen, sweeping with a broom near the windows on the opposite side of the room.

Ash ignored her and crossed the room to the pedestal. Just as she reached out to grab the ring, a hand grabbed her arm from behind and swung her around.

The maid was staring straight at her, with dark, blank eyes. She had pale skin and black hair and could have been a zombie, if only she had been dead and rotting. Well, she still looked dead. Ash didn't scream but tried to pull her arm back. The zombie-woman was strong, though, and she couldn't. Images flashed in her mind of being trapped underwater, but she refused to think about that.

"You can't be here!" the maid hissed, then she pulled Ash over to the nearest window and simply pushed her out, as if it was the easiest thing she had done, and Ash weighed no more than a coin.

Ash screamed all the way down and woke up just in time to stop herself from hitting the ground.

Skylar woke up in her bed and sat up to a room of red crystals. It was both the most beautiful and the strangest thing she had ever seen.

Everything in the room was made of red crystal, resembling rubies; everything, even the walls. Nothing was free of the redness. The walls were almost see-through, and she could see her clothes stacked in her chest of draws.

She stood up, her sheets shattering over her, but she brushed it off and walked over to her full-length mirror beside the window. But instead of seeing herself reflected in it, she saw Phoenix staring back at her.

Of course, it could have been her; they *were* twins, but Skylar had recently dyed her hair, and so it was now obviously Phoenix. Her sister tilted her head, looked into the mirror, and pressed her hand against the glass. She hit it once but then stepped away, deciding that wasn't going to get her anywhere.

Skylar looked away and walked over to the door. When she grabbed the doorknob, the whole door shattered, revealing the hallway beyond. Everything out there was made of the same red crystal. She stepped through the doorway, being careful not to tread on any of the broken glassy crystal. On the other side, however, she didn't find the hallway.

No, she was standing on a street. A dark street with gothic buildings and a full moon hanging in the sky. The moon looked different somehow. She couldn't decide whether it was too big or too small, or whether it was the wrong shape; it just wasn't right. Something about it …

Her steps echoed on the cobblestone road as she wandered, emphasising just how deserted the place was. She walked warily, always glancing over her shoulder and checking all around her. This place was giving her the creeps. She did not like it one bit.

Eventually, with the slow, careful steps she was taking, she reached the end of this empty street and turned onto the next one, which opened up onto a square that she could easily imagine filled with people, but right now, it was empty.

There was, however, a statue that stood in the centre of it.

It was a huge bronze statue of a man with some kind of dragon-like creature. He held a sceptre with a ruby set in the end aloft in his hand, raising it up to the sky in a triumphant pose.

The Sceptre. That was the point of this dream. She could feel it.

How to get it, though?

Skylar looked around, hoping there would be something lying around. A ladder, maybe.

Nothing. Life sure was a whole lot easier for characters in movies.

She looked up at the statue again. The man had a short, cropped beard, and he smiled jovially. His expression was so perfectly captured.

Something moved in the corner of her eye. She spun. Whatever it was ducked behind the statue. She crept around after it. Moving ever so slowly. She found herself back at the start, without encountering anything.

A flash of movement. On top of the statue.

Skylar looked up, as the Sceptre fell.

Too late to move, it hit her.

⸻ ◆ ◆ ◆ ⸻

Phoenix pushed off the covers of her bed, and they shattered all over her, breaking into tiny pieces. She stood up quickly, brushing them off, and saw that her bedroom was made of black crystals. Everything. The whole room and all the objects in it.

She stepped over to the mirror and looked into it, finding Skylar staring back at her. Of course, it was Skylar, and not her. It had to be because Phoenix's hair wasn't black.

She stepped up to the mirror and pressed her hands against the glass, hoping that maybe there wasn't anything there, but of course there was. She hit her hand against it, but it didn't break like she had hoped. She saw Skylar turn away from the mirror and walk out of view.

Phoenix walked over to her bedroom door and took hold of the doorknob, but as soon as she did, it shattered, leaving small shards of black crystal in her hand. She dropped them on the ground and then stepped out into the hallway.

No, wait. She wasn't in the hallway. She was in a city, with tall buildings, and large, sweeping streets. The sun shone brightly, hitting the windows of skyscrapers and reflecting rainbows back.

It was beautiful.

Phoenix wandered, rapt with wonder at her surroundings. The giant, shining skyscrapers surrounded her, and the empty streets, wonderfully clean, were wider than she had ever seen.

A glow ahead of her caught her eye. The source of it was close.

As she approached, she realised she could hear the rush of water. It was loud, roaring around the corner at her. When she saw where the sound was coming from, she halted midstep.

It was a massive waterfall. In the middle of the city.

The water came from under the pavement, as if there were a river flowing beneath the city, and fell into a gigantic rocky hole that disappeared into blackness. Phoenix was staring in amazement when something new caught her eye.

A ruby-studded bracelet was floating in the middle of the falls, as if suspended from an invisible string.

It was the glowing object.

She needed it.

Hands grabbed her from behind. Rough fingers dug into her arms. She tried to pull away, but whoever was holding her was far too strong.

"Goodbye, Princess," a sweet feminine voice said. And then she was hurtling over the edge.

———◆•◆•◆———

Aelana was the first to wake up in the hospital room. She lifted her head from the pillow slowly and instantly sank down. Everything still hurt from the stupid silver jewellery. She moved the covers off her leg slowly and saw a bandage wrapped around her calf. She pulled the sheet back over her just as two girls were brought in on stretchers. She watched from the corner of her eye but couldn't see very well.

They looked to be the same age, and the first had long golden-blonde hair, while the other had long black hair. They looked extremely alike, but it was hard to tell properly from the angle Aelana watched from.

Aelana looked away and saw that there were two other girls already in the room with her. Directly across from her was a girl with short, wavy blonde hair, tipped blue. She was looking back at her, and Aelana saw that she had pretty green eyes that looked almost slightly golden in the light.

Next to this girl was another, with surprisingly long, green hair. It was tied up in a ponytail falling off the side of her bed. She sat up; Aelana caught her eye for a second and then immediately looked away. Aelana couldn't see anything wrong with her so guessed that she was probably sick with something.

A nurse walked over to the side of Aelana's bed and smiled.

"How are you feeling today?" the nurse asked.

"My skin still hurts," Aelana said. The nurse smiled still and brushed a stray brown hair away from her face.

"It's just an allergic reaction, nothing to worry about. You should feel fine soon," she said. "And how about your leg?"

"My leg is fine," Aelana said.

"Okay. Someone will come in soon to check you over," the nurse said and left the room.

Aelana brushed her hair away from her neck and sat up slightly. She flinched as she did and lay back down quickly.

The girl with the green hair was watching Aelana curiously.

"What happened to you?" she asked slowly.

"I, uh, uh," Aelana stuttered. "Actually, I was shot." She moved her sheet away so the girl could see the bandage around her leg.

"Wow," the girl said.

"Wow," Jade said when the girl across the room said she had been shot.

"Yeah, I know. Pretty unbelievable," she said.

"Well, I was kidnapped," Jade replied. "I don't what they wanted with me, but it seemed like more than just for some money. It was like they had a serious grudge against me." It felt good to get the words out, even with how strange they sounded. But she needed to confirm with herself that it was real and it had happened, and saying it aloud helped.

"Wow. Spooky."

"Yeah. Don't know who they were." Jade sighed, sweeping her hair up from beside the bed. "They could have at least kept it off the floor."

"My name's Aelana," the black-haired girl said after a moment of silence.

"Jade," Jade replied and smiled.

"I'm Ash," the blonde in the bed beside Jade said.

Jade smiled at her.

"I'm afraid my story isn't as dramatic as yours," Ash said, with an air of extravagance to her voice. "I almost drowned."

"That still doesn't sound fun," Aelana commented.

"Being shot and kidnapped sounds even worse," Ash replied.

"I guess so," Jade said. "We were all just unlucky."

"Your story doesn't sound like it has anything to do with luck," Ash replied.

"Not really," Jade agreed. "But maybe I was just unlucky in the way that they thought I was someone else."

"Imagine that," Ash said, smiling. "Another girl with long, bright green hair running around. Maybe you have a twin sister you never knew about."

Phoenix opened her eyes; she stared up at the white ceiling and for a moment couldn't work out where she was. The ceiling was different from her bedroom, missing the familiar crack above her bed.

If she wasn't in her bed, then where was she?

She remembered fragments of her dream, of Rachel holding a gun at her, and Skylar, unconscious against the lockers. Then of Amanda shooting her. What an odd dream.

She heard voices and sat up, seeing three other girls and a very unfamiliar room.

Wait, wait, wait. Where am I?

"You know, Ash, you kind of look familiar," one of the girls said. She had short black hair and bright yellowish-looking eyes.

"Excuse me," Phoenix said, interrupting their conversation.

They all turned to look at her, and one of the others was the first to speak. The one with long, green hair.

"Yes?" she asked.

"Where am I?"

"The hospital," the girl said simply.

The hospital? But, that was a dream, right? What if it wasn't?

Phoenix reached down and felt the side of her body, her hands reaching the edge of a bandage wrapped around her waist.

So it wasn't.

2

Aelana thrashed in her sleep, almost throwing her sheets off, finally waking when she kicked out and pain shot up her leg. She opened her eyes and stared up at the ceiling for a moment, before the cold air finally hit her; she pulled her tangled sheets back on with a struggle.

The hospital room was dark around her, and she could just see Jade's sleeping figure, her whole body curled up in her bed, and Ash beside her, lying straight, like a log. There was a slight hum coming from the air conditioner, mounted high on the wall above her head. The curtains were drawn across the windows, but a small sliver of light still managed to find its way past; a slash of moonlight cut across Aelana's bed.

She sat up and saw a card and a bouquet of flowers on the table beside her bed. They were purple and blue flowers that kind of looked like Christmas Bells, but faced up, instead of down, and grew up the stem a bit like wattle. She didn't know what they were called, but they were her favourite. She had always been meaning to find out their name. That they were here meant her parents had been in at one point. She wished she had been awake when they came, but she felt a little better knowing that they had been to see her.

She reached for the card, picked it up off the table, and tried to read it in the dim light, but she could barely make out the words. So she put it back, promising herself to read it in the morning.

She lay back down now, closing her eyes and hoping she could at least get a few more hours of sleep before the sun came up. Just as she was drifting off, there was a rustling in the curtains. She didn't sit back up but rolled over slightly, opening one eye and watching the curtains. They moved again, but she couldn't see anyone or anything, so she guessed it was just the wind; maybe the window had been left open. She rolled back over.

It kept going, keeping her awake every time she almost fell back to sleep, and so she finally sat back up again, squinting in the darkness to see what was disturbing her. From her bed, she couldn't see if the window was open or not. The noise of the curtains blowing around and not knowing whether the window was actually open or not was beginning to annoy her. She needed to know if it was open. She needed to close it if it was.

She doubted she would be able to get up, though.

She doubted that she could walk.

But she needed to know. She just wouldn't be able to sleep until she did. And not just because of her curiosity, but because the stupid rustling had managed to burrow into her mind and keep her awake.

Then another thought struck her.

What if the window was closed? What if there was something or someone in the curtains? She had no idea what had happened to that guy who had shot her in his robbery attempt. Now that she thought about it, she assumed he had been arrested. But what if he hadn't been? What if he had gotten away and had come looking for her?

Now she definitely wasn't going back to sleep.

Wouldn't he have come out by now, though? Or was he waiting for her to fall back asleep?

Aelana's eyes were glued to the window and curtains. When they didn't move for a while, she started to wonder if she was making the whole thing up.

And just as she had convinced herself that she was being ridiculous and was going to lay down, the curtains moved again, and a tiny black cat appeared out from behind them.

The cat sat on the floor beneath the window for a moment, its bright green eyes scanning the room with an unnerving, human-like intelligence. Aelana was mesmerised by the way they seemed to glow. She followed the cat's gaze and turned to see that Jade and Ash were sitting up now, wide awake. The twins, who she had recognised as Phoenix and Skylar Evans, were also up, though far from being able to sit up. Aelana couldn't disguise the enjoyment she found in what had happened to them.

All four of them spotted the cat, and Aelana turned back to see it jump into one of the white chairs underneath the next window, beside an empty bed. Then, before her eyes, the little black cat transformed into a human. A woman. It took a split-second, and Aelana barely registered what had happened.

A woman was sitting in the chair. A woman with long, straight black hair, trailing down her back, and green eyes like that of the cat. She wore a loose white blouse, black pants, and navy-blue high heels.

A woman.

No cat. Just a woman.

The cat had disappeared, and the woman had appeared out of nowhere. It wasn't possible.

Aelana stared. She stared at the woman in the chair and then looked around the room, trying to find the black cat. It had to be somewhere, but that didn't explain where the woman had come from.

When she couldn't find the cat, she decided she was dreaming. When she lay down just before the cat had appeared, she had fallen asleep, and everything after that was a dream.

She would have believed it, except she knew that when you were in a dream, you didn't question anything that happened. Everything in a dream seemed completely normal, no matter how crazy it was. As soon as you told yourself it was a dream, it definitely wasn't a dream. She hated when her mind decided to make sense of things rather than just believing it was a dream.

But this had to be real.

Somehow, she had just watched a cat turn into a woman.

A woman who was now looking at them all, with contempt in her eyes.

She sat in the hospital chair, hands in her lap, waiting for something, it seemed.

After a moment, she shifted in the white, plastic chair and crossed her legs. Then she spoke.

"How are you all feeling?" she asked, her voice soft and velvety, comforting and at odds with the way she was looking at them.

Silence. Aelana was too stunned to open her mouth.

"I'll take that as surprise and not that you all lost your tongues. Otherwise, we would have quite a problem on our hands."

She paused for a second before she went on; Aelana wasn't sure if she was actually expecting an answer or not.

"My name is Shadow," she said, unfolding her legs and then crossing them the other way. "And I'm here to help you all."

"With what?" Jade asked in a small but defiant voice. She narrowed her eyes, regarding the woman warily, clearly not sure whether to trust anything she said. Aelana couldn't help but feel the same way.

"A lot of things," Shadow replied casually. "Magic being the most important one." She said *magic* as if it was obvious, that they should have known who she was and what she was there for.

Although she looked young, maybe in her late thirties or early forties, Shadow carried the air of someone older and wiser, making Aelana believe her when the word slipped from her mouth. Especially after seeing what could only be described as her transforming from cat to woman.

"Magic?" Ash asked incredulously. "You expect us to believe you?"

"Yes, Siren; yes, I do."

"What did you call me?" Ash sat up straighter, staring at Shadow as if the word were an insult. More like she wasn't sure if it was supposed to be or not.

"Calm down," Skylar said softly.

Ash glanced at Skylar and looked back at Shadow, but she didn't say anything else.

"I don't expect you to believe me straight away," Shadow continued, standing up. "But I will give you reason to believe soon enough."

She took slow, elegant steps across the room, her heels making barely a sound, and stopped beside Aelana's bed. Aelana looked up at her, not sure whether to be scared or not, not sure what to expect from this strange person. She was taller than Aelana expected.

"You," she said, gazing down. "Allergic to silver, are you not?"

Aelana could barely nod as Shadow took her arm gently in her slim, pale hands.

"And what mythical creatures are allergic to silver?" she asked the room.

Once again, silence.

"Werewolves," Skylar answered, her voice slightly louder than before.

"Correct," Shadow said, smiling for the first time.

Then she bent down close to Aelana, tightening the grip on her arm, her suddenly sharp nails digging in. "What do you think?"

Aelana didn't know what to think.

Werewolf? Ridiculous.

And yet, somehow, it made sense. For some reason, Aelana really did want to believe her. There was something appealing about the thought of magic and being a Werewolf. What wasn't appealing, though, was the grip Shadow had on her arm. She pulled back roughly, her arm slipping out of Shadow's grip. But her nails left deep scratches in Aelana's arm, blood slowly pooling in them. She clutched her arm to her chest, hissing at the sudden pain.

Shadow turned away from her bed and walked across the room to Ash.

"Ash Blackwood; the last thing I expected from you was drowning," she said. "And yet, even without knowing about magic, you're quite the charmer, aren't you?"

"You could say that," Ash said warily.

"Your Siren abilities shine through naturally in your personality."

Ash didn't say anything this time. She looked blank, at a loss for words.

"And you don't know how you were saved from drowning, do you?" Shadow asked. "It was your friend, Chloe. She's a Shapeshifter. In fact, all your friends have magic." She kept quiet as Shadow moved on from her, stopping beside Jade.

She tapped her fingers along the side of the girl's bed a moment before speaking.

"My parents warned me about you," Jade said before Shadow could open her mouth. "They told me not to trust you."

"So, you do know, then," Shadow replied. "Now tell me, Jade, if I'm not to be trusted and shouldn't be relied on, then why am I the one living happily in my castle while your parents wither away on Earth?"

Jade didn't answer, and so Shadow left her to contemplate the question while she moved on to Phoenix.

"And what are you going to say to me?" Phoenix asked confidently.

"People are drawn to you, aren't they?" Shadow asked as if Phoenix had never spoken.

"Yeah."

"All because of your fairy blood. No matter what, humans will be naturally drawn to you throughout your life. Both in good and bad ways. Like those bullies."

"That doesn't really prove anything," Phoenix whispered.

Again, Shadow didn't react to her.

"Your sister, though." She let the words hang in the air as she stalked across the room to Skylar, who looked like she wanted to be anywhere but here, with that woman's eyes on her.

"Your sister, by some crazy chance, is not fairy; but instead, a Vampire."

Skylar seemed to cower at the words. Phoenix looked surprised. And somewhat scared, Aelana realised.

"Don't you recall the fear those girls who attacked you felt towards you? The way they looked at you like you were a monster? You revealed your true self to them and used magic, without even realising it."

Skylar looked like she did indeed recall exactly what Shadow was talking about.

Without waiting for Skylar to reply, she turned around and walked back across the room to the window. "Rest up," she said. "In a few days, you will see me again. Your training will begin."

Then in a split-second, midstep, she became the little black cat again and disappeared behind the curtains; with a final flick, the curtains settled for the night. But now Aelana was unsettled, even more than she had been before.

Thoughts swirled in her head as she lay back in her bed, staring at the ceiling with the feeling that something monumental was changing in her life. And at the same time, it felt right, like this was what she had been waiting for, and that nothing was any different than before.

3

Aelana did rest up, and a couple of days later, she left the hospital, having healed completely in a third of the time the doctor had expected. She could walk perfectly fine as well, which was also unexpected. She returned to school the very next day after she left the hospital, as if nothing had ever happened. But her head was still filled with the thoughts of Shadow and what she had said. They had never really left.

Was it really possible that she was a Werewolf? No. It couldn't be.

She had debated asking her friends what they thought but had decided against it, as she didn't want to freak them out or have them think she was lying or crazy. The latter being most likely. It definitely would not end well if she told them.

Maybe she should, though. Maybe it would help convince herself that it was crazy and stupid and not real.

Yeah, she would tell them. Somehow. It was just about getting the information out in the right way. In a way that wouldn't make them react the *wrong* way.

Aelana closed her locker and walked out into the schoolyard and the sunlight. It was so nice to be back in the sun. Rachel, Amanda, and Kristy were already sitting at their usual bench beside the lone tree, and she joined them, sitting down beside Kristy.

"Aelana!" Rachel greeted. "How are you?"

"Good," she said, smiling at her friends.

"I cannot believe that you went shopping," Amanda said. "Without us, and on such an exciting day."

"Exciting?" Aelana asked, pulling an apple out of her bag.

"It was so exciting," Kristy said. "You missed out. And maybe you wouldn't have been hurt if you were with us."

"Yeah?" she asked. "So, what exactly happened on this exciting day?"

"Rachel took her dad's gun when he wasn't looking and brought it to school," Amanda said.

"Seriously?" Aelana asked, light-heartedly. "Your dad has a gun at home?"

"He does," Rachel said. "And we scared the hell out of Phoenix and Skylar. It was priceless."

Aelana didn't say anything for a moment, then realised she probably should.

"Really? It was good?"

"You should have seen them," Kristy said, delighted.

"Aren't you in trouble?"

Rachel shrugged off the question. "I mean, my dad's angry at me, but you know he's a police officer. He's making sure I don't get in serious trouble."

Aelana was now thinking back to her time in hospital. About Skylar and Phoenix, in the same room as her, and the story of what had happened to them: an obviously twisted story. They had said it had been some random guy, probably in year twelve. They had lied to her. Of course, they had. Because how would she have reacted at being told her friends had tried to kill them? Probably not well, towards Phoenix and Skylar or her friends. She would have tried to defend her friends in whatever warped way she could think to justify it.

Aelana would admit that she still didn't like either of them. They had their stupid acting careers, and now she was getting magic. But so did they. It wasn't fair, in her opinion, when they already had something special about them. But knowing they had lied to her just to stop her reacting how she knew she would have made her think twice about how exciting it might have been.

"Aelana?" Rachel was looking at her, a hint of concern on her face.

"Hmm?"

"Are you alright?"

"Yeah."

"You just kind of drifted off."

"I was just thinking about something," she said, deciding it was the right time to ask them what they thought. "I had this really weird dream the first night in the hospital."

"Yeah?" Amanda asked, excitedly.

"Okay, okay, so I was in the hospital room, in my bed in the exact space in the room that I was actually in. At first, I thought it wasn't a dream and that I was awake, but it couldn't have been. Because this cat came in from behind the curtains, and then it turned into this woman." She paused for a moment, wondering exactly what to tell them as they stared intently at her. "And she walked over to my bed and … I don't remember exactly what happened, but basically, she said that magic was real and that I was a Werewolf. How crazy is that?"

"So weird," Kristy said.

"Crazy," Amanda agreed, nodding her head.

"Are you sure it isn't because you wish you were a Werewolf?" Rachel gave her a sly look as she asked her question.

"No way," Aelana said. "Like I would want to be a Werewolf, of all things."

"Now I hope it *was* real, just so you have to be something you don't want to," Kristy teased.

"Knock it off," Aelana said. "It was just a dream."

But was it really?

───◆◆◆───

It wasn't until a week later that Aelana finally heard from the mysterious Shadow again. She was at her locker, switching books for classes, when a girl materialised out of the crowd of students beside her.

She instantly recognised her. Lauryn was her name, and by the faint glare on her face, Aelana knew she recognised her too. Not that Lauryn should've had anything to be angry about. She won in the end, didn't she? Bitch.

"It's time," she said, barely keeping the distaste from her voice. Her blonde hair fell over her shoulders in crazy waves as she leant up against the lockers, her eyes partly hidden by her fringe. "Shadow wants to see you."

Aelana wanted to remark that of course she was with Shadow, pretend she knew more than she actually did, condescendingly ask if Lauryn knew of magic. Maybe even ask if Austin knew she was doing this. Instead, she said, "Fine; lead the way."

Lauryn slipped away into the thinning crowd roaming the hallway, and Aelana followed quickly, taking even steps to try and hide her excitement.

Lauryn didn't say another word as she led the way to the school hall. One of the doors was ajar, and Lauryn opened it all the way, holding it for Aelana to step inside first. As she did, Lauryn followed her, and the door crashed closed behind them, sending a shock of fright through Aelana.

The hall was empty, except for Shadow, standing against the edge of the stage, in the same fancy outfit as Aelana had last seen her in. She had her arms crossed in front of her chest, her face blank.

"Hello, Aelana," she said sweetly in her soft, velvet voice.

Aelana didn't say anything, not knowing what exactly she *should* say to this woman.

Shadow passed this off, as if she didn't expect an answer to everything she said but would rather just be listened to. She walked towards Aelana, heels clacking on the wooden floor and echoing slightly around the large, barren space. She stopped barely a metre away and looked Aelana up and down.

"I thought that today we could talk a little bit more about you and magic," Shadow said. "Straighten out some things in need of straightening out. There is a lot of theory involved in how magic works, and there is so much for you to learn."

"Okay …" Aelana said. Her voice sounded weak and uncertain, so different from the confidence Shadow displayed. Aelana wasn't used to hearing herself like that. She wasn't a fan of it.

"I know you told your friends about that night but said it was just a dream," Shadow said. "Believe me, this is not a dream, and you shouldn't treat it as such. Magic is serious business, and the sooner you realise this, the better."

Aelana nodded but didn't open her mouth again.

"You are a very important person," Shadow continued. "More important than even I am now, and I am quite an important person. I won't go into detail about all that yet, though. The most important thing right now is learning about your magic: what it is, how to use it, and how you must learn to control certain aspects of it."

Aelana nodded again, going along with it, but not entirely sure what was going to happen here or if she wanted to be a part of it. This was already more serious than she had been expecting, and she wasn't entirely looking forward to it now. Maybe she should have just gone to her stupid English class. But no, that meant that Skylar and Phoenix would have just one more thing about them that was special, and Aelana would remain with nothing. She needed this. She wanted to be special too.

"Mercury, my dear," Shadow said, looking past Aelana. "Could you please give Aelana here an example of magic?"

Aelana turned around to see Lauryn, leaning against the wall, nod and straighten up. She took a couple of steps forward, and suddenly, all the lights went out overhead, as if someone had flicked all the switches off at once. The darkness that followed pressed in around Aelana, a space just for her that grew smaller with every breath. Then there was a light in front of her, the soft, orange glow of a fire.

The flame hovered in the air, and behind it stood Mercury, the two of them locked away from the world. Mercury took a few quick steps forwards, the darkness rolling around her like mist. Light flickered across her features as she drew close, the flame dying down, shadows playing on her face.

"I'm not going to pretend we like each other, so let me just get one thing straight," she said, voice tight. "This is important to me. I need you to understand the gravity of what you are involved in. Don't tell your friends, don't mess around."

Aelana wanted to snap back at her, but before she could, that all-encompassing darkness drifted away on a phantom breeze, flame sparking out, and Mercury was back against the wall.

Aelana turned back to Shadow, who shot Mercury a warning glance before speaking again.

"Although you will be able to do completely different things," she said with a smile, a smile that was comforting as well as frightening. "Shall we begin?"

Aelana practiced with Shadow, listening to her teach and doing exactly what she was told, for what felt like hours, but in fact, it was only forty minutes: the length of one period. As soon as the bell rang, she was back out the door and on to her next class. The suddenness with which her lesson with Shadow ended left her feeling slightly disheartened, as if she hadn't achieved anything.

Magic was real, though. That she was sure of. More than anything, she was sure that magic was real and that she possessed it. She could use magic. She had finally found something to make her special, to make her different from everyone else. Too bad she couldn't tell anyone. Shadow had told her she simply wasn't allowed to let people know, especially not her friends.

The next day, Mercury brought her again to meet Shadow in the hall. This time, when she entered, Shadow was seated in a row of four plastic chairs, watching the doorway. Another row of four chairs sat opposite her. Aelana could feel those cold eyes on her as she stepped inside and walked across to where Shadow was sitting, waiting for her.

"Before we continue with learning more practical elements," Shadow said, skipping a greeting this time, "I thought I would teach you some theory."

She gestured for Aelana to sit on one of the chairs opposite her.

"Today, you will learn about the origins of magic and see where you fit into the grand scheme of things." She spoke so extravagantly that Aelana couldn't help but be excited. It already promised to be more interesting than normal history, just from Shadow's tone.

"Magic is divided into what we call races, just like how here, on Earth, the people are divided into races. You already know you are a Werewolf. That is your race."

"If magical races are different om race-races, then how come nothing is ever said about them?" Aelana asked. "How come the whole world doesn't know about magic?"

It just came out of her suddenly. She hadn't been expecting to do anything but sit here and listen, but there it was. She had asked it without a hint of doubt or any kind of fear; she just wanted to know.

"Because, Aelana, magic and all the people who possess it do not come from Earth."

"Don't come from Earth?"

"Correct," Shadow said. "Magic comes from a different planet in another universe."

Aelana stared. The words that came out of Shadow's mouth didn't make sense or seem possible.

Another universe?

"What, like an alternate reality or something?" Aelana asked sarcastically, for once feeling confident around Shadow.

"Yes, exactly like that."

Not the answer she had been expecting.

"You're serious? I'm meant to believe that there's an alternate dimension out there where magic exists?"

"You don't have to believe me, but it's true," Shadow said, remaining calm. And just the fact that she was so calm and so sure of herself made Aelana calm down.

"That is just so … crazy."

"We live in a crazy reality."

Aelana wasn't sure what else she could say, but Shadow didn't speak either, not for a long moment, almost like she was assessing if Aelana was ready to hear more.

"Lindreas, for that is the planet's name, exists in its universe in the same spot as Earth. It is placed the same distance from the sun and has the same number of planets in its solar system. The only thing that differs is the planet itself.

"Lindreas has different continents, which are inhabited by different races, and each continent is one kingdom. Because, yes, there are still kings and queens, no democracy like here on Earth, but our system works so much better than any government here.

"Lindreas also has two moons, as opposed to one. One for Werewolves, and one for ampires, whose magic is both dictated by their cycles."

Aelana stayed silent while Shadow talked now, trying to take in everything she was saying. It was so much to think over, but there was something about this information that seemed to make perfect sense somewhere deep in her mind. Like she had known it all along it was just buried within her, where she wouldn't remember it.

"Now, you remember that I said you were an important person?" Shadow asked.

Aelana nodded eagerly.

"That is because you, Aelana, are a princess. In fact, you are heir to the throne of Lupus, the Kingdom of Werewolves."

The words tumbled from her mouth so easily, carried on her velvet voice, as if learning you were royalty to a kingdom you'd never even heard of was completely normal. But the words hit Aelana like a brick. A brick to her face, and they sent her mind reeling off in a direction it had never even thought to go before.

Crazy. Impossible.

"Wait. What?"

"Her Royal Highness, Crown Princess Aelana Nix of Lupus, is your full title."

The words were in one ear and out the other, their importance lost on her from the shock of the others.

"Say that again?"

"Crown Princess Aelana Nix."

Her earlier confidence was completely washed away by those words. Yet they should have made her feel even better about herself, shouldn't they? They should have made her more confident in herself. But no, they made her feel like she had failed at something important, more important than she could imagine. Like the biggest exam of her life, except you weren't told how significant the results would be until afterwards, so you just bludged the whole thing.

Guilt washed over her, dragging her into its depths. Unnecessary guilt, she was already telling herself. It was there, nevertheless.

Aelana stood without a word and walked back to the door, where Lauryn stood. Those words would take time to sink in. And when they had, she had no idea how she'd feel about it.

"It doesn't get any easier to hear, believe me," Lauryn whispered as Aelana passed her on her way out.

Outside the hall it was cool, a lot nicer than being inside, which now felt like every heater in the world had been on in there. She breathed in the cool air, trying to calm her mind. She didn't feel any better, though. Honestly, she just wasn't sure whether she should trust Shadow or not, whether she should believe any of it.

And what was the point of blurting it out like that?

It was all too much.

She needed time to think about this, to really think. This was something serious she was getting herself into. It wasn't just fun and games, like she had at first been expecting. Even after that first lesson, the initial seriousness had worn off a little. But now it was even bigger than she had thought.

You, Aelana, are a princess. In fact, you are heir to the throne of Lupus, the Kingdom of Werewolves.

4

After that, Aelana spent one period almost every day, practicing with the help of both Shadow and Lauryn (who she now knew as Mercury). Learning magic was a slow process for her, as neither Shadow nor Mercury were Werewolves and so didn't share her kind of magic, making it difficult to learn what exactly she was doing.

While having the knowledge that she was a princess and would one day rule a kingdom she had never heard of before, was terrifying, it also meant to her that she was better than Mercury, higher up on the magical ladder, as it were. And that thought was rewarding.

Today, when she walked into the hall, there was a new person with Shadow. A woman with strawberry blonde hair and a friendly smile that instantly made Aelana feel better. She was tall and muscular but had a certain elegance to her stance.

Mercury stiffened at the sight of her but didn't say anything, and took up taking her place leaning against the back wall, beside the door, as she always did. Nothing much more than Shadow's puppet.

"Aelana, this is April Summers," Shadow said. "She's a Werewolf, just like you."

"Shadow said it would help you to get training from someone with the same powers, and I kind of enjoy training people anyway." April smiled. She wasn't looking at Aelana when she did, though. No, she was looking at Mercury.

"Come on, Mercury," Shadow said, heading for the door. "We'll leave them alone to do their training in private. They don't need us for that."

For a split-second an expression passed over Mercury's face, seeming to Aelana that she didn't want to go anywhere with Shadow. But the look passed quickly, and she swung the door opened and followed Shadow out.

"Before we begin," April said, drawing Aelana's attention back to her, "I must warn you not to trust Shadow." She said the words barely above a whisper, like she was scared she'd be overheard. "She will help you with what you need to do, which won't be an easy task, which I understand you don't know anything about yet, – but never let your guard down around her. She has her reasons for helping you, but she could just as easily turn on you for no reason other than boredom or that she found a better way to get what she wants."

April's words rang around in Aelana's head, but she didn't have time to take them all in properly, because April was moving on from her little warning message and what she was really here for. Or maybe the warning was the most important reason she was here.

"Show me what you can do," she said.

"Not much," Aelana admitted. "So far, all I've been able to do with Shadow is grow claws."

"Show me," April said again.

Aelana looked up at her then down at her hands. The first time she had actually grown proper claws, she had been startled by the way they looked and felt. The pain of such a small transformation had been unbearable. Now, after some practice when she was alone, and with Shadow, she didn't really feel anything when it happened.

She watched her hands as her nails grew longer, shooting out from their normal stubby length that barely reached past her fingertips. Once they were the right length, which only took a second, they started to curl in on themselves, wrapping around until they formed a point at the tip, and were solid all the way through.

It was crazy to think that she found this completely normal now, but she did. She had watched her nails turn into claws and turn back again. In barely a week, she was used to this, and that thought was almost scary. Though there was nothing scarier than being told she was heir to a throne. A kingdom.

You, Aelana, are a princess. In fact, you are heir to the throne of Lupus, the Kingdom of Werewolves.

She looked back up at April, who had a comforting smile on her face.

"Very good," she said. "Though you will definitely need to learn to do it faster. But that will come with time and more practice."

And just like that, April transformed, her nails turning into sharp claws faster than Aelana thought possible. She was sure if she had blinked, she would have completely missed it. Then before Aelana could say a single word, April's nails changed back to nails.

"You've got a whole lot to learn," she said. "But I am here to help you all the way."

As soon as Mercury left the hall and closed the door behind her, she walked off. Shadow called out to her, but she ignored her and kept walking until she couldn't hear that stupid voice anymore, carrying her name on a velvet pillow accented with spikes.

Sometimes, she really hated what she had found herself in, but she'd done it to herself and lived with that decision, the stupid but necessary decision weighing down on her every bloody day.

Because Shadow always had something for her to do, somewhere for her to be, treating her like a God damned slave. All she wanted was to help protect the others, but Shadow had already found them before she had a chance to approach them herself. And now she barely had a way of knowing if she would ever misguide them, and she couldn't exactly stop her if she did.

Treated like a slave.

The words echoed around in her head and made her angry; she also wanted to laugh.

Her, a slave. Mercury Winter, a slave. She was capable of so much, but right now, she felt almost completely helpless. She had all this power at her fingertips, – that April had taught her how to use – yet she couldn't use it. Because Shadow had a hold on her. Yep, she definitely felt stupid.

And now, as if it was some kind of cruel joke, there was April in the mix too. Of course, Shadow would do that. Of course. Usually seeing April would have made her feel good, and she would have found comfort with her. But right now, seeing her made her think about how stupid she might have been and how crazy all this was. She knew that if she had a chance to talk to April, all April would say was how disappointed she was. And

Mercury just couldn't take that, partly because she was just as disappointed in herself. But she would see this through until the end.

She had to do it. She had to. This was for everyone. Everyone she cared about, everyone she didn't know, all the nameless faces, and the faceless names. This was for everyone she had a duty to protect and everyone that she just wanted to protect anyway.

Her motives were so like Shadow's yet still so different. Shadow wanted to protect her loved ones and everyone else too, but Shadow just wasn't as reliable to protect everyone else as Mercury was. Shadow didn't have the same strong feeling that Mercury did about protecting innocent people. If Shadow had to or wanted to, she would just make sure her daughters were safe and they would be alright, and let everyone else out there fend for themselves. And nobody knew what could or would make her decide to do that, or when. Mercury really hoped it wasn't too soon.

When the time came, though, all Mercury truly wanted was to make the right choices. That was all that mattered to her. She didn't want people dying if she made a stupid mistake.

But maybe you already have …

When she finally stopped walking, stopped thinking, she was standing around the back of the hall, looking up at a classroom window. A very specific classroom window. She was meant to be in that classroom right now, with her friends, and enjoying not having anything to worry about. But she had everything to worry about.

She could almost see her friends sitting in there right now and imagined what they were doing. Amber was probably arguing with Mel about something stupid or laughing over something equally stupid with Flash. Austin was probably worrying about her, just because she wasn't there, and Jem was convincing him there was nothing wrong yet secretly worrying about her too. And then Seb and Alex would be having a completely different conversation altogether, because they had the least troubles out of all of them. They were, more or less, just along for the ride.

She wanted to be there so badly.

But instead of walking to the door that would lead her to the classroom, she walked back around the hall, back to Shadow, and back to her slavery.

Aelana heard the bell ring and couldn't believe that her lesson with April was already over. She wished it could have been longer, that she could have spent more time learning. Because she was actually learning. She could do so much more than just grow claws now; at least she felt like she could do so much more.

In a way, it also felt like everything was happening so fast. Like she was introduced to something new before she had a chance to process what she'd learnt before.

Half of her was so excited about all this. And the other half worried that she was too excited and not thinking about what was really happening to her.

Now, though, she just wanted the end of the day to come so she could go home, sit in her room, and practice what April had taught her. Maybe she would even come back to school and be able to show off to Shadow how well she had done. Now that would be something.

The most surprising thing she had learnt with April, and the one she wanted to practice the most, was invisibility. Who would have thought that Werewolves would have invisibility? That would most definitely be fun to show off to Shadow. She might even use it to mess with her friends.

She still had two periods to go before the end of the day, though, before she could go home and actually try out all that she had learnt by herself. She sat through these periods with extreme boredom, talking to her friends about completely normal things. Completely normal things that now bored her. That in itself was slightly worrying. Of course, she was still too excited to give it much thought. It was just her excitement causing her boredom, she was sure. The novelty of learning new magic would wear off, and her friends' gossip would draw her back in, and she would never think of it as boring again.

The end of the day was growing close, barely twenty minutes left.

And just when Aelana hoped to finally go home to practice her magic, the most unexpected thing happened. The lockdown bell began to ring.

The first thoughts she had were that the guy from the shop was after her, for whatever reason.

He's back. He worked out where I go to school. He might know where I live. He's coming for me.

Then she told herself she was being absolutely ridiculous, and it was obviously just a practice. Those bells were never rung for any reason except for practicing having a lockdown rather than actually having one.

And why would he care about finding her, anyway?

Stupid. Stupid thought.

Yet something told her that wasn't true, that the lockdown bell was really ringing for a reason. From the look on her teacher's face, whatever instinct was telling her that was right.

"Everyone over on the left side of the classroom, please, right underneath the windows," Mrs Taylor instructed. She was trying to sound calm, but she was obviously very worried and nervous.

Students jumped from their seats and rushed to the wall. Aelana squeezed herself in between a row of desks, next to Danielle. They had been friends once, but that had died out, and they barely ever spoke now. Danielle barely spoke to anyone now, after losing her best friend, Isobel.

"What do you think is going on?" Aelana asked her in a whisper.

"I bet it's Lauryn and her stupid friends," Danielle said, venom in her voice. "They've always been up to something. I wouldn't be surprised if they convinced Austin to do something just so they didn't get in any trouble for it."

And Aelana was quickly reminded why she and Danielle were no longer friends. She had this stupid obsession with Austin that had only become worse when he stopped hanging out with her, Aelana and their friends in favour of Lauryn and Amber.

Mercury. Her name is Mercury.

That gave Aelana a new thought. What if this lockdown really was something to do with Mercury and her friends? Might they know of magic as well? But what would they be doing and how would they have been caught? Why a lockdown? And did Danielle know? Was that why she had always been against Lauryn and Amber, and hated seeing Austin with them?

Aelana wanted to ask but wasn't sure how she could, without giving herself away. And what if Danielle didn't know and was, in fact, just filled with hatred for the two?

The class was beginning to quiet down now, after the initial excitement of the lockdown. Because somehow, it was exciting. Aelana didn't really get that, though, but it did convince her not to ask Danielle more questions, if only because other students would hear.

As the room fell into silence, Aelana heard footsteps outside in the corridor, and her thoughts of the man coming back for her returned. If she had known who it was then, she probably would have laughed at how stupidly ordinary that was.

The footsteps stopped.

Then the door handle started to rattle, but it was locked and didn't open.

There were footsteps again, louder than before.

All of a sudden, the door burst open, kicked down by whoever was outside. And standing in the doorway was someone Aelana had definitely not been expecting, nor anyone that she recognised.

Two people stood in the doorway: a tall blonde woman, no older than twenty, and beside her was a girl who must have been the same age as Aelana, or maybe younger even. She had dark brown hair that wasn't exactly black, but extremely close to it, and a twinkle in her dark eyes, like stars shining on a dark night.

The blonde led the way into the classroom, and the other girl followed her. They both cast their eyes around the room, as if daring anyone to stand up to them. Nobody did. Not the teacher, not a student, and certainly not Aelana.

They looked like they were searching for something. Until their gazes rested on her, and their eyes lit up at finding their goal.

The younger girl hurried across the room towards her, looking excited. The blonde watched, as she knelt down directly in front of Aelana. She tried to back away from her, but she was already pressed against the wall and couldn't move any farther back. She was trapped, with a desk on one side of her and Danielle on the other. Danielle, who shrank away and did nothing to help someone who had once been her friend.

The girl smiled as she knelt in front of Aelana, not a comforting smile, not a nice smile. A horrible, evil smile that made Aelana's skin crawl. Then she leaned in close and grabbed Aelana's wrist. Aelana felt the girl's fingernails digging into her skin, in the same spot Shadow's had been what now felt like months ago.

As blood started to well up beneath the girl's nails, she uttered something under her breath, too quiet for Aelana to hear. Then she was gone.

But so was the classroom.

5

Aelana watched as the classroom morphed into a scene of fighting around her. Of war. She could hear screaming and yelling and even cursing all around her, closing in. It took her a moment to realise that she was holding a sword in her hands. Her hands that had claws instead of nails. Everything was clearer too. She could see better and smell better. She could smell the scent of blood hanging in the air all around, and it made her sick to her stomach.

"Aelana!" The voice came from behind her. A male voice she didn't recognise. "Watch out!"

She spun around just in time to see the axe swinging for her head, and then a black-haired man jumped in front of it to save her. He let out the sound of a wounded animal as it hit him and dropped to the ground. She dropped to her knees, leaning over him.

There was already blood all over him, pouring from the wound that was a slash all the way down his chest and stomach. He looked paler with every breath.

"Kendall, Kendall, you're going to be okay." It was her voice speaking, but she hadn't even opened her mouth.

"Aelana," he said. "Sis, I'm not going to make it, and you know it. Mourn for me later; go fight now."

Every word from his mouth seemed painful, and he winced with every syllable, each sound coming with more air than the last as he struggled.

"But …"

"And tell Aurum I'm sorry for never telling her I loved her." His words died off at the end, but Aelana still heard them clear as day; she couldn't believe what she was hearing from this person she did not know.

Her body nodded its head and stood up again, but she wasn't the one moving it. As she moved through the crowd, ducking and dodging, her thoughts were trapped on one word: Sis.

Did that mean she had a brother? Did she have a brother she didn't even know existed? Had she just watched her unknown brother die?

Kendall. That was his name.

She had a brother called Kendall that she had just watched die, that she had never even known. Maybe she had misheard him. She really hoped she had.

But what was this she was seeing? The future? Had he already died, but she hadn't been there? Surely, she was hallucinating. She didn't have a brother called Kendall.

Her body turned around to look back at him, lying on the ground, covered in blood. The tears in her eyes blurred her vision. She blinked them away, and when they were gone, she was looking back at a classroom full of shocked faces and watching a black boot disappear out the door.

* * *

As if by magic, which wasn't unbelievable, everything around Ash began fading away, forming something new. When it was done, she was no longer looking at a boring old classroom but up at the Eiffel Tower. The Eiffel Tower, plagued by people fighting, wearing armour, and holding weapons. They were all around her, and at first, she felt out of place. But looking down at herself, she found she had her own armour on and a delicately twisted dagger in each hand.

Something about being here, in amongst it all, felt right; it felt good. Ash wanted to fight and be a part of it all. She wanted to use her magic for something other than just practicing with Shadow.

It all felt great, until she saw a flash of pink hair through the crowds. *No. What's Sakura doing here?*

She pushed her way through the fighting people, moving, but not really moving. She finally found her way to Sakura, her best friend. Just in time to see her be swamped by more people than she could possibly handle.

Ash tried to lunge forward and help her but was pulled back by someone. She turned around, swinging for her attacker, knocking them to the ground. It was then that she noticed who it was that had grabbed her.

Riko stared up at her, looked dazed for a moment, and then stood up again quickly before he could get trampled. His eyes shone an icier blue than she had ever seen, and his black hair was cut back off his forehead for once.

"Have you seen Chloe?" he asked.

"N-no," she stuttered, seeing the worry in his eyes.

"Okay." He turned around and pushed his way back, going on with his search.

Ash turned back around herself, intending to go back to her mission of saving Sakura. But with one glance, she realised she was too late.

Sakura was alone now. She was lying on the ground, her armour broken and partly torn off. Her eyes were gazing up at the sky, the life having already left them.

Ash screamed as she looked down at her friend. But her scream was cut off as the dead, lifeless Sakura before her swirled and shifted into real, alive Sakura, looking into Ash's eyes with more worry than she had ever seen.

Skylar watched it all happen. It didn't take her long to realise that whatever she was seeing was some kind of vision induced by the brown-haired girl. The brown-haired Witch. Shadow had taught her enough for her to know, as soon as those words slipped out of the girl's mouth, that she was a Witch. And that meant what she was seeing right now might not actually happen. Hopefully.

Skylar was standing in an office building, behind a desk, although this wasn't an ordinary office anymore. There was obviously some kind of fight going on. But there was a pause in it.

Not for long, though.

A black-haired woman jumped up from behind one of the desks and went sprinting for the window. She wore an elaborate outfit that reminded Skylar of armour from MMORPGs, with intricate patterns and coloured fabrics, though hers wasn't quite as revealing.

She waved her arms frantically over her head when she reached the window and yelled something that Skylar couldn't make out.

The sound of a gun firing broke through the haze that she seemed to be trapped in, and she could suddenly hear properly. Helicopter rotors spinning, quiet shuffling from other people in the room, distant shouts from somewhere outside.

The single bullet that had been fired hit the woman in the spine; she seemed too shocked to scream or make any sound. She swayed on her feet for a moment, and when it looked like she would collapse, the floor broke out from underneath her, and she fell from sight.

"Lithium!" The name was screamed by two people, who went running to the hole the woman had fallen through. One of them was Mercury. The other was a large, broad-shouldered man with flame-red hair. He wore a long coat that flapped in a breeze Skylar could not feel.

Before they could reach the hole in the floor, another gun fired, and the bullet went whizzing over Mercury's head. She ducked so fast she almost tripped over, and that was all Skylar saw as the scene swirled away, the office desks transforming into that of her classroom.

Jade had been terrified when she saw the blonde woman from before enter her classroom, but there hadn't been much time for terror as the girl with the shining eyes had approached, and now she was … here. In a vision, of some sort.

She recognised where she was but didn't really understand. People passed around as if she wasn't even there, and the sound she heard was like muted background noise. The sun was shining down brightly, although there were some clouds in the sky.

At first, it seemed to be a completely normal day like any other, and she didn't understand why this was what she was seeing. But then she turned around and saw a building all the way down the other end of the street, on the beachfront, completely engulfed in flames. Sirens cut through the muted sound she was hearing, but they weren't as close as she thought.

She turned back around, eyes darting back and forth in search of someone who could help, but her gaze stopped dead on the two girls fighting. So that must have been what she was supposed to be seeing.

They were obviously out of place, dressed for fighting, not for a day at the beach. She recognised neither of them. One had short blonde hair, barely past her jaw, and the other had dark red hair, tied up in a high ponytail. She also had claws and sharp, cat-like teeth. The blonde girl had many weapons on her but wasn't using any of them in her fight against the cat girl.

Somehow, nobody noticed them; too captivated by the burning building. Jade watched the people flocking to watch the fire. They were absolutely mesmerised by it.

Jade glanced all around her, watching the people captivated by the flames, and turned back around to the fighting pair, just in time to see the cat girl win. She grabbed one of the blonde's knives from her belt and thrust it into her with speed Jade had never seen before. She then dropped the weapon, sprang away from her opponent, and ran off into the crowd, moving with purpose, as if she had somewhere to be, like the blonde had only been a distraction from her original task here.

Then the crowd of people and flames shooting high into the sky faded away, just as Jade could finally hear the fire truck approaching. But it was gone, the flames and the people, and Jade found herself staring blankly at the wall where the brown-haired Witch had left her.

<hr />

Phoenix, unbeknownst to her, was standing right next to where Jade had been. Phoenix was seeing something different, though.

The street around her was filled with people, all milling about, watching the building alit with flames slowly burn to the ground. She could hear sirens, although they sounded far off in the distance, as though she was caught in some weird, muted haze, like she had cotton balls in her ears.

She watched the people turn to look up at the rooftop of one of the buildings lining the … oh, what was it called? The Corso. That was it. Yes, the people were looking at the rooftop of one shop, and she followed their gaze.

Two women stood on the roof, one with blonde hair and one with black.

The black-haired woman started to speak, and the people became captivated by her rather than the fire. It looked as if she was doing some kind of speech, though Phoenix couldn't make out a single word, just this faint buzzing in her ears.

Then Mercury stood up from a rooftop across from the other two.

She spoke, her voice joining the buzz, glaring at the two women across from her.

For a moment, Phoenix thought that maybe whatever this was she was seeing had become frozen, like a video that needed buffering. There was absolute silence. Then a police officer stepped out of the crowd, yelling up at the two women and directing a few of his words at Mercury. His brow was creased in a mixture of anger and confusion.

And then he burst into flames.

Phoenix almost screamed, but she was too shocked to make a sound. Or maybe she had, and it was just caught up in the sound haze.

She took a few steps back. Her eyes were fixed on the poor man, burning to death, barely noticing Mercury's horrified face or how the blonde woman smiled in delight.

When Shadow had told her she was a fairy possessing fire magic, it had sounded like fun; it had sounding exciting. But watching that man burn to a crisp made her scared of what she might one day be capable of. She never wanted to be able to do that. She never even wanted to think of doing that, just to see if she could. She would never.

As the man dropped to the ground, still burning, he started to disappear, fading away. Phoenix was back in her classroom, no burning policeman anywhere in sight. She sat there, trembling, after that.

6

The lockdown hadn't ended, even after the final bell rang. Still, they sat inside their classrooms, squeezed together in tight spaces. They sat there for another half an hour, until someone decided it was safe to leave, and the deputy came to tell them they could go.

Aelana walked home, her mind a twisted mess. The beginnings of spring twisted around her, leaves blowing past, hair brushed her face. She was in another world, immune to the blossom of colours, the chill still hanging in the air. It didn't matter to her that she left her jacket at school. She was so glad it was the weekend, and as soon as she arrived home, she went straight to her room and just lay there on her bed, staring at the ceiling.

In such a small time, her life had changed so much, and yet not at all. She slept on the same bed every night, in the same room, in the same house she had grown up in. She had the same friends and went to the same school she always had. It was she who was different, not her life. At least, not yet.

It was hard to decide if knowing what she did now about what existed out there made her feel better or worse about herself and the world. At first, she had just enjoyed being special and having something that made her different from the people she was surrounded by, even if Phoenix and Skylar had to share it. But after today, her excitement at the prospect of what she could be and do had faded fast. Now she was confused, wondering if this is what she really wanted.

A brother she'd never heard of?

Princess of a place she'd never seen?

How was she supposed to do this? What did she know about being a princess? Nothing. Absolutely nothing. She didn't know anything about the people she was supposed to rule or what they would expect from her.

That night, just as she was beginning to fall asleep, there was a knock on her window, then she heard it slide open. She rolled over and saw Shadow sitting in her desk chair, wearing a silky floor-length blue skirt and a loose white singlet. An amulet with a thin chain and amber set in the centre sat around her neck.

"What do you want?" Aelana asked in a whisper, not wanting to wake her parents, and sat up.

"I heard about what happened at your school," Shadow said, not bothering to be quiet.

"You only heard about it?"

"I heard about it and decided it was time to tell you exactly why I wanted you."

"And that is?"

"I won't tell you right now, I'll tell you altogether. But we have to go. Get dressed quickly." Shadow stood up and walked to the window.

"Go where?" Aelana asked, finally waking up properly, staring at Shadow like she was crazy and wondering how on earth the woman was in her bedroom.

"To begin," Shadow said firmly, implying that she wasn't to be questioned anymore.

"Fine," Aelana muttered, getting out of bed as Shadow transformed into the little black cat and disappeared out the window.

She crossed her room and pulled a random shirt and pair of jeans out of her drawers, dressed, brushed her hair, and walked over to the window. Even being a cat, getting up to the second-storey window of Aelana's bedroom seemed an impossible task. But Shadow clearly had her ways.

Aelana opened her window fully and looked out. Shadow stood down on the grassy path that ran beside the house, looking up with a hint of impatience, her skirt blowing in a soft breeze.

"Hurry up," Shadow called. "Let's get moving."

"Okay, okay." Aelana stepped away from the window, and Shadow called her name. She peered back out at Shadow, who showed her annoyance by tapping her foot.

"What?" Aelana asked.

"You expect to use the front door?" Shadow asked. "Just jump."

"Jump? Are you insane?"

"Trust me, Aelana," she said. "You'll be fine. Just jump."

Aelana sighed but climbed onto the windowsill and swung her legs slowly over the side. She had never been scared of heights or of climbing things, but she was realistic about what would hurt her and what wouldn't. This would hurt her, unless Shadow had some trick up her non-existent sleeve.

"If I break my legs, I am never speaking to you again," she said and then, with a final quick glance down, pushed herself out her bedroom window.

A rush of adrenaline shot through her, and as her feet hit the grass, she bent low. A second later, she sprang back up and was amazed that she didn't feel any pain. Not a single bit. She was unhurt from a fall that should definitely not have ended that well.

"I said you'd be fine, didn't I?"

"Whatever," Aelana muttered, as Shadow started walking back around the house, leading her over to a nondescript black van parked a few houses away.

Shadow opened the back doors to reveal that Phoenix, Skylar, Jade, and Ash were already sitting in the van: not on seats, but on the floor. Jade was staring intently at her shoes, playing with her laces.

Seeing them now, Aelana was hit with the realisation that they all went to the same school together, albeit in different years. Ash would be graduating soon, she also thought. Then she realised that they would have been there for the lockdown. Had they been approached too? Had they seen things?

Aelana sat herself down with them. Shadow closed the doors, and then they were off, sliding around with every corner Shadow turned.

They finally stopped and were let out of the slightly cramped space; they had arrived at a warehouse. Aelana didn't immediately recognise the area. Shadow unlocked the door and led them inside.

Inside was quite dark, despite all the lights being on. The air felt moist and humid, and Aelana couldn't see into the corners, though she didn't really want to. She wouldn't be surprised at finding dead rats or mould along the walls. The floor was hard, polished concrete that didn't look so polished anymore, but was scratched and worn down after what must have been decades of use. And in the centre of the warehouse floor was this contraption. It was a chair that looked like it might have once been used as an electric chair. Wires sprouted from it everywhere, flopping on the floor and leading to an oval-shaped doorway set at the top of three black steps that seemed out of place, standing in the middle of the room.

Mercury was nowhere in sight, for once.

Shadow noticed them staring at the strange chair, wide-eyed, filled with both wonder and fear. At least, the chair filled Aelana with wonder and fear. Mostly fear. Something about the chair was ominous. Or maybe that was just the eerie feeling of the warehouse. But the chair felt like the source of it.

Shadow reached the contraption, stood in front of it, and faced them. "I am not a Witch," she said. "Therefore, I do not have the ability to send you into visions like a Witch can, without the use of some technology. This is that technology."

"Are you actually going to get around to telling us why we're here, or are we going to have to guess?" Ash asked.

"Patience, Ash," Shadow said. "You shall find out your purpose here right now." She stepped back beside the chair, laying an elegant hand gently on the backrest.

"I've told you all who you are, and your heads are full of thoughts about how special you must be. Of course, there's still so much for you to learn about yourselves, but that's not what this is about right now.

"You all saw Olivia and Raven, the two girls who came to your school in search of you five. Well, they work for a particularly powerful and influential Witch by the name of Marisa Raven. She has always been … a little troublesome to all of us on Lindreas, always opposed to our ways of life and the way of our world. Without seeing any other reason for her troublemaking, we guessed that she just liked to be a nuisance.

"But recent events have brought a new light on this, revealing that she has a plan in play. What her ultimate goal is, no one knows, but she is no longer playing the part of a troublesome child. Her actions have become rather serious."

Aelana was not exactly sure what to do with this information or why they needed to be brought here to hear it. And what was the chair for? That troubled her more than Marisa.

"She has taken something from each of you," she continued. "Important objects that have been in the royal families as far back as our history goes. They are symbols of each of your kingdoms, and without them, you cannot claim your place on the throne. But with them, Marisa could bring ruin to your kingdoms, and all of us, unless we all support each other."

Aelana noticed that as she was saying this, Shadow wrapped her free hand around the amulet hanging from her neck, subconsciously.

"These objects had been hidden away by your parents, in hopes that when you came of age, you would track them down or have someone tell you where they were, before Marisa could find them. But she is a most resilient person and far smarter than we anticipated.

"Now she has hidden them herself, probably in hopes you will never get them back. But I am far smarter than Marisa thought, and I have devised a way of retrieving them for you, which is why we are here and what this machine is for."

Shadow took a few steps so she was standing on the other side of the chair. "Marisa has hidden the objects in your dreams, those dreams you had before waking in the hospital. Yes, I know about them.

"Aelana will sit in the chair, and the rest of you shall step through the portal over there to find yourselves in her dream. You will find the object, a quill, and return with it."

Aelana felt every eye on her as Shadow said her name. She didn't look at them, fighting down the growing fear inside her over that stupid chair. Shadow wasn't worried about it, so she had no reason to be, either.

"How does it work?" she asked, forcing confidence into her voice.

"Magic," Shadow replied, simply.

"If we have to find Aelana's object in her dream, how do we know where to look and what to look for?" Jade asked, seriously.

"You will be taken on the same path as Aelana as you travel through the dream world. Certain elements may change, but you will undoubtedly be brought to what you are there to find. There should really be no trouble with it."

Aelana thought back to her dream and realised she needed to warn them. "There were these …"

"We better get started." Shadow cut her off quickly, not letting the words be heard. "Come, Aelana, sit down. You four, ready yourselves over there."

Aelana reluctantly walked over to the chair. It was wooden and old, close to rotting. When she sat down, something poked into her back. There were straps on the arms and legs, but, thankfully, Shadow didn't touch them. However, she did move the bowl-like thing hanging from the top onto Aelana's head. It was cold and felt weird, and she didn't like it one bit, but didn't say anything, just let Shadow do what she was doing.

No reason to be worried. It'll all be fine. You can trust Shadow, whatever April said. She wouldn't totally endanger your life, right?

There was some kind of switch on top that Shadow flicked, the sound reverberating through the helmet on Aelana's head. When she did, the portal came to life. It started to glow a very faint blue, and an image slowly came into view through the glow.

"Off you go," Shadow said. "Just remember that if you get hurt in the dream world, you will be injured on returning here. So, do be careful, not just for me, but for yourselves."

Aelana watched the image as it came into focus until there was a sharp pain in her head and she had to look away. The last thing she saw before she turned her head was Ash as she disappeared through, the hint of an image in blue beneath her white shirt. A tattoo of some kind.

"Off you go," Shadow said, a tiny smile on her lips. "Just remember that if you get hurt in the dream world, you shall be injured on returning here. So, do be careful, not just for me, but for yourselves." The smile cancelled out any sentiment she was supposedly implying with her words.

Not exactly reassuring, but okay.

Ash looked back to the glowing portal, watching as the mass of dark colours, especially greens, came into focus in the form of grass and trees.

Jade was the first to walk up the steps and face the portal. She was the youngest, yet the bravest, it seemed. She stepped through and disappeared, mixing into the mess of colours on the other side.

Ash followed behind her, walking up the small set of stairs and looking at the portal, standing as close as was possible without going through. Then she did step through, and a tingling sensation ran down her body. On the other side, it became clear to Ash where they were. Or, at least, where Aelana's dream took place.

7

They were standing in a park, just off the path, beneath one of the largest trees around. It was a place very familiar to Ash, as it was somewhere she went with her friends almost every day after school. They would study and do homework, but mostly just play games and procrastinate.

Jade obviously knew the place too, nodding her head in recognition.

Phoenix came through the portal, materialising out of thin air, with Skylar right behind her. Skylar stumbled and ran into the back of her sister, using her then to steady herself.

"I don't see … well, anything interesting," Phoenix said immediately. "Definitely no path."

"I don't think Shadow meant a literal path," said Skylar. "I think she meant more like we'll walk and somehow end up where Aelana did. Like magic." A smile, and with that she was off, leaving Ash, Jade, and Phoenix to follow her, which they did.

Quickly, Ash noticed how more and more trees were sprouting up around them. They couldn't have gone more than twenty metres, and they were almost in a forest; definitely more trees than she had seen before.

The trees towered over them, and they grew closer and closer with every step, until the sun was almost blocked out by the branches spreading over their heads.

"Okay, how is this possible?" Phoenix asked.

Jade surveyed their surroundings, coming to a halt, but didn't supply an answer to the question.

"It must just be how it works," Skylar suggested. "We are in a dream, aren't we?"

"Can we leave the semantics until later?" Ash interrupted. "Let's just get this over with first, and then you can contemplate it all you want."

She pushed forwards and had only gone a few metres when she saw a light shining through the dense woods.

"That's it," Skylar said breathlessly from right beside her and Ash almost jumped out of her skin. Jesus, how had Skylar crept up on her like that? This place was creepy, and she was ready to get out.

Ash forged on, now aware of her companions right behind her. Wow, it was farther away than it seemed. The light grew brighter and brighter, until they reached the edge of a clearing. Ash peeked through, and the first thing she saw was a stone altar, in the exact centre of the clearing. The glowing object was on top of the altar. A feather. The quill.

Lauren Trickey

The clearing should have been dark, but the light from the quill was so bright, it lit up the space as if the sun was directly overheard.

It was then that Ash noticed the people in the clearing. Or maybe not people, exactly. Their skin was pale, and their eyes were sunken but gleaming. They were the same as that maid, and could have been zombies, if not for their co-ordinated movements. No, they were too animated for zombies. And if these ones were like the maid, then they could speak.

There were at least seven of them, guarding the clearing, with one patrolling around and coming awfully close …

Ash pulled her head back to find Jade, Phoenix, and Skylar waiting expectantly.

"Well?" Jade asked, quietly.

"People," Ash whispered, quickly, then decided to add, "Zombie-looking people. But … they aren't zombies. They're more human than zombies."

They gave her puzzled looks.

"See for yourselves," Ash said. "But be careful."

Mercury sat, quite comfortably, on the roof of the warehouse. She had never seen Shadow come here before, had never been asked by her to come here, and it was pure luck that she had been able to follow her tonight.

She'd been watching Phoenix and Skylar's house because apparently, Marisa was in the area somewhere, when Shadow had come to collect them: her lucky day.

So far, she was pretty sure that Shadow hadn't noticed her. In human form, her hearing and sight were diminished – and Mercury was quite confident in her skills – so she should have been unnoticed. That was, until her phone started ringing.

Her favourite song barked into the quiet night air, speaking words in another language, and she rushed to yank the stupid device out of her pocket and shut it off. That's what happened when she was overly confident. Stupid hunk of metal.

"Hello, Mercury," Shadow called up. "I thought I heard you up there. Always forget to put your phone on silent, don't you?"

Of course, it had been her. Of course. Mercury was really going to have to set a different ringtone for her.

"I told you to be careful," Ash said, glaring at her companions. Her stupid companions.

"Define careful," Phoenix said, trying to be funny.

"It means not getting us captured by the creepy zombie-people, who are probably going to kill us now," Ash snapped.

"So not what we did, then," Phoenix replied, still keeping up the act.

"Shut up, would you?" Jade said, just as annoyed as Ash. Not that that was possible right now.

The ropes around her wrists hurt, tied up far too tight for comfort. Not that being tied up with ropes was supposed to be comfortable, anyway. Not when it was the step before your impending doom, as Ash was sure it was to be. At least she could add not smelling like rotting flesh to the list of why those things weren't regular zombies.

The four of them sat in silence, watching the clearing around them, tied up against the altar. The zombie-people had gone off somewhere after having captured them, – all thanks to Phoenix – leaving just one to watch over them while they went off to do whatever they were doing. And who knew what that was. Maybe they had a leader they were bringing back. Maybe that's how they were going to meet their end: at the hands of the Master Zombie.

The zombie-person who had been left behind was the worst possible choice, unless the rest of them were even more useless than him.

Rather than standing still or sitting and watching them, as would have been expected, he wandered the clearing, only glancing at them every couple of minutes. He didn't even turn when they talked or tell them to be quiet, like Ash had been expecting from all the movies she had seen. He didn't open his mouth once, at least not to them. No, he muttered to himself, watching his feet or looking up at the swaying branches. He was a very distracted zombie.

"I think I can get us out," Phoenix whispered, checking if he was turned to them. He wasn't. He was far too enamoured with a colourful bird squawking in a treetop.

"How?" Skylar asked, speaking for the first time since they had been tied up.

"Magic," Phoenix said.

"Don't be all cryptic and annoying like Shadow and have that as your only answer," Jade said, flashing a look that said just how truly annoyed she was.

"I mean, I think I can burn through the ropes," Phoenix replied. "But I'm really sorry if I burn you all as well. I'll really try not to."

"Reassuring," Ash muttered.

"Okay, okay, you can do this," Phoenix uttered softly to herself.

Orange light flashed from behind Phoenix, bright enough to make the guard-zombie turn. Phoenix smiled at him as the light faded to a soft glow. The bird chirped again, and Mr Guard-Zombie couldn't have cared less what they were doing, turning his attention back to its bright body.

Ash turned her head and could just see the tiny fire that Phoenix had created. Its movement was slow and controlled, but it did its job quickly. Phoenix's bindings fell away. It then moved on to Jade and Skylar on either side of her. Skylar was freed first, and Jade a second after her, leaving just Ash.

The small flame worked its way along the ropes around Ash's wrists behind her back until they slipped right off. She could feel the heat against her skin, yet she ended up with no burns; it wasn't painful in the slightest.

A small haze of smoke drifted upwards around them, and the smell of burning drifted with it. Guard-zombie, however, did not notice. He had found a new creature to admire.

Jade stood. Slowly straightening. Then she twisted and leant back, carefully picking the quill from the surface of the stone altar.

Guard-zombie still didn't notice.

Ash stood too, along with Phoenix and Skylar. When he didn't notice them, they stepped around the altar warily, eyes on him, until they were on the other side and sprint into the trees.

"That was crazy," Skylar said when they stopped what they thought was a decent distance away.

"Never. Again," Ash said, slightly out of breath.

"We got it, didn't we?" Jade asked, waving the delicate feather around.

"Yeah, yeah, just be careful with it," Ash replied.

"So, how do we get back now?" Phoenix asked. "Do we have to go back the way we came from? Because I do not remember."

Jade shrugged. "I guess we'll find out soon enough."

It was then that footsteps could be heard. Loud, pounding footsteps. Not walking but running. Not one pair, but many. Coming closer with every footfall.

The four looked at each other; no words needed to be exchanged for them to realise who those steps belonged to and start running themselves.

Of all the places to be chased, it had to be in magical woodland, where the threat of falling or smacking your head on something was greatly increased. Ash cursed as yet another branch snagged her shirt, and she disentangled herself as quickly as possible, trying to keep up with the others. It seemed they weren't having as much trouble as she was.

Eventually, the branches and roots all over the ground started to clear. The trees began to thin, more and more space between them showing, making it easier to run without worrying about falling.

"I can see it!" Skylar cried. "I can see the portal!" She was running out in front, metres ahead of the rest, but didn't even sound out of breath.

A spear whizzed over their heads, planting itself into the ground in front of Skylar, but she dodged around it, and now Ash could see it too: the portal, bright and shining, just beyond where the trees cleared.

Out of the forest and sprinting across open ground. Or as close to sprinting as Ash could get. She had never felt so unfit in her life.

Skylar, of course, reached it first and didn't need to be told to charge through it. Jade was after her, then Phoenix, again leaving just Ash to be saved. She could feel how close the zombie-people were behind her and threw herself through. The portal closed, and the pounding footsteps were gone, leaving a ringing in her ears. How close had she been to not making it?

There was less of a tingling sensation from the portal this time, or she just didn't feel it from how shaken she felt. She landed in a heap on the other side, half rolling down the three short steps. Voices echoed around her, and she looked up to see Aelana still snuggly in the death-chair, and Shadow arguing with Mercury.

After climbing down from her perch on the roof, Mercury now strolled through the doors of the warehouse, trying to appear as though what Shadow had been doing didn't bother her in the slightest. It did, and sadly, Mercury had never been good at hiding her anger.

"Hey, Shadow," she said, trying to sound as bored as possible. At least she wasn't too shabby an actor.

"Mercury, you look simply dashing in that outfit. How come I never see you in it?" Shadow asked with the smallest of smiles.

Mercury hid her smile. It was a lovely outfit. Electric blue pants and jacket, paired with black boots. . Both with deep black accents over the pockets, and two thin black stripes down each side. It felt so nice to wear, and she did look amazing in it.

"Because you never ask me to do anything that requires wearing this," she said.

"What a lovely night, wouldn't you agree?" Shadow asked, changing the subject.

"Seems important," Mercury replied with a light shrug. "What are you doing?"

"Come now, we both know that you know exactly what has been going on down here in my humble warehouse, Mercury."

"How come I wasn't invited to the little party, then?" Mercury asked, walking slowly across the warehouse.

"You simply weren't needed."

She almost laughed but held it in. "Now there's a first."

Shadow was following intently with her eyes, the first signs of annoyance showing on her face. That was enough to make Mercury happy. Never had she thought she could annoy Shadow, although it probably wasn't the best thing to be doing.

"But seriously," Mercury went on. "Why?"

"You'll stop asking questions if you want to stay employed."

Oh yeah, sure. Employed. You employ me to do your dirty work, like killing people, or spying on them and then imprisoning them. Or maybe just hanging around and looking threatening because, let's face it, you're scared of pretty much everyone. But don't you already have someone to do that? Oh right, no, he would be noticed. Or was it that you already killed him? Besides, nobody would ever believe it was me. And you definitely didn't threaten to not help me in the future if I didn't do this all for you.

Despite wanting to say all this, she didn't. That was all for another time, and it wasn't the argument she wanted to start now because it wouldn't get her anywhere tonight.

"I think," Mercury said, "that I'll keep asking questions. Like, when were you going to tell me about this? Isn't this something I should know? Didn't you employ me to help, and protect you? What if Marisa found out and sent her cronies to stop you? But no, I wasn't needed. You could definitely fend them off by yourself." Her voice was simply dripping with sarcasm. "If you could handle them all by yourself, and I'm not needed here, then maybe you just don't need me at all. Have I become redundant?"

She would have continued on her little rant, but the portal began to glow, and then out popped Skylar. Then Jade, Phoenix, and finally Ash, who had a nice little tumble down the steps.

"That's enough, Mercury," Shadow snapped, her anger finally showing in her voice.

"It's only enough when you want it to be," Mercury replied coldly, heading quickly for the door. She exited into the dark night and looked back once, to see Shadow flustered, and Jade with the quill in hand.

Lauren Trickey

8

Although it clearly hadn't been much time since they had gone through the portal, Ash couldn't help but check her phone for the time. The screen was bright, shining the time and date at her: 3 a.m. 14 September 2013.

"What the hell were those things?" Jade asked Shadow, not exactly doing a great job of hiding her annoyance.

Ash couldn't really blame her, though. Shadow had to have known about the zombie-people, or whatever they were.

"So, there were Shadow Lurkers," Shadow replied calmly, as if contemplating it.

"Why didn't you tell us?" Jade asked, clearly trying not to shout.

"It was a test," said Shadow.

"Of what?" Phoenix asked. "Of how much you can freak us out?"

"Of how you would react to the situation and how you would deal with it."

"Because I just love being tested on stupid things like that," Ash muttered, sitting on the arm of the chair, forgetting that Aelana was still seated in it.

"Why on earth would you do that, though?" Jade went on.

"You get tested in school on what you learn there," Shadow said. "I test your magic. On what I teach you. I wanted to see if you would use magic in surprising or dangerous situations. If you think and remember."

"That's no excuse!"

"Stop it! Both of you," Skylar interrupted, not exactly yelling, but speaking louder than Ash had ever heard her. "I don't care if you're angry,

Jade, and I don't care about Shadow trying to justify herself. I just want to go home."

Shadow complied.

Aelana was removed from the death-chair, dazed and confused, but very much alive and unharmed.

"How did it go?" she asked as Shadow led the way to her van.

Jade handed her the quill, and Aelana took it, becoming fixated with it. "This is it?" Jade nodded, but Aelana hadn't taken her eyes off the object. "Wow."

After that, it was the weekend, and Ash and her friends were at the park, the one in Aelana's dream (this time, without the possibility of it turning into a forest or being captured by Shadow Lurkers).

Sitting in a circle in the grass, they really should have been studying, what with the Higher School Certificate (HSC) fast approaching, but instead, they were playing a game that they played maybe a little too much: Truth or Dare. It was surprising that they hadn't run out of questions to ask or dares to do yet.

"Chris, truth or dare?" Riko said, starting off, ice blue eyes gleaming with intent.

"Dare," Chris decided.

"Okay," Riko said, thinking. "I dare you … to go up to a random person in the park, sniff their hair, then run away and come back."

"Oh, man, are you serious?" Chris asked, standing up.

"You chose dare," Riko replied, giving a helpless shrug.

He couldn't argue with that. So Chris, looking very unhappy, started walking off, and they stood to watch him from afar. He did the dare, just as Riko had instructed him to, then dashed off like there was a monster after him.

"I can't believe you made me do that," he said, sitting back down. "Anyway … Sakura, truth or dare?"

"Truth."

"Um … Who's the best?"

"Lame," Riko complained.

"Oh, that's a hard one," Sakura said, pretending to be thinking (and that she hadn't heard Riko's comment). "You."

Ash, Tiger Rose, Chloe, and Riko all groaned in unison, as was necessary for any display of affection from the two.

"Oh, shut up!" Sakura giggled. "So, Riko, truth or dare?"

"Dare!"

"See how long you can hang upside down from that tree."

Riko turned. "That one?" he asked, pointing to the closest tree.

"Yep, go on."

So he did.

Riko stood up, walked over to the tree, and spent about five minutes trying to decide the best place to hang from and how to get there. When he finally did, he was upside down for no more than thirty seconds.

"Wimp," Chloe whispered, smiling.

"Hey!"

He sat down again and looked around the circle, carefully choosing his next target. "Ash, truth or dare?"

"Truth," Ash said, as she always did. She wasn't one for stupid dares; she preferred spilling a little bit of truth at their equally stupid questions.

"Who do you like?" Riko asked.

"No one," she said firmly, keeping her face straight.

"You totally like someone. I can tell," Tiger Rose said, calling her out on her lie.

"I'm telling you, I don't like anyone."

"Oh sure. I totally believe you," Chloe said sarcastically.

"Spit it out," Chris urged.

"No. You're wrong."

"But it's so obvious that you do," Sakura said. "I can tell when you're lying. You *are* my best friend."

"Come on," Riko said. "It's called truth for a reason."

"Fine, if you're all so sure, why don't you just use your magical powers to read my mind?" she snapped. And immediately felt bad about it.

They all stared at her for a long moment, taken aback. But then Sakura snapped out of her daze, and her eyes softened.

"How long have you known?" she asked. "About magic?"

"I found out in the hospital," Ash told them. "The person who told me said that Chloe had saved me, and that you all had magic."

None of them spoke for a long moment, and Ash sensed that they might have known more than they were letting on.

"I know about magic now. You don't have to keep anything from me anymore."

"Don't worry; we won't," Riko said, and she smiled gratefully.

"Were you serious about the mind reading thing?" Chloe asked warily.

"I mean, I don't know if any of you guys can, but … maybe," she said.

"Chris, Riko and I can," Chloe replied. She looked Ash in the eye, tilted her head, and suddenly her expression darkened, and she was getting to her feet, performing a 180 from her previous mood only a few seconds ago.

She glared at Ash as she stood. "Don't you dare. I swear, Ash, if you pull anything! Ugh."

"What?" Tiger Rose asked.

"She likes Riko!" Chloe yelled as she ran off.

Chris, Sakura, and Tiger Rose turned to look at the two of them. And then Ash stood up without saying anything and walked away too. It didn't seem like the smartest thing to do, but she didn't want to hang around and have to talk them. She didn't want to be around them, looking at her like that. They called after her, but she didn't look back.

God, why had she even suggested the mind-reading thing? That was such a stupid idea. She'd been annoyed at all of them, though. They knew she was always truthful, so why couldn't they have seen that if she wasn't telling them the truth, there must have been a reason for it. Why did they have to push her?

And Chloe had *completely* overreacted.

Ash knew how they felt about each other. They all knew. Except for Chloe and Riko, it seemed. They were oblivious to the other's feelings and with how obvious they themselves were being.

She slumped down against a tree, looking up into the branches.

Stupid, stupid, stupid.

Despite it all, though, there was a voice in the back of her head that, for some reason, was telling her this wasn't at all stupid, and its argument was sounding pretty good.

Lauren Trickey

Chloe sat down on a park bench, staring at the grass around her feet.

God, just when she was beginning to think that Riko actually liked her and something might happen, Ash had to find out she was a Siren and would probably now ruin her chances with him.

Sure, Ash was all special, but Chloe already hated her with magic and was starting to wish she never needed to find out.

And Ash was special. Even worse.

Just typical. Of course, she wasn't going to get to be with Riko after all this time. Of course.

What if they were soulmates? Couldn't Chloe at least have a chance with Riko to find out whether they were meant to be or not? But no. Ash knew about magic now, so that was never going to happen. Because Ash was just so … Ash. She didn't even need magic to make people fall in love with her. Now she just had extra strength to her influence and charm. And Chloe just knew Riko would fall for it.

"Chloe? Chloe?" Riko's voice snapped her out of her thoughts, and she looked up.

"What do you want?" she asked.

"I just wanted to see if you were alright," he said slowly. "You seemed kind of … upset about the Ash thing."

"Oh, it's really nothing," she said, knowing she sounded unconvincing.

"Are you sure?" he asked.

"I'm fine."

He didn't move for a moment, standing by the bench, as if he was unsure what to do.

He couldn't really be that oblivious, could he? Well, if he didn't want to say what they were clearly both thinking, then fine; Ash could have him.

"I'm fine," she repeated, not looking at him. "I'd just like to be left alone."

"Alright …" She heard him turn and then his retreating footsteps across the grass.

Riko left Chloe where she was, sitting on the bench, and went off to find Ash.

He should've said something to her then. But the words wouldn't come. And he still wanted to check on Ash. He wanted to tell her that he didn't feel the same about her before he told Chloe how he felt about her. Maybe confessing the first would make the second easier. He was hoping. He also wasn't going to push Chloe if she wanted to be alone.

Ash had to be around here somewhere. This was where she had gone, wasn't it?

'Go away, Riko,' a voice inside his head said.

'Ash?' he called out.

'I said, go away!'

'We need to talk for a moment.'

'Talk later.'

'No, Ash. Talk now.'

If she wanted to go with telepathy, he could play her game.

'Just leave me alone.'

'We need to talk.'

'Fine! Let's talk!' As the words entered his head, she appeared in front of him.

Riko jumped back, stunned. Ash with the ability to actually use her magic was a little bit terrifying. It would definitely take some getting used to.

"What are we talking about, then?" she asked, face as calm as always.

He took a deep breath and looked down at his feet, then back up at her.

"Look, you're a great friend, but I don't feel the same way about you that you feel about me. I don't like you in that way. I only see you as a friend." He said it as quickly as possible, trying to get the words out before he thought about it and messed up, before he had a chance to stumble and stop. It was out there now, and although he felt kind of bad about having to say it, it needed to be said. He was glad.

"Are you sure about that, Riko?" a voice in the back of his mind asked.

No, he wasn't sure, now that the voice mentioned it.

"I was expecting that," Ash whispered. "Look, I never expected you to like me. Chloe's liked you for ages, and I wasn't going to get in the way of that when you so obviously like her too."

"Really?" He was obvious? That obvious? But then again, nothing ever made it past Ash. She did notice everything.

"I think now might be a good time to make a decision. Simply stay or leave."

"But Chloe told me to leave her alone."

"It doesn't matter where you go if you leave, you just don't stay."

"But you're still my friend, Ash. I still want to be here for you."

"Tough."

Riko looked around. This was simple. He would leave and go back to Chris, Sakura, and Tiger Rose. That way, he'd made his decision. He'd choose Chloe. Even if Chloe didn't know it yet.

"So?"

But there was that voice in the back of his head, telling him he shouldn't leave, he should choose Ash instead.

"Just give her a chance," it said.

"Kiss her! Kiss her! Kiss her!" it screamed at him.

There was a slight, almost unnoticeable smile on Ash's lips. Riko, being oblivious like he was, didn't take it into account.

He couldn't fight it. The voice in his head was somehow stronger than his own reasoning. Wasn't it his own reasoning though? No, that voice was different to how he sounded in his head. But where else could it come from? It didn't sound like Ash, either.

Then, without really meaning to, Riko leant forward and kissed her.

There was this kind of nagging in the back of Ash's mind, giving her a sense of guilt about causing Riko such inner turmoil when he was so sure of his choice. But there was a much stronger feeling flooding her: using magic was fun. That was the first time she'd used her Siren influence on anyone, and wow, it was cool.

He stared at her with this horrified look, and she just smiled back. Then he backed away, turned, and left in an awkward half-jog, half-run.

Ash had no intention of continuing to mess with him like that. She wasn't a monster, she wasn't going to cause a divide within her friends, she just wanted to finally try out these new powers she had.

She felt like she had accomplished something.

The next day, Chloe didn't speak to Ash.

Or the next day.

Or the next day.

Or the next day.

Ash didn't know what to feel about it.

So she acted like it didn't worry her, like it wasn't happening. This had never happened amongst their friends before, so she wasn't sure how she should react or what she should do.

That was when Chloe finally spoke to her.

"Are you even taking this seriously?" Chloe asked as they stood at their lockers.

Ash looked at her but didn't open her mouth.

"I don't even know what to think of you anymore, Ash," Chloe continued, looking away. "Magic has changed you."

"What can I say," Ash said. "I don't disagree at all."

There was silence.

"Thank you for saving me, by the way."

Chloe looked up sharply at her.

"It takes you that long to say it?"

"I said it, didn't I?"

Chloe didn't speak.

"Look, Chloe, I'm sorry for getting to you like that," Ash said. "I thought you'd trust me."

Chloe still didn't speak.

She was silent for so long that Ash almost walked off and left her.

"You're right, Ash; you've always been a good friend. I'm sorry for not trusting you."

9

Ash was beginning to find her lessons with Shadow boring and useless. Every time, as Mercury stood by the wall, Shadow blabbered on, trying to teach a new power that Ash could do in about five seconds. She wouldn't be surprised if she could teach herself magic.

She could teleport, albeit only small distances at the moment. Telepathy was easy. And she was getting better and better at summoning different types of weapons. The only thing she had yet to do was become a mermaid in water. But she doubted that would be hard, when everything else was so easy.

Ash was about to voice her complaints, but Shadow was quick to cut her off before she could even open her mouth.

"Since you're so able with magic," she said, "I think it's time you learnt something new."

Shadow glanced at Mercury, who pushed off from the wall. She looked back at Ash with the tiniest of smiles.

"Time to fight. It will help you greatly if you are to encounter more Shadow Lurkers."

Mercury slowly walked across the hall to Ash, who wasn't sure what was going to happen. Her footsteps were even and her face almost blank, half-hidden behind her fringe and waves of hair. Ash thought she caught the faintest of smiles on the other girl's lips.

When Mercury reached her, they stood facing each other for a few long seconds; Ash had no idea what to expect. At "fight," she had imagined fists flying at her and her having no idea how to defend herself. But Mercury was calm, that faint smile playing across the corners of her mouth. She was also smaller than Ash, shorter by about half a head.

It was then that Mercury dropped; Ash's legs were swept away from underneath her, and Mercury stood again, suddenly towering over her as she lay on her back on the wooden floor. Mercury lightly placed a sandaled foot on her chest and looked at Shadow, that faint smile disappearing instantly.

"Alright, Mercury," Shadow said, and she stepped away.

Ash stood, slowly, feeling more than a little dazed. What exactly just happened? Well, she'd have to answer that question by learning herself. Finally, something that was a challenge.

If there was something Ash learnt in that lesson, it was that Mercury could do more than stand against a wall. A lot more. She was definitely going to have bruises tomorrow. Now Ash understood why Shadow kept her around when she had never seemed to do much.

She'd say she wasn't looking forward to it again, to the prospect of landing on her back a billion more times and all the bruises she was sure to acquire, but she would be lying. This was something she couldn't learn in one lesson, let alone five seconds, and especially not against Mercury. It was exciting.

All that excitement disappeared, though, when she came out to meet her friends at lunch. Chloe did not look happy, and Ash didn't have to guess why. Chloe approached her before she even reached the table.

"I can't believe you, Ash! You tell me I should trust you, but then I find out that you kissed Riko! What the hell?"

"Have you ever thought that maybe reading people's minds isn't really helping anything?" Ash asked. It wasn't hard to work out that was how she knew. Of course, Riko could have just told her. But knowing Riko, he wouldn't have.

Chloe stared at her. "You're the one who suggested it in the first place!"

Ash shrugged and started to walk past her. "I can see now that it was a bad idea."

Ash went to sit down, and Chloe started walking off.

"Where are you going?" Tiger called.

"Away," Chloe yelled. "I don't want to be around her!" With a pointed glance at Ash, she rounded the corner, into the building.

"Ash …" Sakura began.

"Save it," Ash said.

"It's not about that," Sakura said. "It's your eyes, Ash."

"What?"

"Your eyes are looking awfully … well, gold."

Ash looked at her and tilted her head.

"Yeah," Sakura said. "Definitely not green."

When she said that, Ash looked at Tiger Rose, Riko, and Chris, silently asking them for confirmation. They all nodded, fixated on her eyes, which had apparently changed colour.

She stood up and started walking to the bathroom. She had to see this for herself.

She pushed the door open, then the second one, and walked straight over to the large mirror on the wall. Sure enough, her eyes were mysteriously golden.

Ash didn't know what to make of it.

She stood in the bathroom, looking at herself in the mirror, looking at the crazy gold eyes that couldn't possibly be hers. After a moment, she noticed the black flecks speckling the gold. Such detailed colouring couldn't possibly be explained. It wasn't lost on her that the colour of her eyes matched the stars patterned around her wrists and ankles.

The tiny, golden stars were sprinkled around both her wrists and ankles and had been done barely a week after the dark turquoise treble clef that took up much of her back, plastered right in the centre.

She wasn't quite sure whether she liked her eyes or not. Of all colours, though, why gold?

As she exited the bathroom, she dug her sunglasses out of the bottom of her bag and put them on. She didn't exactly want people noticing and starting to wonder or question (or even freak out). Most would probably assume they were contacts, but then they'd question why she was wearing gold contacts.

She was definitely going to be asking Shadow about this.

"What beautiful eyes those are, Ash," Shadow said when she entered the hall the next day.

"Yeah, about that …"

"You're wondering why it happened," Shadow interrupted. "Don't worry; there is nothing wrong. With the use of magic, your real looks are revealing themselves."

"Real looks?"

"Magic is a very clever thing," Shadow began. "Never doubt that it can have a mind of its own.

"When you never used it, and weren't exposed to a magical environment when you were young, it disguised itself by changing simple things like your eye colour. Your eyes have always been gold; they just appeared green as a disguise to the human world."

"Huh."

"It is the same with Jade's green hair, and her ears; you must have noticed they are becoming pointed. Or Skylar's hair as well. It may just seem to be dyed now, but it will stay black. Her eyes will most likely change colour too. They are probably gold, like yours. And Aelana as well. Her eyes will change. Yellow for Werewolves."

Ash was both awed and confused. That was amazing. Gold eyes. She had gold eyes. Skylar would too. That was crazy cool. And she *had* noticed Jade's ears.

10

There were fifteen minutes left of the day.

Ash sat next to Sakura and Chris at the back of the classroom, doodling in her notebook and glancing up at the clock about every twenty seconds. She should definitely have been listening to what the teacher was saying. It was some last message about being prepared for the HSC, but Ash couldn't have cared less. She was just simply too bored to listen. And she'd heard it all before.

After the week had gone by, Chloe still wasn't talking to her; in fact, she completely ignored her. Ash hadn't been worrying about that, though. She had been focused on her lessons with Shadow and when it might be her turn to finally sit in the death-chair. She also hadn't seen Shadow for the last three days and was wondering about her next lesson, considering the holidays were only fifteen minutes away.

The clock ticked on.

Ten minutes.

"Hey, Ash, are you going to be busy after school?" Sakura asked.

"Am I ever busy?" Ash replied.

Sakura smiled. "Great. Because we're going shopping."

Ash tilted her head and smiled. "Since when is Sakura the one to ask me to go shopping?"

"Since I want to go shopping," Sakura said simply.

"Well, I definitely won't get in your way."

"Why, thank you, best friend."

"No problem, best friend."

Five minutes.

"Could it take any longer?" Chris groaned.

"It's not that much longer," Sakura said.

"I'm with Chris," Ash said. "Why can't school be over already?"

"Both of you, quit whining," Sakura said. "Such babies." She shook her head with disappointment.

"Goody two-shoes," Ash replied.

Sakura smiled kindly at her. "What was that?"

"Goody two-shoes," Ash repeated.

"I'm sorry, I can't hear you," Sakura said. "Your voice is this little whine in the background."

"Oh, is that because your giant shoes are blocking your ears?"

"Sorry?"

Ash nodded. "Alright, alright. I see."

The bell rang.

It was surprising sudden at that moment.

"Time to Let's go shopping," Sakura said, jumping up and grabbing Ash's hand.

------◆◆◆------

Mercury couldn't wait for the end of the day.

The last three days had been some of the most peaceful she had experienced in ages, and she was looking forward to the holidays, bringing plenty more. Although that wouldn't necessarily happen.

"Fifteen more minutes," she said aloud, after glancing at her watch.

"Do you always have to do that?" Mel asked, giving her an annoyed glare.

"You know I do," she replied.

Mel sighed, an amazingly dramatic sigh.

"Hey, you wanna be friends, you've gotta deal with it."

"Do I want to be friends with you?" Mel asked.

"Why, of course you do," Amber cut in.

"Are you sure?" Mel asked.

"Yes," Mercury and Amber said in unison.

"Well, you're better than Danielle," Mel admitted. "And Aelana and her friends."

"Of course, we are," Amber said.

Mel gave her a look.

Mercury would admit, it was still weird having Mel around.

After knowing her so long as Isobel, one of Danielle's cronies, it was weird being her friend, knowing her by her real name of Melancholy Ever, and, more importantly, knowing that they were sisters. Which was crazy, given the fact that Melancholy Ever was a name that, in Mercury's mind, had always belonged to someone she considered an enemy. She had never met the person, but she had heard the name plenty of times. Melancholy Ever was supposed to be a fearsome Vampire high up in Marisa's ranks. It wasn't until they finally met each other, introduced by their real names, that all that was changed.

"How much longer?" Jem asked.

Mercury checked her watch. "Ten minutes."

And then there was Jem. The best half-brother anyone could ever ask for. He had promised to be the overprotective older brother he hadn't had a chance to be when they were younger. Even though he was the younger sibling. His mousy brown hair was never too long, never too short, never hanging in his eyes. And he was a gentleman, which Flash was particularly fond of.

"Are we planning to do anything after school?" Alex asked, his blond hair, so unlike Jem's, hanging straight over his eyes. He looked at it, furrowed his brow, and brushed it aside.

Mercury looked around. "Well? Any suggestions?"

"Wasn't someone trying to organise an end-of-year party?" Mel asked with a pointed look at Amber.

Amber held her gaze. "Indeed, I was."

"Well?" Alex asked. "Is there a party?"

"Indeed, there is," Amber said.

"Oh! Yay!" Flash said, overhearing and coming over to join them from where she sat with Austin.

"So, Amber came through on her promise of a party," Austin chimed in, joining them also.

By this point, the teacher had given up on trying to control them until the end of class. Instead, students were sitting on chairs and desks, even on the floor, talking or looking at their phones. The room was lively, filled with the excited chatter of teenagers anticipating the school holidays.

"Uh huh."

"So tell us about it, then," said Austin, his American accent always sounding so different from the rest of their Australian ones, no matter how much they heard it. "What are we doing?" He stood behind Mercury, hands hanging loosely around her shoulders.

Amber looked at him strangely for a moment. "Sometimes you're a real dork," she said, without any real reason. Those two were just like that though. Partly best friends, and partly sworn enemies.

"Hey!"

"Anyway," she went on. "My place, 5:30. Don't be late, or you'll meet your doom."

Ordinarily, that could be taken as a joke, but coming from Amber, it was better off to believe her. She could break you down with both words and actions.

Amber had dark brown hair and eyes to match. She was smart, she was pretty (gorgeous, some, like Alex, might say), and she was the queen of organisation. She knew how smart and pretty she was, too, and wasn't against using it to her advantage. Just add magic, and you had yourself one formidable Shapeshifter. It was definitely one of the reasons she and Mercury were best friends. That, and because they were just as weird as each other.

"Although it isn't really the end of the year," Jem pointed out.

"Stop being pedantic," Mel replied.

"It's the end of year eleven, so it's the end of the school year," Mercury said, then added, "I agree with Mel; stop being pedantic."

"What will this fabulous party of yours be like?" Seb asked, ignoring the sibling argument in his usual calm fashion, and finally deciding he wanted to speak.

"Why, fabulous, of course."

Ash and Sakura wandered around the mall for what felt like hours. In reality, it was no more than an hour and a half, but time flies when you're having fun, and they always had fun together.

It was just when they were leaving that Chloe arrived.

"Chloe, hi," Sakura called to her from across the entryway.

Chloe walked over, shifting uncomfortably from foot to foot when her eyes met Ash. She looked away quickly, focusing on Sakura.

"Hi, guys," she said.

"Hi," Ash said.

Chloe gave her a weird look, like she couldn't believe this was happening. Couldn't believe they were being so normal. Couldn't believe that she was being civil when the look in her eyes said she wanted to tear Ash apart. Maybe not just with words.

"Leaving, I see," Chloe said.

Sakura nodded. "What about you?"

"Need a new soccer ball," Chloe said, shrugging. "What did you come for?"

Sakura held up her bag proudly, smiling like a maniac. "New dress. For my date with Chris."

Chloe smiled. "Oooh. I want to see."

Sakura patted the bag. "Don't worry, you will."

"I bet you'll look great," Chloe said. "As always."

"What about Riko?" Sakura asked.

Chloe glanced quickly at Ash before answering.

"We're going to see a movie on Saturday," she said.

"Oooh," Sakura said. "Have a good time."

Ash felt awkward standing there, only listening to their conversation. They hadn't exactly directed a question at her, but like Chloe would. And even if Ash did open her mouth and add something, it would probably just make her situation with Chloe worse. Better to keep quiet.

"Anyway, we've got to go now," Sakura said. "See you later."

Chloe said goodbye, they all waved, and then Chloe walked off to get her soccer ball, and Sakura and Ash left the mall.

"Holy crap, that was awkward," Ash said as soon as they were outside.

"Chloe really doesn't like you right now, does she?" Sakura asked, sounding genuinely curious.

Ash shook her head. "Nope. Not at all."

"What the hell did you do?"

"You don't know?" Ash asked. "You didn't hear Chloe yelling at me?"

"No, I did not," Sakura said. "I was more focused on you and how you were going to react. Because nothing like this has ever happened with our friends before, and I was really hoping you weren't going to make it worse."

Ash smiled at her friend. Oh, she probably had made it worse. "I may have sort of accidentally on purpose kissed Riko …"

Sakura's eyes widened. "You did not!"

"Maybe."

"Jesus, Ash. No wonder she's so mad at you."

Ash shrugged. "I know I should feel bad about it, but for some reason, I just don't."

Sakura sighed. "What will I do with you?"

After walking home with Sakura and waving goodbye when they reached her house, Ash continued to her beachfront abode.

Rather than walking through the front door, Ash walked on the sand around to the back door, just as she always did. Her mother had paid a lot of money to have the house built on the sand.

Ash still remembered when she saw her for the last time and when she had been left with the house and all that money. She still wondered why she had been allowed to live all alone in the house as a minor. With access to the money, no less.

She left the door open behind her as she entered, letting the breeze in, and stepped down into the living room to find Shadow sitting on her lounge.

She stared for a moment, shocked. Then she wondered how Shadow had found a way into her home. The door was always locked, Ash made sure of that.

"How have you been, Ash?" Shadow asked in her usual deceptively light tone.

"Fine," Ash replied, not moving from where she stood. "What do you want?"

"I can't drop in and make sure you're okay?"

"That's not really something I'd expect from you," Ash said.

"You should learn to expect the unexpected."

Ash sighed then turned away from Shadow and walked into the little kitchenette. Whatever; Shadow could do whatever, but this was Ash's home, and she was not going to let Shadow ruin her comfort in her own home.

She put her bag down on the curved bench, poured herself a glass of water, and finally turned back to Shadow, who still sat on the lounge, watching with disinterest.

"Well, you know how I am now," Ash said, taking a sip of water. "Is there anything else, or are you planning on leaving soon?"

Shadow smiled but didn't say anything straight away.

She didn't get a change to reply because, just then, someone appeared at the top of the stairs. The stairs that led solely to Ash's bedroom.

Ash narrowed her eyes, not knowing what to say or do.

The girl at the top of the stairs looked like she didn't know, either.

Shadow glared up at the girl, who stood frozen, eyes flashing from Shadow to Ash. And then before Ash's eyes, Shadow transformed, but not into a cat. No, she became a different person altogether: a young man with blue-black hair and quite a few piercings.

"Rogue," he ground out.

"I'm sorry, Tyler," the girl whimpered; she started to descend the stairs, her movements stiff and eyes watering, as they fixed on the young man.

Ash was too stunned to move. "What the hell are you doing here?" she managed to say, hand tightly gripping her glass of water.

The girl's auburn ponytail swung behind her as she jumped down the last couple of steps and quickly made her way over to Tyler.

"Like I said, Ash, just checking up on you," he said, in a sickly smooth voice.

"Get out," she said, glaring at him, her voice hard. "Get out of my house."

"Sure thing, sugar," he said as he stood and guided the girl, Rogue, towards the open back door.

Rogue stumbled on the step up to the door but caught herself and then rushed out, Tyler following her. He turned as he walked out and gave her a sleazy grin.

"Don't call me sugar!" she yelled after him as he disappeared onto the sand.

11

She sat in the confines of the old stones, worn with age, but not quite covered in moss. Despite the time it had been there, the castle was in good condition. Once, it had been neglected, but now, it stood proudly once more. And she intended to keep it that way. There was still some work that needed to be done, but she would get to that. All in due time.

"Marisa!" Tyler's voice echoed down the corridor to her, and she exited her room to watch him approach, with Rogue in tow. The corridor was dark, with torches hung in brackets on the wall. No electricity here. Not that they needed it just yet. Soon.

"Did you find it?" she asked him.

"It wasn't there," he said. "She didn't have it."

Marisa narrowed her eyes. "Are you sure?"

Tyler remained confident. "I'm sure. She doesn't have it. We searched every inch of her house."

Marisa stood silently for a moment, thinking. "One of the others, then."

Tyler and Rogue were still, watching her. Rogue looked extremely nervous. She had been a nervous wreck ever since Marisa had found her and recruited her. It almost made her smile, the effect she had on people. But instead, she turned and headed down the corridor, walking into the shadows.

"We need to stop Shadow before she gets any further," she said, hearing Tyler and Rogue's quick footsteps as they caught up with her. "She may only have succeeded once, but it proves that she can, and she will try to again."

She reached a door at the end of the corridor and opened it with force, slamming it against the wall; the two girls in the room spun around to her. They stood up from their seats, and their smiles grew.

This room was bright, with big windows looking out onto a forest of lush green grass that surrounded the castle. This room was so different from all the rest. Luxurious cushions covered the stone floor, and decorative lanterns hung from the ceiling. It could have been out of *Aladdin*, not that Marisa was interested. The two girls were, though.

"Yes, Marisa?" the black-haired girl asked. The blonde, however, stayed silent.

"You two are going to be doing something very important for me," Marisa said.

Tyler and Rogue stood in the doorway behind her, looking in warily but not daring to enter. Nobody but Marisa dared to enter this room; she was the only one who wasn't fearful afraid of these two girls. They were her two second in command, after all.

"It's time," she said, and the girls' smiles only grew. She didn't have to tell them exactly what she meant. They already knew. They had been waiting for this, just as she had. They were the only ones who knew of her full plan. The others waited for their orders, just glad to have a part in her grand scheme and hoping they would play an important role.

Marisa turned back to Tyler and Rogue in the doorway, both of them standing stock still and just peeking into the room around her. When she faced them, they looked only at her.

"You are going to get Raven, Fate, and Zach, then I will tell you exactly where you will be going and what you will be doing. Shadow will not be continuing on this little quest of hers."

Marisa did smile then. Her smile was wide and full of a strange, twisted happiness.

12

Ash needed to talk to Shadow. She needed to see her now.

But she didn't have any way to contact her.

She was still shocked from those two strangers in her house. Those two magic strangers. At least she guessed that they both had magic. The girl hadn't done anything that seemed magical, but Tyler definitely had.

With some sense back now, she decided to go upstairs to see what Rogue had been pocking around in and if she had stolen anything.

Her room looked surprisingly untouched. She had expected her belongings to be everywhere, but they were all in place. Either Rogue hadn't searched very well, or she had the sense to put back what she touched. Probably because they were planning to leave before she arrived home and didn't want her to think anything was wrong. Even her bed was made, which she didn't usually do. Rogue had gone to a lot of trouble to make the room nice, nicer than even Ash bothered to leave it.

She sat down on the end of her bed and pulled out her phone, opened her contacts, and scrolled through them, wondering who she was going to call. She couldn't talk to Shadow, so she needed to choose the next best person.

Sakura.

It would always be Sakura.

"Hi," Sakura said cheerily, answering the call. "Didn't we just see each other recently?"

"Yeah, yeah," Ash replied. "Need to be serious for a moment, though."

"I'm listening."

"There were people in my house," Ash said. "Magical people."

"Wait, what?"

"I don't know who they were, but the guy was sitting on my lounge looking like … someone else, and then he changed and became himself. Well, I think it was himself."

"Shapeshifter," Sakura said, "like Chloe."

"Chloe can do that? Ugh."

"Yeah. She used to do it a lot. Before, uh … before we met you."

"Seriously? You just stopped using magic when you met me?"

"We all knew who you were," Sakura said, adding quickly, "Princess." Ash sighed.

"We knew the rules too. Everyone did. Don't tell the princesses who they are. And then all the rulers started dying, and, well, no one wanted to say anything because they didn't want to break those rules."

"Wait, wait, wait. Dying?"

"Yes," Sakura said. "The rulers of Lindreas started dying. Some people suspect they were murdered, but others say they were just old, and they definitely were. Of course, nobody wanted to do anything about investigating if they were murdered or not, except Queen Shadow."

Ash stood up at the mention of her.

"Shadow? Shadow is a queen?" She started pacing around her bedroom.

"Yeah. Queen of Noctiuagus."

Ash stopped. "What?" she asked, utterly confused.

"I didn't come up with the name, okay? It's just what it's called. Her kingdom. She's Queen of the Night Walkers."

"Night Walkers?"

"You really don't know a whole lot about magic, do you?" Sakura asked, sounding slightly exasperated. "Night Walkers. Cat people. Cats that can turn into people. There's a guy at our school who's one. Austin Perry in year eleven. Why do you think he's so popular? It's just how Night Walkers are. Riko and Chris are, too, though they try to fly under the radar more."

"Oh. Him," Ash said bluntly. Of course, she knew who Austin was. Practically everyone did. He was "the most attractive boy in the year, practically in the school," a certain someone in his year liked to say. Now she knew why. "I only know about my own kingdom. That's all Shadow really teaches me about."

"You know Shadow?" Sakura asked, stunned.

"Yeah … She's the one who told me about magic, about you, and she's been teaching me."

"Queen Shadow is training you?" Sakura asked, and Ash couldn't tell if she was awed or worried.

Mercury arrived on her best friend's doorstep and didn't bother to knock.

She let herself in, and Austin followed behind her, giving her a look that silently questioned her actions.

"Amber won't mind," she said. "Trust me."

"Sometimes I wonder whether I should …"

She looked back at him, raising an eyebrow. "Oh, really?"

It was then that Amber came out of her room and saw them. "I thought I heard voices," was all she said, continuing past them to the kitchen.

Mercury and Austin were heading for the backyard when Amber's voice rang out: "Since you're here, would you mind helping me?"

So they walked back to the kitchen to help Amber take her plates and bowls of various foods out to the tables in the backyard. Once they had her array of snack foods and drinks out there, Amber brought out her speakers, which she placed in the back corners of the yard.

5:30 rolled around just as they were finishing up, and the rest of their friends started to arrive.

When Jem spotted Mercury, he walked straight over to her.

"Decided to leave me behind, did we?" he asked.

She shrugged. "Sorry. Sacrifices had to be made." She offered him a smile that said "What can you do?"

"Glad to know that I'm expendable," he said. "Nothing better than knowing that your queen is willing to sacrifice you for the greater good."

"Oh, shut up. You know I wouldn't do that."

He shrugged this time and then smiled. "Just making sure." He wandered away then, over to see what food Amber had to offer.

Sakura arrived at Ash's house, having left straight after their phone conversation. Ash didn't really need her to come, but Sakura had insisted, and so here she was, standing in the back room, looking at the ocean and the setting sun as Ash poured drinks.

"What did they look like?" she asked.

"The guy had black hair and lots of piercing, and the girl was short with reddish hair," Ash answered, coming to stand out with her and handing Sakura the lemonade she had asked for.

"Tyler Orestas," Sakura said. "Not sure who the girl is."

"Her name was Rogue."

"Rogue? Never heard of her. If she's with Tyler, she works for Marisa Raven, though."

"How do you know about Marisa?" Ash asked.

Sakura stared at her. "You really don't know anything, do you?"

Ash shook her head.

"Allow me to give you a quick history lesson, then," she said with a smile. "Marisa Raven has been the cause of two wars in Lindreas. Although nobody really knows her true motives, she seems bent on bringing ruin to all the kingdoms and our whole world. She never showed interest in ruling herself, more like she just likes causing havoc. Or at least that's the way I've heard it."

"You are right, young Vampire," came a familiar voice. "Although I know what her motives are."

Sakura spotted Shadow over Ash's shoulder, and her eyes went wide, then she did a small curtsy and stood up straight.

Ash turned to see Shadow standing just inside the back door, her face serious.

"Tyler Orestas and Rogue were here?" she asked.

"Yes," Ash said slowly, wary after her encounter today.

Shadow seemed to think this over for a minute. "No matter. It is time to continue, Ash."

Sakura looked between the two of them, trying vainly to understand.

Ash turned back to her. "I have to go," she said. "Stay here if you want. I'll see you soon."

Sakura looked too stunned to reply. She only nodded her head and took a step back, placing her glass on the kitchen bench. "I might go too," she said softly but didn't move as Ash headed for the back door and left.

Ash followed Shadow around to the front of her house, where the van awaited.

✦•◆•✦

The sun was beginning to set over Amber's little party. It was a warm night though, as they were finally into spring. And they could see the stars, as there were no clouds. It was the perfect night to begin their holidays, and the perfect night for their party.

Mercury was returning to the yard with more snacks that Amber had asked her to get, when something hit her in the back and she fell, dropping the bowl. She landed in the broken shards of bowl and chip and rolled onto her back, wondering what exactly had knocked her over. It had sure felt like a foot, but there was no one there. But nor was there any other object that could be the culprit.

She stood up, peering down the corridor, brow furrowed, but couldn't see anyone and so turned back to the mess she had created.

"Amber," she called.

No response.

"Amber! There was an accident!"

Footsteps.

Amber joined her in the hallway and immediately saw the remains of chips and the bowl on the floor. "What happened?"

"I don't know," Mercury admitted. "I guess I tripped. Somehow."

"Duck," Amber said suddenly.

Mercury ducked.

Whispers from the air told her it was an arm swinging over her head. Belonging to a female. She sprung up and spun to face whoever it was.

A black-haired girl she didn't recognised glared at her.

Although she didn't know who the girl was, Mercury immediately recognised her as a Vampire.

"Amber, back please," she said, her tone serious.

She heard Amber's footsteps behind her and started walking backwards, eyes firmly on the girl in front of her. She had no idea who she was, but she didn't like Vampires (except for Mel, of course).

The girl kept glaring as they backed up and tried lashing out at her again. Mercury dodged, barely. The hallway was too tight to fight in, which was why she was making her way to the backyard. Also, her friends were there. This girl wouldn't want to fight all eight of them, and if she thought she could, she'd be sorely mistaken.

They reached the backyard, and Mercury heard struggling behind her. She turned for a split-second to see what was going on, and the vampire took the opportunity, punching her in the jaw. Hard. Mercury stumbled, and her gaze flicked straight back to the girl, whose face remained hard, glare fixed in place.

"Behind you!" someone yelled. Alex.

Mercury ducked as another fist came at her from behind, then spun and kicked out at this second attacker. Her foot hit squarely in their chest and they stumbled but did not fall. It wasn't one of her best kicks.

He straightened, and she scanned his features quickly.

Werewolf.

Hands grabbed her from behind, arms sliding easily under her own and hauling her backwards. The Vampire hissed in her ear, then Mercury heard that small, wet sound that accompanied growing fangs.

Oh, God. No, no, no.

Mercury immediately began to struggle. She knew she was panicking and she knew that she shouldn't be, but that wasn't going to stop her now. Her mind was stuck on those fangs, inches from her neck. She couldn't see them but she knew they were there. Could almost feel them, sending shivers down her spine. The werewolf boy watched in amusement as tears started to well in her eyes.

She was about to be bitten. Her biggest fear was about to come true. She was going to be bitten. The girl would drink her blood. Her fangs would be in Mercury's neck. It was going to happen. This was it.

Those tears started rolling down her cheeks. No, no, no. The werewolf boy laughed, but Mercury didn't care because this was it. This was it; she was going to be bitten. She couldn't stop it; she was too panicked, not in the right mind to even try and get away. She still wriggled and struggled, but what was that going to do?

And then her saviour came to her aid. The Vampire girl's jacket caught fire, flaring into a bright blaze. Tearing away from Mercury, she slid out of the flaming jacket as fast as could, and Mercury almost fell to her knees in relief. Oh, magic, what would she do without it?

The smouldering jacket lay on the ground, and the Vampire cradled her arms, which had also been burnt, the fire instantly melting through the fake leather. She snarled at Mercury, who was getting as far away as she could.

She stepped over to Austin, who effortlessly wiped the remaining tears from her eyes. "Merc, you're okay," he said.

She nodded, closing her eyes and taking a deep breath. She was definitely going to have to work on that. That was not an acceptable way to react to Vampires. She could see that *now*.

After she was sure she was alright, she turned from Austin to see what had become of the party. Their friends stood around, holding back others. Amber had restrained a Witch by the name of Raven Duskrose, and she realised that the Werewolf was Zach Tinder. Mel was nowhere to be seen.

There was an eerie silence hanging over the backyard now. Nobody moved. Then the black-haired boy appeared, stepping out of the hallway and from behind the Vampire girl, who was collapsed on the grass, still cradling her poor arms.

"What do you want?" Mercury asked, stepping away from Austin and standing straight.

The black-haired boy's expression didn't change from the peaceful one it held, but it looked like he wanted to smile. "Nothing important," he said.

"Then leave," she said firmly.

"We can't, I'm afraid."

She glared. "At least introduce yourself and your friends, then."

"Tyler Orestas," he said, doing the smallest bow possible. He nodded his head to the Vampire girl. "Fate Whisper. Rogue." He nodded to the girl lying unconscious near the table. If he felt bad for her, he didn't show it. "And then I know you know Raven and Zach."

"Tyler," she said slowly, deliberately taking her time, rolling his name off her tongue. "Get out."

She recognised his last name. Orestas. It was the name of one of the Varietean islands. What was he doing working for Marisa, if his family was the main landholder of an island? Rebellion, Mercury guessed. Wanted to be different from his rich, important parents.

"We are out," he said.

"Don't make me ask twice," she replied, her voice lightening.

He didn't move, nor did he speak.

"Tyler, do you feel like dying today? Because it can be very easily arranged if you decide not to leave now."

"By your hand?" he asked, rather smugly.

"If you wish."

"Oh no, really, it's not necessary." A smug grin had pulled onto his face.

Mercury gave him an equally smug look, then fire swirled around her hand, and from it appeared a knife. A hint of fear appeared on Tyler's face when he saw it. Despite that, he kept up the act, offering the same smile.

"Oh, Mercury," he said. "Fear doesn't always work, you know. Keep at it long enough, and it isn't scary anymore. I've heard about you, of course I have, and I've heard about how much you think of yourself. You're supposedly more special than anyone else. But you can't do everything, and you can't scare me away with a little knife."

So that's what he was going to do: try to make her think less of herself. She had seen his fear; she knew it was there. His acting skills weren't exactly the best. So she smiled kindly at him, lifted her arm, and threw the knife. It flew by his head, almost clipping his piercing-filled ear, and stuck between two bricks in the wall behind him.

He dodged out of the way, but if she had been trying to hit him, he never would have been fast enough. Honestly, where did Marisa find some of her lackeys?

"Would you like a second warning?" she asked.

He didn't answer. His eyes were wide, and he was no longer trying to hide his fear, nor could he hide his utter surprise at how close he had come to having a knife in his forehead. Sure, he had heard of her, but the stories clearly didn't do her justice.

Fire swirled around her hand again, this time moving slowly around her hand and wrist; Tyler backed over to the doorway, almost tripping over Fate, the Vampire, still on the ground.

The fire dissipated as he steadied himself, and a second knife sat snuggly in the palm of her hand.

"So what's it going to be?" she asked, tightening her grip on the knife.

He blinked a few times, looking around the yard, eyes flashing across Mercury's friends, then to her eyes and finally the knife in her hand.

His earlier expression of confidence settled on his face, with a hint of disinterest.

Mercury threw the second knife.

It flew past him on the other side this time and stuck between bricks again. Mercury would have to apologise to Amber later for ruining the wall.

From where she stood, she could see Tyler wobbling, shaking, like his knees were about to give out. That confidence hadn't lasted long.

"Do you need any more convincing?" she asked.

"Marisa sent Revenge and Tempest after Shadow!" he blurted. Then his knees did give out and he collapsed beside Fate in the grass.

Fate shot him a furious glare and whacked him, whimpering from the burns on her arm. Raven tore herself from Amber's grip, but Mercury was off. She jumped over both Fate and Tyler and rushed for the front door.

Revenge and Tempest, of course. Wasn't Shadow just lucky that Mercury knew where to find her"

"Merc, wait," Jem called, but she didn't. He could catch up.

13

Once again, they entered the warehouse, and a shiver went up Ash's spine as she spotted the chair.

It was her turn. So soon it had come.

She walked slowly to the chair, both excited and insanely nervous. Her stomach was twisted in knots, yet she also wanted to sit in the chair, to experience it. Aelana had lived. Aelana was fine. It couldn't be that bad.

She reached it and sat down, closing her eyes against the sudden wave of anxiety. She wasn't used to feeling anxious. About anything.

Shadow placed the bowl on top of her head and flicked a switch, the sound ringing in Ash's ears. To her left, the portal began to glow, and as an image started to form in it, she felt a stab of pain and had to look away.

Skylar approached the portal. She approached it without a hint of fear or wariness. She was surprised by how much she wanted to do this. She wanted to step through the portal and see what was on the other side. Last time she had been nervous, so nervous that she had wanted to back out, but this time, she was ready. The butterflies in her stomach were from excitement, not nerves. She was ready this time.

A sprawling city started to take form before her eyes. Flat, squat buildings of sandstone, similar to that place in that Indiana Jones movie. Skylar couldn't remember the name of it. Dark fabrics hung from windows, and clotheslines stretched between buildings in tight alleyways.

"Well, go on," Phoenix said behind her and she jumped, startled.

She looked back and saw that her sister was waiting behind her, and so were Jade and Aelana.

She turned back to the portal and stepped in, without hesitating.

The tingling sensation went through her body as she came out the other side, tiny storms of sand kicked up by her feet. Before her stood what must have been the castle. She saw a moat surrounding it, with a lowered drawbridge spanning it.

She only had a moment to admire it, though, because suddenly, she was on the ground, a great weight on top of her, her face pressed into the sand and dirt.

"Sorry," Phoenix said, and the weight disappeared. "I tripped."

Skylar stood up again and moved to the side, away from the portal. After Jade and Aelana joined them, they crossed the drawbridge.

On the other side was a wide, arched corridor; the portcullis was raised, allowing them to walk through. The wide corridor opened onto a beautiful courtyard with a stone fountain in the centre, of a mermaid holding a triton up, from which the water spurted out. The courtyard floor was red, gold, and grey hexagonal tiles that were perfectly clean, without any cracks, as if they had just been lain. Not a speck of sand or dirt on them, and gleaming in the sunlight.

Skylar had been expecting them to get lost, but there was only one doorway off the courtyard, apart from the entrance, so there didn't seem to be any chance of that.

The castle that stood around them was as flat and squat as the other buildings in the city, with light sandstone walls. There were many windows the walls that looked out onto the courtyard, but they were too high up to reach.

Jade glanced around the courtyard back at them, then headed for the door, taking the lead. Skylar followed quickly after her.

When Jade reached the door, she tested it, and it swung gently open. Darkness lay beyond. Darkness so absolute that not even the sunlight behind them could penetrate it.

"So," Phoenix said, looking into the darkness, "should we …?"

Skylar looked at her sister and then back into the darkness. Except it wasn't so dark anymore. Well, no, it *was* dark. But she could see.

Right. Vampire. She had to remind herself.

Her eyes adjusted to the darkness, and she could see a long hallway stretching away from her, curving around a bend.

"Did the hallway get lighter, or is it just me?" Aelana asked, stepping up beside her and peering into the darkness.

"It's just you," Jade answered. "And Skylar."

"Should we go in there?" Phoenix asked.

"I guess so," Skylar said.

She stepped in through the door and looked around.

The hallway was extravagant beyond belief. If it had been lighter, Skylar was pretty sure that the ceiling would have been a light blue. Gold then bordered the blue in elaborate swirling patterns, with flecks of soft pink throughout. The walls seemed to be white and rather plain, although she couldn't be certain.

Aelana followed her into the hallway, and Skylar watched surprise dawn on her face. Whether it was because of what she saw or simply that she could see so well, Skylar didn't know. Jade and Phoenix joined them; Jade, all clad in black, was a little hard to see, while Phoenix looked around, blinking, trying to make her eyes adjust.

"Lead the way, sis," Phoenix said, and so Skylar turned to the hallway opening before them and did just that.

The floor was equally as extravagant as the ceiling, made of tiles all the colours of the walls and ceiling; the rubber soles of Skylar's shoes made awkward squishing sounds with every step, almost as if the floor were wet.

She was more than a little shocked to realise that she didn't feel a sliver of doubt about her ability to lead them down the hallway in the dark. The dark felt good. The dark felt right. It was quite comforting in a way.

The hallway was long, bending around, and surely crossing over itself. She was beginning to think that maybe they had become lost after all, when she saw light. Only a faint trickle, but light. Skylar's first instinct was to shy away from the light and stay in her comforting darkness.

Quit it. Don't be stupid.

Phoenix shot past her, racing into the light and around what was hopefully the last corner.

"Oh, glorious light, how I missed you," Skylar heard her say.

She came around the bend and saw her blonde-haired twin, kneeling at the bottom of a flight of stairs. Lying in the sunlight pouring in from the opening, in her floral singlet and white shorts, she definitely looked the part to be a fairy.

"Knock off the theatrics," Skylar teased, starting up the stairs and purposely almost stepping on her sister's hand.

"Hey!"

Skylar continued and looked back when she reached the top.

"Get up," Jade said bluntly, but not without humour, following Skylar.

Aelana glanced at Phoenix as she ascended the stairs, and finally, Phoenix pulled herself up and followed after them.

Skylar was first through the doorway at the top of the stairs, and she wandered cautiously into the round room that greeted her. She had been right about the colour of the walls and the patterns on the ceiling, she found, now seeing them in daylight.

There was no one in the round room. It was empty, but for the grey stone pedestal standing proudly in the centre.

"So far, so good," Phoenix said, though her voice was soft, wary.

Skylar, for the first time here, felt nervous. Only slightly. She had an inkling that something didn't feel right, nagging in the back of her mind, a tickle on the back of her neck.

Jade approached the pedestal. It was a rather plain, unadorned thing, but it didn't need to be decorated. Because it wasn't important, only the object on it was.

Ash's ring.

Jade glanced around herself with every step, careful, but taking long strides that only her long legs could handle without looking ridiculous.

When she reached the pedestal, she snatched the ring up and quickly scanned the room again. No secret traps set off. The ceiling didn't descend on them, poison darts didn't shoot from the walls. There was no secret door flung open, hiding Shadow Lurkers inside.

Jade turned to them and smiled, then the door slammed closed behind them.

Skylar stumbled away, turning around to face the gold patterned door. Aelana, who was closest, grabbed the handle and tried pulling it open; her feet slipped on the floor. It didn't budge, and she let go, defeated, with wide eyes.

"How high are we?" Phoenix asked, looking over at Jade.

Jade stowed the ring in the pocket of her shirt (she always wore fancy button-up shirts, usually in black) and then walked over to one of the many windows on the opposite side of the room and peered out.

"Pretty high," she said, looking back at them with a grim expression.

Skylar rushed to join her and check for herself.

They weren't just pretty high. They were very high, higher than any part of the castle they had seen. It didn't have any towers that Skylar had seen, yet they were most certainly in a high tower. The moat stretched out below her, meeting the sandstone wall of whatever non-existent tower they had somehow found themselves in.

"How is this even possible?" she asked, backing away from the window a few steps.

Aelana and Phoenix made their way over then, clearly needing to see for themselves.

"What the hell?" Phoenix said, staring down at the moat and sand, what felt like miles below them.

"Impossible," Aelana breathed, still with her wide-eyed expression.

Jade shrugged. "Any ideas?"

Phoenix looked ready to speak, but she didn't get a chance to say what was on her mind, because it was at that moment that the Shadow Lurkers finally made their appearance.

They arrived through the windows, swinging in on ropes as if they had rappelled down from the roof. They landed past where the four girls were standing, filling the space and leaving them cornered by the windows. There must have been thirty of them—more than last time—and they closed in quickly.

The leader pushed her way to the front of the group and signalled the rest to spread out. She was pale, of course, and looked the part of a zombie, just as the others did, but for the rotting flesh. Somehow, she seemed different from the rest of the group. Her hair was bright compared to the others, strawberry blonde, and her eyes shone with intelligence that the others lacked. She was short but curvy in all the right places, and she wore clothes that stuck tight to her body.

She stared straight at Skylar, who felt as though she was meant to know who the woman was or, at least, who she had once been. Then Skylar noticed the dagger she held in her hand and suddenly didn't care who the woman was, she just didn't like the way she was stalking towards her.

"What are we going to do?" Aelana asked nervously.

Skylar looked around, taking her eyes away from the woman with the dagger.

Shadow Lurker, she mentally corrected herself.

Her gaze stopped at the window, the window they were being pushed towards; the Shadow Lurkers hung back but slowly advanced at them, keeping them near it.

"The window," she said aloud.

"What?" Aelana asked. "You mean jump out the window? Are you crazy?"

"Good thinking," Jade said, before Skylar could reply.

"Either you're insane, or I'm missing something," Aelana said, her voice gaining speed.

"Oh, I get it!" Phoenix said, smiling knowingly at her sister.

Jade, who was closest, turned from the Shadow Lurkers and sat on the sill, then swung her legs up onto it. She stood up slowly, placing her hands along its frame for support. She gave Skylar a smiled then pushed herself out and disappeared from sight.

Aelana stared, then looked back and forth between Skylar and Phoenix. "Did she really just do that?"

"Yep," Phoenix said, hoisting herself into the window next.

She copied Jade's movements, sitting, swinging her legs up, standing, and using the window frame for support. She looked down, smiled back at Skylar and Aelana, and then she too disappeared.

Aelana was too stunned for words this time, terror making her wide-eyed expression stick around, unable to comprehend how her companions were throwing themselves out the window with a smile.

The Shadow Lurkers watched too, understanding no better than Aelana how they were so willing to fling themselves out, yet smiles crept onto their faces. They seemed to believe that they had done their job, and were watching the girls throw themselves to their demise.

Skylar found herself sitting on the window sill next.

She swung her legs up, imitating both Jade and her sister, placing her hands on the frame in the same spots as them, and getting her feet beneath her, balancing in the window. She looked down to where she could see Phoenix and Jade, swimming in clear water for the bank.

"It's the moat," she said to Aelana before she took a breath and jumped.

Her hair flew around her face as she fell, and the sensation filled her with a strange enjoyment that made her want to laugh. It was only for a second, though, because then she hit the water, her feet ploughing through and waves closing up over her head.

It was warmer than she had been expecting and amazingly clear, she found, as she blinked her eyes open. She surfaced just as a huge splash erupted next to her, then Aelana surfaced beside her a few seconds later, her face white.

"Oh, my God," she said, a smile slowly pulling at the corners of her mouth. "Wow."

Skylar smiled back at her and then looked around to find Jade and Phoenix, who were now standing on the sandy ground at the edge of the moat. Phoenix waved them over, and Skylar started swimming.

"Climb out over here," Jade instructed when she reached the edge.

There was a wall of smooth sandstone higher than Skylar could reach up, but there were also marks in it where Jade and Phoenix had scrabbled to get out. Skylar pulled herself out of the water, and Phoenix grabbed her hand to haul her up.

Aelana was right behind her, and she slipped on the sandy wall at first but found the right spots to use, and then Jade reached down and pulled her out too.

Now that they were all safely on the bank, they looked back up at the tower that had materialised out of thin air. It was different from the rest of the castle, made of large grey stones, rather than the smooth sandstone of the rest of the city.

Skylar noticed the portal was now open again, hovering at the end of the drawbridge, and she pointed it out to the others.

"Do you still have the ring?" Phoenix asked as they walked over.

Jade nodded, pulling it from her chest pocket and then slipping it back in.

They reached the portal and returned through it, one after the other.

<hr />

Mercury edged up to the doors of the warehouse with Jem right behind her, footsteps light, trying to stay as silent as possible. The doors were only open a crack, a sliver of light spilling into the night, and Mercury inched over and peered inside.

Revenge and Tempest weren't there.

As soon as she realised this, she straightened up and walked in; Jem followed behind her, glancing around warily.

Shadow turned to them as their footsteps echoed but did not speak, regarding them coolly. Probably waiting for Mercury to explain why she had turned up accompanied this time.

Maybe Tyler had lied, had found once last lick of confidence in himself.

Standing just a few metres into the warehouse, Mercury looked around, making sure she hadn't missed anything. Her eyes flicked over Ash seated in Shadow's weird contraption.

Everything seemed fine. No danger that she could detect.

Then she was blown off her feet.

She flew forwards and tumbled to the ground, rolling as she hit the floor and coming up in a crouch, facing the door. Revenge and Tempest now stood there, Revenge smiling smugly and Tempest as straight-faced as ever. Jem rocked slightly as he made it to his feet, and Mercury stood too.

"I just knew Tyler wouldn't be enough to stop you," Revenge said, walking forwards. "Foolish of Marisa to trust him."

Mercury didn't say a word. Partly because she had nothing to say yet, and partly because she was wondering what cruel fate had befallen her to have to deal with two Vampires in one night.

Revenge continued forwards, a harsh smile playing over her elegant features, until she was stopped suddenly, as if she had run into an invisible wall. A flash of confusion replaced her smile, but it was back after a second, and she looked Mercury in the eyes.

"Simple tricks like that can't stop us," she said and looked back at Tempest, her black hair swinging over her bare shoulders. Revenge always wore the stupidest of outfits, Mercury thought.

She felt the wall of air she had placed in front of Revenge drop, Tempest overriding her control.

"Girls, I'm only going to ask once," Shadow said, reminding Mercury that she was there. "Please leave, or we will be forced to make you, and it will not end well for you."

Revenge laughed, showing her fangs. "Oh, please," she said. "You can't stop us, Shadow. And as much as she thinks she can, Mercury can't, either."

If it were anyone else, Mercury would have had some kind of witty remark. But this was Revenge Frost. A Vampire. Mercury hated Vampires. In a terrified sort of way.

"Nothing to say, Mercury?" Revenge asked.

"Nothing really on my mind," Mercury replied, trying to act with her usual confidence. She wasn't feeling it now, though. Not when she was speaking to Revenge.

"Now, that's surprising; I've heard you like to make a few jokes," Revenge said, then started pacing. "Well, it's been nice talking, but we really have to get down to business now."

And then she disappeared.

Stupid Vampires with their stupid invisibility.

There was a sound behind her, but before she could turn to see what it was, a wall of fire came rushing towards her. She dived out of the way at the last second, the fire nipping at the soles of her boots.

"That was never going to work," she said, facing Tempest, who was now standing inside the warehouse.

Tempest walked calmly forward, and as she did, the floor started to roll, as if waves were passing beneath it, then giant obelisk-shaped crystals began to spurt from the ground all around her, and she stumbled away from them as they did, shock forming on her normally emotionless face. When she regained her balance, she glared at Mercury, and suddenly, there were shards of ice shooting towards Mercury's face. They melted before they reached her.

Tempest looked mildly annoyed but started towards Mercury once again. Mercury didn't move, waiting for her to come closer. Her powers may have been stronger than Tempest's, but they were both Sorceresses, so there was no point in trying to fight with magic. It wasn't going to get them anywhere.

She waited, until she felt something on her ankles, climbing up her legs. Looking down at the vines rising out of the ground and crawling up her body, she sighed, and they caught fire and burnt away.

"This is all just games," she said, watching the remains of the vines drop to the floor.

When she looked up, Tempest had reached her, and she was holding a sword. She swung, and Mercury dodged back, creating some distance between them, then Mercury reached back over her shoulder and unsheathed her own sword.

Mercury attacked, and the situation quickly became all too familiar. She'd fought Tempest like this before, just after she became friends with Austin. No, they hadn't even been friends yet.

They fell into a rhythm of clashing swords, Tempest's scimitar against Mercury's katana. Once, Tempest had been more skilled than Mercury, but that was years ago. And Mercury had continued training since then. For a moment just like this. She would have liked to hit Tempest at least once. It would have been so very satisfying after what the two had been through, but keeping her distracted was enough.

Skylar came through the portal behind Phoenix and ran straight into her.

"Hey, what is it?" she asked.

Phoenix didn't answer. Neither did Jade.

Aelana ran into Skylar as she stepped through the portal last, but Skylar didn't even react because now she saw why Jade and Phoenix had stopped on the steps.

Mercury was here, with a boy with mousy brown hair. One of her friends. Jem something. He was fighting a woman with black hair, while Mercury was sword fighting with a woman with blonde hair, both of them with different swords. Mercury had a katana. While the woman she fought had a sword that Skylar was sure she'd seen in *Indiana Jones*. She remembered using one in an episode of her show a couple of months ago.

The warehouse had undergone some changes since they'd left.

Over by the door, there were these great, big crystals of all different colours, protruding from the ground, almost completely blocking the doorway. There were vines growing out of the walls and floor, looking as if they'd been physically ripped apart by something trapped inside. Burn marks littered the floor, and drops of blood were sprinkled on the dirty ground in a trail leading to Jem.

It was only after she noticed all these things that she realised Shadow was standing right beside the portal.

"Girls, quickly, get away from here," she said, ushering them down the steps.

"Where should we go?" Jade asked her, watching around them rather than looking at Shadow.

"There's a back door," Shadow said, gesturing vaguely behind her.

Skylar looked over her and saw the door, set into the wall, hidden behind a pile of boxes. They started towards it.

"Ah ah ah," said a voice from behind them. Skylar turned.

The black-haired woman was the one who had spoken. Jem was lying on the ground behind her, reaching for a short sword just out of reach.

She gave Skylar the same feeling as the Shadow Lurker, the feeling that she should know who she was or know something about her. Skylar couldn't quite put her finger on it.

"Tempest," the woman called.

The blonde turned when her name was called and immediately spotted them. Mercury saw them too. A wave of heat exploded out from behind Skylar then, and she turned to see the boxes alight, the flames radiating off them and blocking the door.

Well, great.

There was silence but for the crackling fire, then a cry of pain rang out, and everyone looked around, searching for the source.

The blonde was backing away from Mercury, a hand to her side, and her sword dropped on the ground. Blood dripped off the end of Mercury's sword, and she couldn't seem to hide her smile.

The black-haired woman hissed, an animal sound, and stalked over to Mercury from where she left Jem on the ground. Her hand closed effortlessly around Mercury's neck, and she lifted her up in one swift movement. Mercury's legs kicked for a second, but then she was still, looking down at Revenge with undisguised fear.

"You think you're just so amazing and perfect," the woman spat at her. "But you'll break. Soon enough, you'll fall apart. You don't understand what you've walked into, and you'll break when it comes crashing down on you. And you know where you'll be then? Your kingdom will be in ruins, and I'll have dumped your body in a ditch after draining your blood."

Of course. She was a Vampire. That's what it was.

She let go of Mercury after her little tirade was done and headed for the warehouse door. The blonde followed her, dripping a trail of blood behind her. They snaked their way through the giant crystals quickly.

Mercury was on her knees on the warehouse floor, watching them go. She was shaking, so much so that Skylar could see it from half way across the warehouse.

The blonde glanced back before she disappeared into the night, and just when Skylar thought it was over, something exploded.

14

Skylar opened her eyes and slowly lifted herself off the floor, sitting up. They were scattered everywhere. Even Shadow was sprawled on the ground, white blouse singed and ruined.

Skylar noticed that she was the first to pull herself up. She stood, getting her legs underneath her, but they wobbled, and she sat back down. Her head was spinning. Her companions began to rise around her, but watching them was making her feel sick, so she brought her knees up, hugging them, then stared down at the floor through them, listening rather than watching.

"Jem, are you okay?" Mercury asked, and it was the first time Skylar had heard her sound worried.

"I'm fine," Jem grunted. He didn't sound fine to her.

Skylar pulled her phone out of her back pocket, and the screen flashed to life, the time and date shining back at her: 12:02 a.m., 21 September 2013. First day of the holidays. First day of the holidays, and she was in an abandoned warehouse, dizzy, after being attacked by two women, including a Vampire.

"Excuse me," a voice said over her.

She looked up from her phone to see Jem offering his hand; surprisingly, he was uninjured. She took it.

"Jem Foxshadow," he said as he pulled her to her feet. She didn't let go of his hand straight away, waiting to see if she felt like she would fall over this time.

"Thanks," she said, letting go.

"What happened here?" Phoenix asked.

Skylar turned to see her standing by the portal and couldn't help but notice that the edges of her clothes were singed.

"More importantly," Jade said, "who were they?"

"Revenge Frost and Tempest Sanguine," Shadow answered, dusting off her clothes. "Marisa's left- and right-hand women."

"What did they want?" Phoenix asked.

"Me," Shadow said. "No doubt Marisa knows what we are doing and is trying to stop us. Trying to stop me from helping you."

"So what? Is she going to come after us now?" Jade asked.

"Unlikely," Shadow said. "I am her biggest problem. She will try to get rid of me first, even though you are definitely the easier targets."

"Great," Jade muttered. "So, she will come after us then." She started to wander away across the warehouse floor.

These were great questions, sure, but Skylar had something else on her mind. "What exploded?" she asked.

"Petrol," Mercury answered from a corner.

"There used to be cars and boats stored in here," Shadow supplied.

"Mercury, are you done looking around?" Jem asked. "At whatever you're looking at?"

"Yes," Mercury answered, walking over.

"Good," Jem said, yawning. "Because I would really like some sleep."

"You could leave without me, you know. I can get home by myself."

"You know I wouldn't," he replied.

"Oh yeah, but what if I was expecting you to go home and plan my birthday party?" Mercury teased.

Jem yawned and laughed. "I think I need sleep first. And besides, you wouldn't let anyone plan anything for your birthday party but yourself."

"You've got me there," she replied.

"So can we go now?" Jem asked.

"Yeah, let's go," Mercury said, and they headed for the door.

"Can we go too?" Skylar asked.

"Soon enough," Shadow said. "But first, we have to pack up the equipment."

"What? Really?" Phoenix groaned.

"Do you want them coming back?" Shadow asked. "Knowing where we are?"

"I guess not," Phoenix mumbled.

"Shouldn't we be going to a hospital?" Aelana asked, with her usual mix of fear and confusion.

"You will heal," Shadow said lightly. "You are walking and talking, aren't you?"

Aelana nodded.

"Then it is nothing that your body, aided with magic, can't handle."

After what they'd already seen, Skylar didn't see a reason not to believe what Shadow said, and Aelana was too stunned to bother arguing.

After Shadow disassembled her contraption, they helped her carry it out to her van, which they had then had to sit in the back of with, and Shadow delivered them back to their homes.

15

Marisa was waiting. Seated on her old throne, long abandoned, moss covering the once-gleaming arms. She liked its state of disrepair. It was one of the few things she did like.

They entered the old, abused, and forgotten throne room, halfway through being restored to its former glory; most of them were unharmed, except for Tyler, unconscious, and Tempest, a deep cut in her side. They were taken away to be looked after and patched up.

"Duelling with Mercury again?" Marisa asked. She didn't even have to inquire, but the question rolled off her tongue anyway.

"We would have had them, and we would have had the ring," Revenge informed. "If Mercury hadn't turned up with her brother."

"Blaze?" Marisa asked, surprised.

"No. Jem Foxshadow. The half-brother."

"Oh. Him."

"I'm not sure if Shadow knew we would be there and contacted them, or if they were the ones who knew, but they were there when we arrived."

"They knew," Fate grumbled.

Marisa turned to the little fourteen-year-old. Fate always had a dark expression; Marisa didn't think she'd ever seen the girl smile. No, one time, when Marisa asked her to join her just a few short months ago. Fate was committed and the kind of fearless that Marisa wanted.

"How did they know?" she asked.

"Tyler told her," Fate said angrily.

"Did he?" Marisa's eyebrows shot up, and she sat straighter in her throne. A cold smile relaxed onto her face as she contemplated this, silently furious inside.

Fate nodded.

"Well, well, well."

She stood without another word, stalking past Revenge, Fate, Zach, Raven, and Rogue. Rogue stood sheepishly near the door. She was going to be paying Tyler a little visit.

His room was one of the smaller ones on the ground floor; a small window was hewn from the stone on one wall, a small bed with plain white sheets sat parallel to it, and there was a small oak chest for his clothes. He was just waking when she entered.

"Marisa," he said blurrily, sitting up.

"Tyler," she said. "Fate has just told me a little story about you."

He stiffened. "Y-y-yes?"

"Forgive her if she's wrong, but she told me that you told Mercury our plans."

He didn't answer straight away.

"Well, uh, maybe."

"That's not a good enough answer, Tyler."

"I …" He sagged. "I told her."

"That's alright," she said.

"Really?" He looked up hopefully.

"No," she said, shaking her head.

She crossed the room, looked out the window, then turned back to Tyler.

"This act is unforgivable," she continued. "How can I trust you not to reveal more to her? Or to anyone else? I can't, and I never will. And I do not need someone I can't trust working for me.'

"I'm sorry, Marisa. I'm so sorry. It's just that nothing you told me to do worked on her. She surprised me, and I wasn't ready. What can I do to prove to you I'm trustworthy?"

"There's nothing you can do," she said.

His eyes widened.

"Wait. Please."

His dagger, an ornate family heirloom, sat on his bedside table; Marisa picked it up and tested its weight, towering over Tyler in his bed.

"This isn't necessary! I won't do it again! I promise."

She didn't reply.

"Marisa … Oh, Gods please!"

She just watched him for a moment as he tried to scramble out of his bed, desperately trying to throw the sheets off and instead getting all tangled up in them. He was too slow to untangle himself, but he never actually had a chance of getting away. Marisa lodged the dagger deep in his neck.

"I do not take traitors lightly," she said. Then she turned away from his bed and exited, leaving him to contemplate his actions in his last moments, gurgling for life, which seeped out and stained his white sheets.

16

Skylar was not sure how she was expecting her parents to react when she came down the stairs in her new outfit, but comforting smiles was not it.

She *had* been thinking there would be disapproving scowls, faintly veiled, and maybe even an "Oh, Skylar, you cannot go outside in that!"

Phoenix had insisted on going shopping earlier that day, and she had encouraged Skylar to try on all sorts of clothes, until she finally came across the combination she now wore. Even then, she hadn't wanted to spend any money, but her sister had insisted. And so here she was, standing at the top of the stairs with her parents smiling at her, just as encouraging as Phoenix had been.

When they had arrived home, Skylar, finally excited about her purchase, had rushed upstairs and changed, regarding herself in the mirror for longer than necessary, admiring her new look: black shorts, heeled black ankle boots with yellow eyelets, and a black crop singlet with gold accents, but the plaid shirt she wore over it was by far her favourite. The stripes were green, blue, and pastel pink, and thin black ones few and far between.

It was most definitely different from the patterned T-shirt and frilly skirt she had been wearing all day, but wow, she liked it so much more. The skirt and shirt flung in the corner of her room suddenly felt tacky. Why had she ever worn them?

"We're having people over for dinner," her mum said when Skylar reached the bottom of the stairs.

She may as well have just turned around and gone back up.

"Who?" she asked, trying (but failing) not to sound annoyed.

"The Thompsons."

She groaned and rolled her eyes.

"Why them? Why always them?"

"Because Dave and Mary are lovely."

"Sure, they are. To you and Dad. Not to me or Phoenix," she said. "And their kids are even worse. They seem incapable of any thought or speech other than 'Let's make fun of Skylar and her ratchet sister.'"

"Language!"

"I didn't say anything," Skylar protested.

Her mum was silent for a moment.

"Please," she said. "I'm not saying that you do anything wrong, but please don't provoke them, and don't react to their comments."

"You know I won't." She glanced sideways at her mum. "Probably."

Her mum smiled. "I know."

The Thompsons arrived for dinner, and at the sight of them, Skylar was just about ready to hide in her closet and never come out. She didn't say anything as Dave and Mary and their three evil kids, Sophia, Anna, and Ryan, walked in. She closed the door behind them and tried to act like she cared they were here. They sat down at the table, Skylar somehow ending up next to Sophia, the worst of them.

Neither of them spoke at first.

Dinner was still cooking.

Her mum talked to Dave and Mary.

Her dad cooked.

Anna and Ryan talked.

And Sophia sat next to Skylar, glancing at her every so often in a sneering sort of way.

Skylar was about to punch her.

In the face.

With the hardest thing she could find.

Like a brick.

Or maybe just her fist would do. She'd do it exactly how Mercury had taught her.

"What's with that outfit, anyway?" Sophia finally asked.

Skylar looked at her, deciding whether to answer or not.

"I'm guessing you don't like it," Skylar said, looking away. "I knew you wouldn't be able to appreciate my style."

"Style?" Sophia asked, seemingly taken aback by Skylar's answer. "That's not stylish."

"Maybe not to you."

Sophia was speechless.

"I didn't expect you to understand," Skylar said.

It was like Sophia didn't know how to react when Skylar was so outward and direct to her. She was used to quiet, shy Skylar, and she was getting the complete opposite. Skylar was quite enjoying her surprise.

"What, is this meant to be some kind of statement?" Sophia asked.

"Uh huh."

"Of what?"

"You wouldn't understand."

"Whatever," Sophia huffed as their dinner was finally served.

When both families were finished eating, the talking resumed. Skylar, with her now improved hearing, couldn't help but listen to the conversation her mum was having with Mary.

"What is that horrid outfit she is wearing?" Mary asked.

"What? Skylar?" her mum asked. "Oh, I don't like it either."

"My girls would never be caught dead in anything like that. They'd never want to wear such a thing."

"I'm not a fan of it, but I couldn't just tell her not to wear it," her mum said. "I mean, she's finally finding her self-confidence, and if wearing that boosts her confidence, then I couldn't take it away from her. What if that one act could completely reverse it all and make her shy again? I wouldn't want to do that to her."

"Yes, but those are horrible clothes," Mary said. "She couldn't have chosen anything better? Why don't you persuade her to wear something else?"

"What she wants to wear is not for me to decide."

"Whatcha listening to?" Phoenix asked.

Skylar jumped. Phoenix was so good at catching her off guard. Everyone around the table stared at her for a second and then went back to their various conversations.

"Just Mum backing me up," she said with a smile.

"By the way," Phoenix said, "I like the new look."

"Thanks."

As dinner finally came to an end and their guests were getting ready to leave, Skylar's phone rang, and she answered quickly.

"Hello?"

"Hi," Mercury said. "I don't mean to alarm you, but your dinner guests aren't who they seem."

Skylar didn't answer but backed into the hallway. She grabbed Phoenix's arm and dragged her sister out with her, then held the phone out so they could both hold their ears to it to listen (she didn't dare put it on speaker).

"Mary—as she has so endearingly called herself—is Marisa Raven. You know, the one Shadow warned you about."

Phoenix and Skylar looked up sharply. First at each other, then back into the living room where Marisa was standing.

"How do you know this?" Phoenix asked, her voice barely a whisper.

"I promise I'm not hiding in the bushes in front of your house," Mercury said. There was a slight sound of rustling in the background. "Although I am here if you need me," she then added. "Just be careful. Hopefully, she'll leave without any trouble. Nice outfit, by the way."

Then she hung up before either could reply.

Skylar and Phoenix walked back into the living room to see Mary and her family getting up to leave. They stood as close to the wall as possible, both watching warily, Skylar hoping she would get out as fast as possible.

"Thank you for the fantastic dinner," she was saying, like she had nothing on her mind other than how wonderful it was to spend time with another family.

Skylar couldn't help but wonder how she could stand there and be so pleasant when she was bent on ruining a world that Skylar and Phoenix had only just learnt about. And were supposed to rule in.

"No problem at all," their father replied.

Skylar decided the scenario was far too similar to something she had once seen on the internet: a picture of Hitler holding hands with a little girl and walking as if he hadn't a care in the world. The image had irked her, and by the comments all over it, it had struck plenty of people the same way.

"Well, we'd better get going now," Dave said, slowly heading for the hallway.

Goodbyes spread across the room, with Skylar and Phoenix joining in so as not to stick out. As Mary made her way over to them, they both froze in place, unconvincing smiles plastered on their faces.

She bent down to bid them farewell, and it struck Skylar just how tall she was; easily over six feet.

"It was lovely to see you both," she said. It seemed harmless at first, but then she leant in closer. "Don't worry. I know you were talking to Mercury just a minute ago. She's not as subtle as she thinks. I know you know who I am, but I'm not here to kill you just yet. Aren't I allowed to enjoy time with my family and friends every once in a while? Have a nice night, you two." Then she stretched up to her surprising height and headed for the door, followed by her husband, daughters, and son.

Only when the front door closed behind them did Skylar feel like she could breathe again.

Phoenix headed to the door, and Skylar decided to follow her. They stepped outside, just a couple of metres down the front path, and Phoenix looked around while Skylar still felt stunned. Marisa's voice had made her insides go cold. It wasn't even the words, really, just the way she spoke, the way she *knew* the words would get into Skylar's head.

"A promise is a promise," a voice said from behind them. Skylar snapped out of her daze.

The twins turned to see Mercury sitting on the roof, almost blending in to the darkness of night, but for the bright blue slashes of her clothes and her bright hair that was tied off her face; still, a few strands of hair wafted around her cheeks. She was a pale smear against the dark backdrop. Her legs dangled over the edge of the roof, and after a second, she pushed herself off. She landed gracefully on the lawn, as if she had jumped off a metre-high box and not the roof of a two-storey house.

"So what happened?" she asked, a playful hint to her voice.

"Nothing," Phoenix said. "She came, ate dinner, and left."

"She knows you were here," Skylar added.

"Shouldn't we, like, go after her or something?" Phoenix asked.

"Sure, if you want to get yourself killed," Mercury said, plainly.

"Why are you here?" Phoenix then asked. "What is Shadow's point with this if Marisa wasn't even here for anything?"

"Shadow isn't exactly happy with me at the moment," Mercury said nonchalantly. "This was my own idea."

Skylar tilted her head. She didn't understand Mercury.

"Why?" she asked. "If you're just Shadow's … assistant, then why help us like this?"

Mercury smiled. "I'm more than just Shadow's stupid assistant. I'm just like the two of you. I'll let you decide what that means." Her eyes shone, like a flame danced in their cores.

Skylar didn't know what to say to that. Both she and Phoenix were silent. Honestly, Skylar found herself admiring this girl.

Really, she hadn't thought much of Mercury ever since they'd met. She'd quickly thought back to what she knew of Lauryn from school, though that wasn't much, since they were in different years. Mercury hadn't stood out to her as an interesting figure, just standing against the wall, almost like Shadow's puppet. But she wasn't. Or so she said.

It made her wonder what she could possibly be doing, working for Shadow. What was the purpose behind it?

Why?

And why come here to see them because of Marisa when Shadow hadn't sent her?

Did she actually care about them? But why would she? She certainly wasn't a vampire or fairy, so it wasn't about protecting them because of any sort loyalty to her kingdom; that part was still hard for Skylar to grasp.

"Why don't you two go back inside?" Mercury said, breaking the silence. "I'll see you tomorrow."

Phoenix and Skylar nodded, not knowing what else to say.

They watched as she crossed the front yard and mounted the black and blue motorbike parked on the street. Neither of them had noticed it until then. Skylar distantly thought about the colour scheme Mercury had going. As she put on her helmet—black with a startling neon pink horizontal stripe—she waved backed to them. Then she started the bike and was off down the dark street before either of the twins could react.

17

Skylar sat on the hard wooden bench, licking her ice cream in the forming spring heat and watching the people pass her by. She looked down at her phone sitting on her leg. Still nothing. She picked it up and opened it, reading the text from Mercury again:

"Meet you in the park. That bench by the fountain."

That was it. No time.

Skylar glanced over at the fountain again, at a little boy trying to reach one of the carved dolphins in the centre. Then she slipped her phone into her back pocket, and when she looked away from the boy about to fall into the water, Mercury was sitting beside her. Denim shorts, colourful T-shirt hanging off one shoulder, floral boots, hair as blonde and wavy as usual, with her fringe out of her eyes for the first time since Skylar had known her.

Skylar had sensed a tingling in the back of her mind as Mercury sat down. Something about the other girl brushed up against the new reach of her senses she was learning to find.

"Took you long enough," Skylar said, the words spilling from her mouth before she could even think of what she was saying.

Mercury smiled. "Don't you just love spring? Because I do. People feel happier in spring."

The comment perplexed Skylar. Never had she thought Mercury would make such a statement to her. Never had the thought even occurred to her that Mercury might have a favourite season or that she would want to share it with her.

"Why did you want to meet?" Skylar asked, instead of answering the season question. She was far too stunned by how arbitrary it was to even realise Mercury had, in fact, been expecting an answer from her.

Mercury didn't lose her pleasant smile but turned on the bench seat and folded one leg up on it so that her whole body was facing Skylar. "Have you heard from Shadow lately?"

"No," Skylar said immediately. Too quickly maybe, but it wasn't a lie.

The thought had been on her mind for a while, actually. Well, the past week. She hadn't heard anything from Shadow at all and had been wondering what could have happened to her. Especially after that visit from Marisa.

Mercury shrugged. "Just making sure. She has a habit of leaving me out of things. Even though she says she wants my help."

"You don't seem too worried about it."

"Shadow can look after herself. I'm more worried about you," Mercury said. "You and Phoenix and Jade, Ash and Aelana." Her voice dropped away on Aelana's name, a sign Skylar knew well, that she had a deep distaste for the girl.

"Why? Could what April said be true? Could she just be abandoning us?"

Mercury stiffened at the mention of April, but her shoulders dropped quickly, and the smile was back on her face. "It's possible," she said. "But I doubt it. Shadow still has something to gain from you. She's probably just assessing her options. What I'm worried about, though, is that while she's off deciding what to do with her life, Marisa could try to target you instead."

Skylar didn't speak. Somehow, she hadn't even thought of that. Hadn't Marisa been in her house just last night? She could have walked in there and snatched them away or killed them on the spot. Shivers tingled up her spine, and she forced her mind away from that train of thought.

Mercury stood up. "Wanna walk?"

Skylar stood up as well and, in that moment, realised that her ice cream was melting on her hands. She wiped her hands with the napkin, threw the ice cream in the nearby bin, and followed to catch up with Mercury.

"Why is it that you care?" Skylar found herself asking, falling into step beside the other girl.

"I care about people," she replied. 'That's kind of my thing."

"Your thing?"

"Yeah," she said. "Everyone is the hero of their own story, right?" Skylar nodded. She supposed that was true. "That's what makes me a hero in my story. I'll do what I can to help. There's no use discovering you belong in a world of magic and doing nothing with it. I have the opportunity to … well, maybe not change things, but make a difference in the lives of others, so I will. I'd rather that than sitting around, not knowing what to do and being too scared to try."

Skylar nodded again. She didn't say it aloud, but Mercury seemed to be talking about herself as if she were the main character of a book or movie, thrust into a strange scenario that she wasn't prepared for, and dragged along on a terrifying adventure. Except Mercury didn't seem frightened at all; it seemed like she actually wanted it to happen.

"And as horrible as it is to think, Marisa is the hero of her own story, making you, me, and Shadow villains to her, while she's the villain for all of us."

"Hmph. I'd never really thought of it like that." Yes. Mercury was far too eager. She liked the prospect of danger. She talked as if she were discussing the plot of some movie and smiled as if it was the best story she had ever heard.

"Overthinking is also my thing."

After that, the conversation descended into something more friendly and inconsequential. They walked and talked and left the park, and were still talking a couple of blocks from Skylar's house.

The buildings on this street were mainly tall apartment blocks, stretching up to the sky, all closely packed, meaning they'd have to go around in a big arc.

"I know a shortcut," Mercury said, leading the way between two of the buildings down a little alleyway.

The sunlight was cut off by one of the impossibly tall buildings, plunging Mercury's shortcut into dim shadow. The shade was welcoming after all that time in the sun, though, and Skylar strolled down the path, glad to be out of the heat.

They had nearly reached the end, the sun ready to welcome them to its warmth again, when Mercury stopped. Skylar came to a stop behind her; she peered over her shoulder, relaxed after their friendly small talk. A blonde woman blocked the way. Not Tempest, but she had a look in her eye equally as threatening.

"Hello, Mercury," she said. She spoke with an accent Skylar didn't recognise. It was like nothing she'd heard before. Her vowels were shortened in places but all the wrong places, while they were more pronounced in others.

"Hi, Olivia," Mercury replied curtly. "Having a nice day, are we?"

"You know me, always having a good day."

"That's nice," Mercury said. "Stop right there, Martin. I would almost think you were trying to sneak up on us."

Mercury kept her eyes on Olivia but Skylar spun around, looking for this Martin.

A blond man stood behind them, no more than five metres away.

Martin laughed. "What would make you think that?" He spoke with that same strange accent. His voice was deeper but similar in tone to the woman's.

Mercury, still looking at Olivia, said, "Oh, just the way Olivia here was clearly acting as a distraction. Sometimes, I think you take me for a fool."

"Well, we won't be making that mistake again," Olivia said, and lunged, just as Skylar turned back around.

Olivia and Mercury went down, and Skylar spun again just in time to catch Martin's fist with her face. She stumbled back, hit the wall, and slid down to the ground. She blinked as spots spun in and out of her sight. But she scrambled back up, wobbling on her feet, her vision focusing as Martin came at her again. She dodged past him this time as he swung and spun quickly, lashing a kick into his lower back.

Just do what Mercury taught you.

Martin turned and glared at her, and next thing she knew, there was something grabbing her from behind, pulling her into the wall. She looked down at her arms and legs and saw the dark vines wrapped around them, pulling her back. She hit the wall and the vines began to tighten and she didn't know what to do.

Magic. Use magic.

But before she could try, the vines started to loosen, and she saw Mercury standing just behind Martin. Relief washed over her, and then Martin's elbow cracked back into Mercury's face, and she wheeled back, clutching her nose.

The vines tightened again.

Then Olivia appeared and grabbed Mercury, spinning her around so they were facing each other. Olivia stared at her with a look of concentration on her face; Mercury didn't move. She stood stock still, as if she didn't even want to help Skylar anymore.

A vine latched around her neck, and suddenly, she couldn't breathe.

"What do you want?" she managed to choke out as Martin loomed over her.

"You."

18

Yesterday, Marisa may have not been in the mood for trouble, but she had woken up this morning and decided it was the right day. Skylar couldn't be much of a problem, but Marisa wasn't going to take any chances. Maybe it hadn't worked on Jade, but Skylar was different. She was fragile, in stature and mind. And Marisa herself tied her up in the dungeon.

She came back upstairs to find Olivia and Martin sitting in the newly appointed dining room at the large oak table they had procured. They chatted away, clearly happy with their work.

"Well done," Marisa said, giving them one of her rare smiles of actual happiness.

They both smiled back.

"It was too easy," Olivia boasted. "Mercury's not as tough as she's made out to be."

"It was almost easier than kidnapping Jade," Martin said, agreeing with his sister.

"Now, now," Marisa scolded, "don't get cocky. Do I need to remind you that little Miss Windrunner is still very much alive and, I daresay, not scared of either of you?" She paused, her smile turning cold, the kind of smile only a confident sociopath like Marisa could possibly pull off. "I could almost say you failed there. In fact, I might."

Their own smiles dropped, that hint of fear seeping into their eyes. Marisa loved when that happened, when they had that look where they knew she was far more powerful than them.

"You didn't want her dead, though," Olivia said.

"No, I did not," Marisa agreed. "But your plan did not work."

"Oh, calm down," said a new voice, silky and soft.

Marisa didn't bother to turn and see Melancholy as she entered the room. The Vampire girl strode past her and took a seat at the end of the table, assessing the ornate carved legs for a moment before crossing her legs elegantly, then sweeping her long, black hair – down to her knees – behind her back.

"Their plan was perfectly fine," she said. "We just didn't realise what effect it would have on Jade."

"So you have decided to join us again," Marisa said.

Melancholy nodded. "I could say that I love it here and only leave because I have other commitments, but that would be a lie. Really, I just don't want to rot away in this place like the rest of you. Maybe when you actually finish your renovations, I'll feel more inclined to stay." She spoke with the easy confidence that only someone like Mel could have. It came from a mixture of good looks, strong magic, and knowing that Marisa couldn't do without her.

"Oh, of course," Marisa replied. "But since you are here, I have a job for you."

"Yes?" Melancholy perked up, eyes gleaming.

"Olivia and Martin recently captured for us one Skylar Song, and I would like you to … Do I even need to explain?"

Melancholy stood, a cruel smile growing on her perfect, pale lips. "Just point me in the right direction," she said, with the kind of intent that only Marisa could replicate.

Skylar sat on the wooden chair, arms tied behind her back, ankles fastened to the front legs, and tried not to freak out. Like that was an easy thing to do.

The room was dark. Probably darker than she perceived it as, she realised. The walls were stone, covered in moss, and there were no windows, nor a lightbulb on the ceiling. The only light in the room was filtering through the gaps in the wooden door across from her.

Sitting in the darkness, no idea where she was, she tried to focus on magic to keep her mind calm. She concentrated on what she could hear and see, though that wasn't much.

Footsteps echoed in the hallway beyond the door. Then that door opened, and the sudden light was blinding; Skylar looked away, closing her eyes as someone stepped into the room with her.

The person leant down beside the chair, and Skylar flinched away, only to find that they hadn't touched her. No, they were undoing the ropes restraining her. It took barely a minute for them to undo them all, and then they stood.

Even with the door open, the room was still dark, and Skylar could only see part of their face: young, pale, female. Vampire?

"You have to get out of here quickly," the girl said, speaking softly.

Skylar nodded, standing, unable to speak.

"Go right. You will see a set of stairs that leads up. Two flights up is a door to your left that leads outside. Get away as fast as you can. To the forest."

Then she left, and a moment later, Skylar did too, following her instructions.

She wasted no time getting out, didn't stop to marvel at the stone staircase with the gargoyles on every landing. Right, up the two flights of stairs, then left, to a small, rounded door that did indeed lead outside.

She stepped out onto rough stones, creating a courtyard among trees. They weren't very tall trees. Well, they probably were, but after what she had seen in Aelana's dream, trees would probably never seem tall to her again.

The stones became a path that she followed, which led to an old, stone staircase, worn with time and millions of footsteps, leading down to God only knew where. Skylar started down them, seeing no other option.

There was a voice gnawing in the back of her mind with each step, asking her if she knew where she was, if she could find her way home, if she thought she had any chance of finding someone she knew in this strange place. She ignored it. Fear wasn't going to get her anywhere right now.

Hurrying down the steps, enclosed on both sides by more trees, she passed under a crumbling arch with moss and other plants growing out of its stones.

Sun filtered through the leaves, creating a warm, welcoming vibe to the strange forest and stairs. Tree roots grew over the path and Skylar hopped over them.

She must have been descending the stairs for five minutes when the trees began to thin out. Another minute, she guessed, and she had reached the bottom, stepping onto soft grass. She was greeted, however, by more trees. These ones far more foreboding than the others.

It only took her a few seconds to realise she knew these ones. These were the ones from Aelana's dream world. Shivers shot down her spine, and her hands started to shake. But whoever had freed her had told her to go this way. Would somebody be waiting for her somewhere in there? Or was this a trap? Why release her just to send her into a trap?

Surely it would be better than being locked up in a dungeon, she decided, and so she delved into the forest and didn't look back.

It only took Melancholy two minutes to return to Marisa, a scowl on her face.

"She wasn't there," the Vampire said.

Marisa didn't show her surprise. "She wasn't?"

"Nobody's there," Melancholy said. "Either she wasn't tied up tightly enough, or somebody freed her. I say it was Tyler."

"Tyler didn't do it," Marisa said immediately.

"Are you really so sure?"

"I don't take betrayal lightly," she said, and by the look on the girl's face, she instantly understood what Marisa meant.

There was silence.

"You know I question your loyalty," Marisa said. "Let's not pretend that you aren't aware of it."

"You can question my loyalty as much as you want; it doesn't worry me. I don't feel the need to prove myself to you. I'm sure *you* are aware of *that*."

Marisa could never tell whether Melancholy really was just that confident, or if she was faking. And she could never tell if the girl was just that prissy, or if she mostly stayed away because she was a traitor and didn't want to get caught. Because if there was one thing Marisa *was* certain of, it was that Melancholy knew what the consequence of that would be.

"Are you going to send someone out to find her?"

"No," Marisa said. "We'll let her go back to Mercury and Shadow, tell them that we had her. Make them worry. Let them know that we can take them any time we please. It's all just an elaborate game, my dear."

"I don't see how they'll be worrying when she's either going to tell them that she easily escaped, or that someone freed her," Melancholy said, then turned and walked off.

<hr />

Skylar felt like she'd been walking for hours. Her feet were sore, toes kicked on countless rocks and roots. Soon her legs wouldn't be able to hold her up any longer. She was really wishing that she had a watch right now.

She stopped, sitting down on a nice flat rock, took a deep breath and suddenly felt how her heart was beating. It was so, so slow, like it was barely working, yet she didn't feel tired, didn't feel out of breath.

She remembered what Shadow had said:

"Vampires aren't dead, their hearts just beat slowly, and so their bodies work slowly, but this isn't a hindrance on their abilities, because of magic. Magic keeps them going when their bodies can't keep up. Magic sustains you at an equal amount to the processes of your body."

She could feel it now. She could actually *feel* what Shadow had been telling her.

There was a growl from the bushes behind her.

Skylar jumped up and started backing away. A creature emerged.

The first she saw of it was white, the colour of bone, and then it came fully into view, and it was ... a skeleton. It was the skeleton of some kind of big cat.

She was too stunned to even think of running or dodging when it came at her. The only reason she wasn't slashed to pieces was because when it leapt at her, she tripped backwards in fright.

She crumpled to the ground, and the skeleton cat circled around, getting ready to pounce again. Her brain kicked into gear, and she scrambled to her feet, backing up slowly, trying to think of something to do.

The big cat stalked forwards, and just as it was about to leap at her a second time, there was a flash of steel, and its head toppled to the ground, followed by the rest of its bones.

A boy stepped out of some tall bushes, sheathing his sword at his hip. He looked down at the collection of bones and then over at her.

Skylar noticed instantly how bright his blue eyes were. They shone, and he flicked his hair out of his eyes. Dirty blond hair.

"What are you doing here, Vampire?" he asked, concerned.

"I-I-I …" She couldn't speak.

"You're …?" He dipped his head, tilting it to the side in a questioning manner.

"I'm, I'm, I'm lost."

"In the Dark Forest?"

She nodded.

"What's your name?"

"Skylar," she said. "Skylar Evans."

A hint of understanding dawned on his face.

"Evans? You're not still going by that name, are you?"

She frowned. "What?"

"Nothing," he said quickly, then, "Tyrel Silverblade."

Oh, right. Song is my name, isn't it?

"Thank you for saving me, Tyrel," she said.

"No problem," he replied. "Her Highness has been looking for you."

The words sounded harsh coming from his mouth, his tone changing with the mention of Her Highness'.

"Oh," she said, not sure what else to add.

"Well, come on, it's a long way back to Elpidas," he said and turned to start walking.

"Where?" she asked.

He started into the trees. "The capital. If you could call it that."

"Of?" she asked, heading after him.

"Of Elementum."

"Where?"

"Lindreas," he said.

Oh.

So that's where she was.

"How long is it going to take us to get to …?"

"Elpidas."

"Elpidas?" she asked, knocking a fern frond out of the way as she followed him.

"Hopefully, it will only take two days."

"Two days?"

"If we walk quickly."

"Two days?" Skylar repeated.

"Yes."

She had nothing else to say, and it seemed that neither did Tyrel, so they walked on in silence.

19

The sky was dark, but at least they were finally out of the forest. Skylar had never been happier in her life.

Their trip through the Dark Forest had been mostly uneventful, though he had warned her that it had been unusually calm. They had run across more of those skeleton creatures, in the shape of bears, leopards, monkeys, and things Skylar couldn't recognise. But Tyrel was good at steering them clear of the many animals lurking in the shadows, and when he couldn't, he easily dealt with them with his sword.

"It shouldn't be too far now," he said from up ahead. "Twenty more minutes, and we should reach Duchcast, where we'll stay for the night."

The thought of sleep urged Skylar on, and she nodded, even though she knew he couldn't see her make the gesture, walking behind him as she was.

A few hours ago now, Skylar had contemplated how old Tyrel was. He couldn't have been much older than her, maybe eighteen or nineteen, yet there he was, wandering the Dark Forest. Then again, she had been too. He couldn't have been looking for her, though, could he? She hadn't wanted to ask.

It was almost twenty minutes later when over the hill Skylar could see light; fires burning in windows. At first the fires surprised her, but then she wondered what she had been expecting. The small town looked just like it was out of any number of fantasy stories. Really, it was what she should have been expecting.

Tyrel led the way down a grassy hill and onto the main street of the village, which they followed until they reached the town square, passing a mismatch of houses that were all jumbled together. They resembled in style the kinds of cottages in movies set in medieval times, with thatched rooves, and rounded, wooden doors – some with knockers and some without. Many of them were one storey, small, and they couldn't have had more than four rooms, but there were some of two, and even three storeys.

The only way they differed from medieval movie cottages was in colour. They were painted in vibrant colours: reds and greens, purples and oranges, blues and pinks. They were not boring buildings, despite their nature.

Skylar and Tyrel reached the town square, which was busy for the time of night. Nobody paid them attention until Tyrel stepped into the centre of the square, beside its fountain, and announced, "We're here on business from Her Highness."

Absolute silence.

Absolute silence, and everyone in the vicinity turned to look at him, eyeing him up and down, assessing him sternly. Maybe trying to pick if he was lying.

"We would appreciate somewhere to stay for the night," he continued, voice sure, unwavering.

The crowd of watchful citizens parted as a beautiful young lady in a lilac tunic and navy-blue jeans approached Tyrel.

"I have a spare room I could offer you," she said. Her eyes glistened, and her tone was firm but welcoming.

"Thank you," Tyrel said, waving Skylar over. She joined him by the fountain as the woman started walking, and they followed her, leaving the square and heading down a maze of streets.

"My name's Viridis," she said.

Skylar detected that she had an accent. Similar to Olivia and Martin's, though not as pronounced.

"Tyrel," he introduced. "And this is Skylar."

Skylar tried to smile, but she had no energy left to care. She was just happy she was going to get to sleep. Sure, it would be in a strange house in a strange town in a strange kingdom in a strange dimension. But it was sleep, and she could really do with some. Or a lot.

Viridis led them down another street with a cobblestone path, just like all the others. She stopped at a doorway with elaborate carvings, retrieved a key from her pocket, and opened the door, letting them inside.

The house was warm. It was the first thing Skylar noticed.

Until then, she hadn't realised how cold it had become outside and how exposed she was in her short shorts. She rubbed at the goosebumps on her legs slowly traversing the room.

Lanterns hung from the ceiling, small but intricate, bright firelight spilling out of them. A digital clock hung on the wall, opposite a small but modern television with three armchairs arrayed around it.

It was almost midnight. No wonder Skylar felt exhausted.

A moment later, it struck her as strange: the combination of lanterns and fire with electronics.

"Sit," Viridis instructed. "I just have to make the beds and then you can both get some rest."

"Thank you," Tyrel said, and Skylar echoed him softly as Viridis strode away down the hall.

"How are you feeling?" Tyrel asked gently.

"Alright," she said, her voice barely above a whisper.

"I'll get us to Elpidas tomorrow," he said. "But we'll have to be up early."

Skylar nodded, his words barely sinking in.

Viridis had only one spare room in her house, but thankfully, it had two beds.

Skylar collapsed on hers, not even bothering to take her shoes off. She curled up, closed her eyes, and was asleep instantly.

She had an uneventful sleep with no strange dreams and woke up the next morning utterly refreshed.

Lifting her head from the pillow, she found Tyrel's bed empty. She rolled off her bed, barely getting her feet underneath her, and stood.

She heard voices as she exited the room and found Viridis and Tyrel talking and eating breakfast.

Skylar joined them at the table, sitting down and realising that there was a plate in front of her with toast, waffles, and strawberries piled on it.

"She awakes," said Viridis. "The mysterious Skylar Song finally joins us."

Skylar managed a smile, then looked back at the food.

"Well, go on, eat," Viridis said.

Skylar looked up at her then back at the food and dug in.

She chose a strawberry first, and it was the best strawberry she had ever eaten. It tasted so fresh, so perfect. She would never settle for a normal strawberry again.

Once breakfast was finished, Tyrel and Skylar headed off again, leaving Viridis and Duchcast behind. They walked a combination of cobblestone streets and dirt roads, and every so often, they passed people on horses and people with carts. But no cars. It seemed that was one piece of technology they didn't possess.

"I said I'd get us here," Tyrel said, but Skylar didn't see anything yet. And then she did.

The sun was beginning to set when she saw the steeple over the treetops. Light glinted off the gold, shining with the last rays of sun.

"You say it like it's a big achievement," Skylar scoffed.

"If you had been by yourself, it would have taken at least a month. And that's if you knew the way," he replied. "Without my magic, you would be barely a few hours out of Duchcast, yet here we are, halfway across the continent."

Skylar didn't have anything to say to that. Magic sure was strange.

They passed only a few houses and cottages on their way, and then suddenly, it was there.

A stone castle rose out of the trees with high steeples tipped with gold, and a stone fence with a wrought iron gate bordering it. It was polished, shiny new, and yet so, so old. The castle exuded power and yet sat humbly, all on its own, surrounded by trees.

Tyrel led the way to the gate, where a girl with dark hair, in jeans and a leather jacket stood beside a small guardhouse, face tilted into the dying sun.

"Hi, Tyrel,'" she said, sounding professional.

"Hi, Ignis," Tyrel replied. "I have a … gift, for Mercury."

Mercury?

"Finally," Ignis said, all her professionalism draining away in that word. "She's been really worried."

"Well, I guess I shouldn't keep her waiting any longer," Tyrel said, the venom back in his voice.

Ignis eyed him. "I know that tone," she said. "No mischief."

"I promise," he replied, and the gate opened.

Ignis stayed where she was, and Skylar followed Tyrel into the courtyard.

It was even grander than the one in Ash's dream.

Although there was no fountain in this one, the floor was of great sandstone tiles that met steps, which led up to two massive oak doors. The stone walls surrounding the courtyard were high, with plants growing over them, creating a hedge-like effect. There was only one slab of stone that stretched the whole height of the wall completely plant free, and it had swirling patterns etched on its surface.

Tyrel didn't seem at all concerned with how fabulous their surroundings were. He stalked to the stairs, taking the three of them in one stride. Skylar hurried to catch up with him. She couldn't help but notice that his shoulders were tight; he wasn't relaxed, like he had been seconds ago.

A boy stood at the top of the stairs. He was on the short side, but kind looking, with light brown hair and bright brown eyes that matched his smile.

"Names," he said, with an impish grin in Tyrel's direction.

"Do we really have to do this every time, Fabian?" Tyrel asked, sighing.

Fabian tilted his head slightly. "Yes. I enjoy annoying you. Also, your hair is weird, and I enjoy bothering you for that too."

Tyrel glared. Skylar stifled a laugh. Fabian turned to look at her.

"Princess Skylar finally arrives," he said.

"Can we get on with this?" Tyrel asked.

Fabian lost the smile. "You're just no fun."

"Watch it, Rose."

"I'll try to, Silverblade." He pursed his lips. "Just doesn't have the same ring to it."

Fabian's smile returned, and he pushed the giant doors open with ease.

On the other side was a huge entrance hall, painted sapphire and silver, with hints of red. It was long and wide, glittering with the firelight of ornate, crystal chandeliers hanging from the ceiling, a few storeys above their heads.

Fabian led them to the sweeping staircase at the other end, with steps that could have been made of gold. At the top of the first flight was a set of doors that were almost too simple for the rest of the castle. Fabian opened these doors, stepping in.

"May I present Her Royal Highness, Princess Skylar Song, and Mr Tyrel Silverblade," he announced.

Through the doors was what could only be known as the Throne Room.

Skylar walked into the throne room, which matched the door in being plainer than the rest of the castle. The walls were dark, with large windows that would let in mass amounts of light, if the sun hadn't set.

At the far end of the room sat a young woman in plain clothes on a spiralling throne of wood and bronze. She sat with her elbows on her knees and her chin on her hands. She was restlessly tapping the nails of one hand on her cheek.

She looked up at the sound of Fabian's voice, and Skylar saw her face.

Mercury.

Mercury sat on the throne.

She stood up, descended the steps of the platform her throne sat on, and walked across the length of the throne room to them. She walked quickly but neatly, hurrying, but not looking like she was. She wore clothes that Skylar was used to seeing her in: denim jeans, colourful shirt, boots, and blonde hair falling in a mix of ringlets and waves.

"Skylar," she said, "I'm really glad you're okay."

Tyrel cleared his throat.

"Tyrel," she acknowledged.

"Your Highness," he replied, his voice still full of that venomous hatred.

She smiled coldly. "It doesn't matter how you say it, I'll never get sick of hearing it." Her voice was no less venomous than his.

She turned back to face Skylar.

"So what happened?" she asked, her tone back to caring.

"I'm not even sure," Skylar admitted.

Mercury tilted her head.

"I was freed," Skylar said. "I'm not sure by who."

"What did they look like?" Mercury asked.

"It was dark," she said. "I didn't really see them properly, but it was definitely a girl. A Vampire. At least I think so."

Mercury nodded, thinking this over.

"It could only be Revenge or Fate, but that definitely isn't something Revenge would do. It must have been Fate, as ridiculous as that seems." She uttered the words softly, and Skylar couldn't tell if she was speaking to herself or not.

"Uh."

"I mean, I guess it makes sense. She could still feel some kind of loyalty to her kind and didn't want anything to happen to you."

"I guess."

"Fate," Mercury whispered.

She turned away and then back to them.

"Thank you, Tyrel, for finding Skylar and bringing her here. You may leave," she said.

He bowed in a mocking gesture, turned, and left. Fabian watched him go until the door closed.

"Can we go home now?" Skylar asked. "Phoenix is probably wondering where I am, and my parents … Oh, my God, my parents!"

"They think that you are perfectly safe," Mercury said, calmly. "They …" She paused and took a deep breath before continuing. "Look, Skylar, they … they aren't your real parents," she said slowly.

Skylar stared. Sure, it made sense if she thought about it, but … why?

If they were her real parents why weren't they here, running their kingdom? Why were they living a normal life on Earth? Even so …

"What?"

"Your real parents … I don't even want to say this." Mercury had tears in her eyes. "Your real parents are dead. That's why Shadow came looking for you in the first place. That's why you're important, because right now, your kingdom is being run by a bunch of losers who think they know what they're doing when they really don't."

"Dead," Skylar repeated, her brain latching on to that word.

"Your foster parents know who you really are," Mercury continued. "They don't have magic, but they know of it and promised to keep you safe. They know where you are; don't worry."

"Dead," she said again.

Mercury looked solemn. "You can go home now."

"Do the others know this?" Skylar asked.

"If Shadow hasn't told you already, then I wouldn't think so."

Skylar nodded, staring off into space.

"Okay, I'd like to go home now."

20

Mercury took her hand. The world flashed, and they were on Skylar's front lawn, the sun high in the sky.

Skylar stepped away from Mercury and stumbled, her head spinning. She blinked and realised she was lying in the grass. Soft, green grass. Mercury stood in front of her and looked back.

"Having fun down there?" she asked.

Skylar didn't understand how she could suddenly be so cheery again when only a moment ago, she'd had tears in her eyes, telling Skylar her parents were dead.

She was strange.

Skylar sat up slowly. She put her hands on the grass and pushed herself up, bending her legs and kneeling for a moment. The grass was wet with dew, and she brushed her hands on her clothes as she stood.

She walked to the front door; Mercury stayed where she was. She opened it and, just before stepping inside, looked back. Mercury was gone.

The door closed, and Skylar walked up the hallway and into the living room. Phoenix was sitting in the armchair, holding her hand out. Fire danced in it.

Focusing on what she was doing, she didn't notice Skylar until she blew out the flame.

Phoenix looked up. "'Hey!'"

Then she and saw who it was.

"Oh, my God! Skylar! Where have you been?"

She jumped up, and next thing Skylar knew, they were hugging.

"Around," Skylar said, smiling.

Phoenix let her go and didn't talk for a moment.

"Around? That's all you have to say?"

"I was on Lindreas," she said.

Phoenix's eyes widened. "What was it like?"

"Weird and amazing and scary."

"Why were you there?"

"Um … kidnapped?" Skylar said, like it was merely a suggestion.

"Wait … seriously?"

She nodded.

"Tell me all about it. Everything."

So they sat, and Skylar did just that. She told Phoenix everything. She told her about meeting Mercury and Olivia and Martin, and about how she was freed from the dungeonby a mysterious person who Mercury thought was Fate. She told her about the Dark Forest and Tyrel; Phoenix seemed interested by him until Skylar told her how weird he'd been around Mercury. She told her about Ignis and Fabian, and even the thing which she'd almost forgotten about:

"There's one other thing," Skylar said as her story was reaching its end.

"Yeah?" Phoenix asked, still excited.

"Apparently our parents …"

"Yeah?"

"Our parents are dead."

Phoenix didn't speak. Her face went pale. She lost her excitement.

"They just went out shopping …" Her voice dropped away at the end.

"Not those parents," Skylar corrected. "Our real ones. The ones who were king and queen."

"Our … real parents," Phoenix said slowly.

Skylar only nodded.

Phoenix looked at her and then looked away. At the doorway, where their parents were standing.

"We knew you would have to find out eventually," their mum said. "We never planned on hiding it from you forever."

Skylar had never really thought about it, until now, but neither she nor Phoenix looked much like the two adults sitting with them. Their mother was a tall, kind woman with auburn hair, and their father was also tall, with dark brown hair. And they both had startling grey eyes, so different in looks to their supposed children.

Phoenix was silent.

"Did you know our parents?" Skylar asked.

"We never met them directly," her dad answered. "But we knew of them."

"Your parents were apparently beloved in their kingdoms," her mum said. "We heard many stories about them."

"Kingdoms?"

"Yes. Otherwise, you couldn't both be heir to thrones." Her mum smiled the tiniest smile when she said it.

"King Somber of Lamia, and Queen Aima of Alae," her dad supplied.

"If Aima was a fairy queen, why does her name mean 'blood'?" Phoenix asked, finally speaking.

"Who knows?" their father said.

"Wait, how do you know that?" Skylar asked, turning to her sister.

Phoenix shrugged. "I don't know," she admitted. "I just did."

"Since when have you been learning Greek?"

"Since when did you know it was Greek?"

Now it was Skylar's turn to shrug. "I just do."

"It's all a part of magic," their mother said. "Apparently because Lindreans are responsible for humans existing, you can pick up our languages very easily."

"Lindreans are responsible for humans existing?" Phoenix asked.

"We really aren't the best people to be asking this," she said, a little flustered. "But there are stories. As every culture and religion has stories about how the world was created, so do Lindreans. They have stories of creation and gods and human existence. Of how magic came to be and how everything came to be. I don't know them well, though."

"Shadow will," Skylar said.

Her parents paled.

"We were warned to keep you away from her," their dad said.

"She's been helping us," Phoenix insisted.

He looked sceptical.

"We've been told not to trust her," Skylar said quickly. "And anyway, we haven't heard from her in a while."

"I know I won't be able to persuade you away," their mother said, "so please be careful."

Skylar awoke that night to the gentle sound of her phone buzzing.

She rolled out of bed and picked it up off her desk. Someone was ringing her. A number she didn't recognise. Half-asleep, she answered without thinking.

"Hello, Skylar," Shadow greeted. "Please get your sister and meet me outside." Then she hung up.

Skylar groaned. She wanted to crawl back into bed. She didn't want to go somewhere with Shadow. She wanted to sleep. Properly sleep. After her mini adventure and all.

She didn't, though. She dressed and walked down the hall to Phoenix's room. She knocked on the door and let herself in.

Phoenix looked up. "What do you want?"

"Shadow called," Skylar whispered.

Phoenix groaned. "What does she want?"

"Us. Now."

"Okay, okay," Phoenix said, getting up. "I'll meet you out there."

Skylar left the room. She waited in the hall for a moment, making sure Phoenix was actually getting up, then headed downstairs. Phoenix appeared at the top of the staircase, stumbled down, and then they were out the front door, careful to be quiet.

Shadow's van sat on the road outside their house. They walked over and let themselves in, finding Aelana, Ash, and Jade already sitting in the back. Jade was fidgeting with her shoelaces again, as she always did in the van.

Skylar watched out the window as Shadow drove.

They wound their way through the suburbs, not seeing any other cars, then they crossed the harbour bridge and were in the city. The van stopped outside the Powerhouse Museum.

Skylar jumped out of the van first, anticipation now clawing at her.

Shadow led the way inside, opening the doors without alarms going off.

They could be silent, Skylar thought.

But Shadow seemed too confident.

No. She's done something.

Skylar had been to the Powerhouse Museum a few times, and she had good memories of running around it with Phoenix and her parents, enjoying the weird and crazy objects found inside.

Now, however, it was dark, making the place take on a creepier feel, with the long shadows coming off contraptions and installations they passed. It was like wandering a maze that only Shadow knew the way through.

Skylar was still awed by her newfound abilities as a Vampire, and revelled in the experience of being able to use her 'night vision' – as Phoenix called it – to see all around her, even in the near pitch-black darkness they were engulfed in.

They descended a set of stairs single file, walking out onto a large floor, filled with odd contraptions. Skylar remembered from her visits that this was where the chocolate-making machine was located. They didn't pass it, though.

Shadow stopped abruptly. They fanned out around her and saw that the portal machine with its death-chair stood before them, albeit a little more compacted than before.

"Isn't this a little … conspicuous?" Jade asked. "A little too obvious? What if someone realises it's not right?"

"It has a sign," Shadow said.

And indeed, it did.

A little sign sat off to the side of the machine, stating that it was the prototype for a time machine created by someone Skylar had never heard of, with a name she could never hope to pronounce.

Well …

"'Skylar, if you wouldn't mind." Shadow gestured to the chair.

She stepped up to the chair, eyeing it warily. There was a lump rising in her throat. She didn't know if she wanted to sit down.

But she did.

She squeezed her eyes shut as she settled into the chair, feeling the bowl lower down onto her head, a cool sensation following.

Then the portal began to glow. She could see it against her eyelids.

21

Phoenix looked over at her sister, eyes tightly shut in the chair, then back to the portal, where an image was swirling into existence. Jade stepped up to it, looked back, and then jumped through. Phoenix hurried to follow, glancing back to Ash and Aelana before they disappeared, and she was through.

She was in a city.

A city of dark, gothic buildings, with tall spires and cobblestone streets, bathed in moonlight.

Jade stood a few paces away, staring down the empty street they were on. Aelana and Ash joined them quickly, their entrances echoing against the buildings.

"So," Phoenix said, breaking the eerie silence. "Where to?"

Jade shot her a look that said "Are you trying to get us killed?" Phoenix flashed her a smile in return.

"Does anybody see any glowing?" Ash asked.

Jade looked around, Phoenix shrugged, but Aelana had seen something. She pointed off behind them. They turned to look.

Sure enough, a glow emanated from the end of the street. It was faint and barely noticeable, but it was there.

"Let's go!" Phoenix called out, then started to skip away. She could almost feel Jade rolling her eyes. She laughed.

Phoenix knew that people thought she used comedy as a way to hide her fears and insecurities, but she didn't. She just liked being silly. She wasn't scared at all right now. Let the Shadow Lurkers come. She could use magic now!

When they reached the end of the street, the glow was brighter, coming from the left. They followed. They followed the glowing all across the city, until they were standing in a large paved square. In the centre of the square was a large bronze statue of a man and a creature that might have been a dragon, or might have been some kind of creepy demon. In the man's hand was a sceptre.

The sceptre was long and black; it seemed fragile. Whatever strange material it was made of twisted and curved, thin strands wrapped around each other again and again, rather than one solid piece. At the end—which the man held raised to the sky—sat a tiny ruby that shone despite the lack of light. Rays of tinted light seemed to shine from it, illuminating the ground around the statue.

"How do we get it?" Aelana asked.

Phoenix stared up at the sceptre. "I can get it."

They looked at her.

"How?" Jade asked.

"Magic," she said.

"Elaborate," Jade replied.

Instead of answering, Phoenix smiled. She'd been waiting for a chance to do this.

She felt the wings as they sprouted from her back. It didn't hurt, like she had been expecting at first, but was a rather relieving feeling. Like scratching an itch in the middle of your back that you just couldn't reach.

The first time she'd successfully been able to transform, she had admired herself in the mirror, so she knew well what it looked like.

Although her clothes remained the same, her hair grew in length and darkened to a strawberry blonde. Her wings were round and coloured orange, blue, and pink, in a pattern of many tessellating shapes, with bright red circles in the tips of the top two and a border of blue.

Phoenix did a little hop, and when her feet left the ground, her wings did one great flap, then started to buzz quickly, like a hummingbird's. As this was only a half-transformation, her wings were smaller in proportion to her body than they would be for a full transformation.

She was only a few inches off the ground, but she was flying. Or hovering.

She broke out in a big grin.

They all stared for a moment, but Aelana's eyes were the biggest. Jade started to smile.

"Nice," she said. "We're finally going to use magic."

Phoenix nodded as she looked up at the statue. Now came the hard part.

Being able to transform was one thing, but she'd never actually flown anywhere before. Her room wasn't really big enough for that. This would be a wonderful learning process.

Her wings buzzed. She drifted upwards. Slowly.

She came in line with the sceptre.

Now, forwards.

Flying was not as easy as it looked in cartoons. It was much harder to control.

Somehow, Phoenix managed to get herself moving forwards. The challenging part of flying was that sometimes she had to make a physical and mental effort to move her wings, and then sometimes, it was like they had a mind of their own and just knew what she wanted.

She reached the statue.

But she was moving a little too fast and banged against it, catching the arm at the last second so she didn't go tumbling away or fall to the ground.

Phoenix hung from the statue, finding that the metal was warm. Her wings buzzed, and she righted herself and began hovering again.

The sceptre was right there. Her hand closed around it. It slipped easily from the statue's grip. She held it tightly and drifted back to the ground. Her feet touched the pavers, and the shadows burst to life under the full moon.

The Shadow Lurkers were here. Better late than never.

Phoenix sprung back into the air, her wings catching her as her feet left the ground once again. The Shadow Lurkers poured down the street at them, circling around them and backing them up against the base of the bronze statue.

Well, all of them, except for Phoenix.

She floated just above the heads of the zombie-like creatures. Some of them reached for her feet, but she lifted her legs away when they did.

"Well, are you going to help us or not?" Jade asked, backing up. "Your wings are great, but if you could actually use them for something other than looking pretty, it would be appreciated by us ground-dwellers."

"Ground-dwellers," Phoenix repeated, smiling. "Phoenix is to the rescue."

Her next move took a little extra concentration.

Her body started to shrink. She shrunk down until she was barely the size of her own thumb. Her clothes morphed on her body, becoming things more fitting to a fairy: a sparkling orange singlet and miniskirt. Her shoes changed too. Rather than shoes, they became black vines tangling up her legs to her knees. She shimmered. She glowed. She was the size of a dandelion. She was a fairy princess.

It was the first time she'd done this.

The world looked weird. Everything suddenly so big. It was all new to her from here on. The one thing she did know, however, was what Shadow had told her: her powers were stronger in this tiny form.

A practice fireball confirmed this.

It wasn't just any old fireball; it was bigger than her body as it was now, and burned brightly, taking out a Shadow Lurker as it shot away from her. *Sweet.*

She floated back down to the ground, in amongst greying legs and feet, and when she touched down, fire shot away from her in all directions. She could tell it was going to take some time to get control of her powers.

For her tiny size, her power was definitely strong. It was almost too easy to ward away the Shadow Lurkers.

She cut a nice swathe through them with a flare of fire, making them back up and part. The perfect opportunity for Jade, Ash, and Aelana to escape.

They ran.

Phoenix chased after them by air, flying faster than she would have thought possible. And surprisingly well. She had better control of her wings like this. She didn't even need to think about it; she just flew. She ducked and weaved through the air, spinning and gliding.

It was tiring, though.

She caught up to Jade and landed on her shoulder.

She heard a sound. A deep, rumbling sound. A voice. "Are you alright?" it asked. Jade asked.

"I'm fine," Phoenix breathed.

She leaned against Jade's neck to catch her breath, almost getting tangled in her silky green hair.

When she felt better, she pushed away, into the air and tried, for the first time, to transform back.

A tingle went through her body.

And she grew. Her limbs lengthened, her hair shortened, her wings disappeared, and she was back to normal, blonde Phoenix again.

And they were back. Back in the real world. That had been easy.

But where was the Sceptre?

22

Phoenix looked at her empty hands.

It was gone. She'd dropped it.

But when?

She tried to think of when she could have let go of it. Had it been when she'd transformed? It would make sense. She was sure she'd had it, though. Really, it could have been at any point.

"Wait, where's the Sceptre?" Aelana asked.

Phoenix looked up, sheepishly.

Jade was shaking her head. Ash was glaring.

"I take it that you haven't returned with the Sceptre," Shadow said.

"You didn't get it?" Skylar jumped out of the chair, tripped, stumbled, regained her balance, and looked down at her sister, astonished.

"I did get it," Phoenix explained, "but I dropped it."

Skylar looked like she didn't know whether to cry or be angry. Phoenix hated it when she looked like that.

"You'll have to go back for it," Shadow said. "It will be much more dangerous, though. You can only do this so many times, and now that the Shadow Lurkers have seen you, they will know you are coming for it."

"Any advice?" Jade asked.

Shadow sighed, showing her first sign of annoyance. "I am going to send Mercury with you."

She stepped away and took out her phone.

Mercury's phone buzzed.

Ugh, why hadn't she turned it off?

It created the most irritating sound as it vibrated on the nightstand and she finally picked it up, not being able to ignore it.

"What are you doing?" Austin asked from beside her.

She clutched the phone to her chest and closed her eyes. "Wishing I didn't have to answer this."

"Who is it?"

"I don't know."

Sighing, she opened her eyes and lifted her phone, turning it to see the screen.

Shadow.

This had better be good.

"I don't want to answer," she said, looking at Austin.

"But you have to," he replied.

She nodded and answered the phone, lifting it to her ear.

She could thank a Werewolf by the name of Luna Grim for the call coming through. It was her invention that allowed interdimensional cell phone coverage.

Mercury," Shadow began, "I realise it is late, but we have found ourselves with a dilemma and would be grateful for your help."

"What is it?" she asked, annoyance seeping into her tone.

"Skylar's Sceptre has been … left in the dream realm," Shadow said, clearly choosing her words carefully.

"And now all the Shadow Lurkers know that you're coming back for it, and by you, I mean them. You need me because none of them are near trained enough, but you're willing to throw them to the sharks in the first place, as long as the element of surprise is there. But now that you've lost it, you need my help."

"Calm down," Austin whispered.

"Correct," Shadow said stiffly.

"Fine. Fine," Mercury said. "I'm coming."

She hung up.

The phone stayed in her hand for a moment, before she twisted and placed it back on the nightstand.

"I have to go," she said, hating the words as she said them.

"It's alright," Austin replied, smiling at her.

She smiled back as she removed herself from the nice, warm bed. Her nice, warm bed.

She dressed inside the huge walk-in wardrobe that was now hers: dressed, laced her boots, and tied her hair up. Then she settled her sword across her back, fastened to her jacket with pieces of itself, metal clips that melted into the jacket. The last things were her daggers, slid into her boots.

When she was done, she crossed the room, picked up her phone, and stood over the bed. After waiting a second, she leaned down to kiss Austin. He smiled his beautiful, bright smile at her and then pulled her down. She laughed.

"Have fun," he said.

"Yeah. Fun."

He let her go and she stood back up, walked to the door; it opened without a creak, as if it hadn't been standing for countless millennia. She turned and waved as the door closed behind her.

It took her twenty minutes.

Even from inside the building, they all heard the sound of her motorbike, circling around the building, until she pulled to a stop and shut it off. Another two minutes and she was before them. She was dressed in a jacket and cargo pants of deep, electric blue. On both these items, two thin, black stripes made their way down the sides. Her blonde hair was tied back in a plait, fringe sneaking into her eyes.

She carried a weapon too: a sword across her back.

She didn't look happy. "Let's get this over with."

Phoenix stood. She'd found herself a nice spot on the floor, leaning against the steps connected to the portal.

Mercury surveyed them. "I don't want to take all of you with me," she said. "Phoenix, Jade, you can come. Ash and Aelana, you stay here."

Phoenix watched their faces fall at this decision. Well, Ash's did; Aelana looked relieved.

Mercury came over to her, walking easily in her heeled boots, boots that reached over her knees.

Shadow went to set up the portal once again, Skylar sitting back down.

An image started to form, showing the same street as before, with the full moon high in the sky. Except it wasn't deserted this time. People lined the streets. No, not people. Shadow Lurkers.

Mercury cracked a smile. "Looks like we're in for some fun," she said drily.

Mercury was through the portal first. As soon as it spat her out in the crude interpretation of Elis, she ducked around the corner, out of sight.

Phoenix appeared right behind Jade, both of them joining her quickly.

She stood with her back to the wall and peered around the building.

There really weren't that many of them, easy to get rid of with magic. The problem was that she didn't see the Sceptre.

"Plan?" Jade asked in a whisper.

Mercury looked at her. "I really wish you had a bow."

Phoenix didn't seem to understand, but Jade did.

"Me too."

She was referring, of course, to the Elves' ability with a bow and arrows. There was some kind of magic behind their amazing aim and second nature ability, but Phoenix didn't know what. The point was, Jade would have been a lot more helpful to Mercury with a bow.

"You should start carrying one," she said.

Jade nodded. "Noted."

Mercury looked out again. Then turned back.

"Alright, Phoenix, you need to transform again, because I've been told that you can. Try not to go too crazy with the fire, because I want you to look for who has the Sceptre," she directed. "Then Jade and I will go fight the Shadow Lurkers. Find it, and we'll come and get it."

"We're going to fight them?" Jade asked. She didn't sound scared.

"We certainly are. Ready?"

"Yep," Phoenix said, then, in just over the blink of an eye, she shrunk down, becoming a glowing ball of light, hovering in the air. As soon as it was done, she zipped away.

Mercury peeked once more.

She saw Phoenix as a tiny glow, disappearing over heads. Then she was gone.

"Time to shine," Mercury whispered.

Then she stepped out from behind the building.

The Shadow Lurkers didn't notice her. Well, she hadn't made a sound, so why should they?

Jade followed warily, and Mercury removed a dagger from her boot, handing it to her.

Jade took it, held it confidently.

Mercury had the insane urge to whistle. But it was probably the stupidest thing she could have done, so she didn't.

Instead, she sent vines growing out of the ground, cracking and distorting the cobblestones. They wrapped their way around whatever was closest, and the Shadow Llurkers began to realise she was there. Too late.

It took concentration on her part to keep it going, to direct those vines up the sides of buildings and twisting amongst the mass of bodies. Then they sharpened at their tips and grew thorns, digging into the bodies they held, piercing heads, abdomens, arms, and legs.

Curiously, there was no blood.

She hadn't expected any.

Her little trick hadn't dealt with of all of them, though. It did, however, create a nice little maze for the rest to have to find their way through. It reminded Mercury of the story of Sleeping Beauty and that wall of plants that grew back even when cut down, or however the story went.

Fantastic.

Jade stood rooted to the spot beside her, awestruck.

The first Shadow Lurker popped through the vine wall in front of them. It was a man, with short, silvery hair and what were once the brightest of yellow eyes. Mercury recognised who it was but didn't say a word. It wouldn't be fair to mention. Not now, anyway.

She had known this man when he was alive, when he had a soul in his body and blood in his heart. She had met him once, and he had been nice to her, which made it hard when her sword took his head. She had to remind herself that it wasn't him anymore.

She sheathed her sword across her back once more, watching the Shadow Lurkers find their way through, the crude excuses for life. Not zombie, but no longer living, either. Real people who had happily been dead, with their bodies reanimated, forced into life without their soul, the thing that made them who they were.

Magic was the easiest way to get rid of them, for they no longer had any.

Each one that crawled through the vines was greeted with a blast of fire or ice, burning them away or freezing them in place.

A light appeared overhead. Phoenix had returned.

"I found the Sceptre," she said, her voice a barely audible squeak.

"Lead the way," Mercury replied.

Phoenix started to float off, and Mercury followed, with Jade behind her. The vines parted for them, clearing a path through the maze, allowing them to walk easily to the other side of the wall of vegetation.

Phoenix stopped. Mercury and Jade halted behind her glow.

"One of them has it over that way," she chimed, a tiny arm reaching out and pointing away.

Mercury looked around and saw the unmistakable glow that marked their prize.

"Good work," she said softly.

There weren't many Shadow Lurkers left. Just a few, milling about, already forgetting about the possible danger. Sometimes, they were so stupid. They couldn't be blamed for that, though.

Fire this time.

As she walked, fire spread out, emanating from her like the glow did from the Sceptre (except she was far deadlier).

Shadow had dragged her away for this? Something that Shadow could have easily done herself? She may as well have been the Queen of Bad Timing.

When she saw how many Shadow Lurkers were there, she felt like she had been dragged away from her lovely evening because Shadow just liked to screw with her. Phoenix could have done it. Ash could have done it. They all could have done it together.

Her fire flickered around her, and she heard its playful voice in her head, asking who they were getting next.

That one, she told it, eyeing the Sceptre in the hand of one of the remaining Shadow Lurkers.

It jumped out, racing through the air, and striking the woman. It caught to her clothing and hair, and burned around her. It snapped hungrily at her form.

Mercury watched it, amused, as she walked over, snatching the Sceptre from the woman's grip as she fell.

A smile crawled onto her face as she held it, the fire flickering and fading.

She turned and raised an eyebrow at Jade and Phoenix (who was back to human), her smile becoming a sly grin.

Phoenix didn't take her eyes of the Sceptre until they were back in the Powerhouse Museum and she was sure Mercury still had it. It was such a relief to see it still in her hand when the portal dimmed.

23

Her earphone swung down beside her, and finally, Phoenix could tell that the incessant ringing was, in fact, the doorbell.

She stood from her desk, leaving behind the schoolwork that she hadn't started yet (she was still mad about having work to do in the holidays), and made her way downstairs.

The heavy front door swung open as she pulled it back, and standing on the doorstep was Scarlett. As in, Scarlett, her best friend (not counting Skylar, of course).

Scarlett stepped inside quickly, pushing Phoenix back as she did, and then closed the door just as quickly.

There went the other earphone, coming loose from the push, and then falling from Phoenix's ear as she regained her balance. She reeled in the swinging wires and stuffed them in her pocket as Scarlett turned to face her.

"What the hell are you doing?" Scarlett asked, her usually calm face red.

Her light brown hair was unkempt, and Phoenix had the thought that this wasn't her friend. Hadn't Ash mentioned a Shapeshifter before?

"What do you mean, what am I doing?" Phoenix replied.

"I mean, what on earth do you think you could be gaining from Shadow?" Scarlett asked. Her eyes blazed with repressed anger, bright green fire.

"Knowledge? Learning about magic and who I am?" Well, it was no secret that Scarlett knew of magic, if she knew who Shadow was.

"You weren't meant to find out yet." She spoke in the hardest tone Phoenix had ever heard from her. Which was saying something, since

Scarlett had never been one for niceties and was always first to tell the blatant truth, no matter how hurtful.

"When was I supposed to find out, then?" Phoenix asked. "And why do you even care?"

"I care because I'm your protector," Scarlett said harshly, a hair off yelling. "I'm supposed to protect you from people like Shadow and anyone else who might harm you."

"My what?"

"Protector," Scarlett repeated, calming down and smoothing her hair. "My sole purpose in life is to keep you from harm, to act as a personal bodyguard."

"I have a personal bodyguard?"

Scarlett nodded.

"So you're a fairy?"

Scarlett nodded again. "You weren't supposed to know for a couple more years. You weren't supposed to be put in danger until you were old enough to understand the responsibilities placed on you and could deal with them properly."

"But you can be in danger?" Phoenix asked. "All this time, protecting me."

"It's my purpose."

"You sound like a robot."

Scarlett flashed a smile. "Oh, I'm definitely not a robot. It's just the easiest way to explain."

They sat on the lounge in the living room, a bowl of chips between them and each holding a cup of lemonade.

"I like your hair," Phoenix said.

The top layer of Scarlett's hair was pulled into a bun, sitting neatly at the back of her head. There were small strands of stems and flower petals strung through it. Phoenix also realised now that it was not unkempt but teased.

She tilted her head back and forth for Phoenix to see, then said, "Traditional fairy look. I was in a meeting. It looked better before."

"So if you're my personal bodyguard, then what other positions are there? And does everyone have a protector?"

"By everyone, I assume you mean royals," Scarlett said, laughing lightly. "And only the Crown Prince or Princess has a protector."

"As for other positions, the only other one nonroyals are born into is Seer."

"What do they do?"

"They see the future. Well, glimpses of it. But they're also in charge of record keeping, the Portal, and a few other things."

"The portal?"

"Each kingdom has a portal. It's a way for royals to travel quickly between castles without having to go dimensionally between Lindreas and Earth."

"Who's our Seer?"

"Her name's Frost Stone. She's an ice fairy. Very quiet; I haven't spoken to her much."

"What kind of fairy are you?"

'Crystal fairy."

Instantly Phoenix thought of that night with Revenge and Tempest, and how those crystals had grown from the warehouse floor, partly blocking the door. Mercury must have done it, as she was the only one who could. That was one thing Shadow had taught Phoenix.

Fairy and Sorcerer magic were similar, but while Fairies only controlled one element, Sorcerers controlled all of them. But "controlled" apparently wasn't exactly the right word to use for Sorcerers when talking about magic. For Fairies, it was simple, they used gestures and some thought to control the element they were born to. Sorcerers didn't. They communicated with the elements, asking them or telling them what to do, as if they were living things that could think, even without a brain.

According to Shadow, they were. They had minds of their own and acted how they wished, but Sorcerers were the only ones able to hear what they were saying; that was the nature of their magic. Not so much the controlling of elements, but the ability to communicate with them, to hear what they said and talk back.

"So, if the Crown Princess and Prince have protectors, then who is Skylar's?"

"A guy called Jack Danger," Scarlett said, pulling a face. "I've never liked him, and I wouldn't trust him around Skylar."

24

Mercury stood, resplendent in white.

She wore a simple dress. It was a reasonable length, just above her knees. The skirt was loose but the top was tight, with thick shoulder straps.

The grass felt nice between her toes; the sun felt nice on her skin. It was a beautiful day, not a cloud in the sky.

She heard the chatter of people around her, of her friends and family, but she was separated from it, in her own little bubble, watching Austin walking over to her.

He was wearing a suit, even though he didn't need to be.

In fact, everyone was dressed up for the occasion, despite it not being at all necessary. They wanted to be dressed up. Because that's what people did when they celebrated something important.

Austin reached her, and now they were both in the bubble, away from everyone else.

He looked good in a suit, she decided, even though he was barefoot.

His brown hair was tousled, as always. He smiled, and his eyes became a more vibrant green.

"I know it doesn't really mean anything," he said. "But I got you this anyway."

He produced a ring. It was a simple ring. Rose gold, with a sapphire set in it.

Mercury was speechless. She grabbed his arm tightly, feeling like she might just fall over.

"You didn't have to," she finally said.

"But I wanted to," he replied. "It might not mean anything to you today, but it means something to me."

He lightly took her hand from his arm and slid the ring onto her finger.

She had tears in her eyes as she stepped forward and wrapped her arms around him.

"I love you so much." Her voice was muffled in his shoulder.

"I love you, too, Merc," he replied.

The space around them exploded with life.

Their friends had found them.

Amber, Jem, and Flash greeted them.

"Oooh, nice ring," Amber said upon seeing it, as Mercury straightened. "Where'd you get the money for that, Austin?"

He just smiled at her.

"Are you guys really getting married?" Flash asked, giggling.

Mercury was startled by how she looked. Her usually scruffy, brown hair, with its bright blue and purple streaks, was brushed beautifully and tied back. And she was wearing a dress. A green one with a knee-length skirt. Mercury wondered how Amber had managed to get Flash to agree to it.

"It's not a wedding, Flash," Austin said, kindly to his best friend. "It's more of an acknowledgement that we're soulmates and will stay together. You'll have this with Jem one day."

Flash giggled. "If we're soulmates."

Mercury laughed at the look on Jem's face. It was the "if" that caused it. He looked startled, his eyes wide, like he wanted to say something but wasn't sure what.

"Of course, you are," Amber said. "Why wouldn't you be?"

Flash considered this. Just as she came up with an answer, she turned and saw Jem's face. She started laughing. His eyes grew wider.

Soulmates was the term for two people who were, well, destined to be together. It was linked to the fact that every Lindrean had a soul. These souls were born into people and could be responsible for lots of their characteristics, like their physical appearance or their personality, the one that was always determined by their soul. Souls lived life after life, retaining memories and connections with other souls (though they never shared these memories with their host). Soulmates were then two souls that had a romantic connection that existed throughout each life they lived. Therefore, the people the souls inhabited would always find each other and fall in love. They would be different people each time, but they were always the same souls. The longer the souls were around, the easier it was for them to find their mate, and the faster the two connected.

And today, they were celebrating that Mercury and Austin were soulmates. Mercury's older brother, Blaze, would be conducting the ceremony. There wasn't much that he needed to say, though.

She could see him now, across the large opening in the forest, standing with Lithium, his soulmate, who had become like an older sister to Mercury.

Any minute now, he'd call everyone together to begin.

Mercury spotted someone else across the clearing, standing by herself, near Blaze and Lithium. It was Zafeiri.

"I'll be right back," she said to her friends and started over to join her.

Zafeiri was human, meaning she had no magic and no place here. She was a good friend to Mercury, though; she had accidentally spilled to about magic when she first discovered it. It had been easy to tell her, despite them only seeing each other once a week in dance class. Mercury thought that it was because they only saw each other once a week. Her theory was that it provided a kind of detachment, meaning if she messed up, she didn't have to be around Zafeiri every day, and so it was easier to talk to her, because she didn't have to be as worried about saying stupid things. She wished she still did dance. But other commitments had arisen. Zafeiri, however, was still her friend.

"Hi," Mercury said as she reached her.

Zafeiri smiled as soon as she saw her, making her nose round, and her eyes crinkle in a way that made her look so sweet. "Hi."

Zafeiri naturally had brown hair, but as she'd been saying she wanted to do, her hair was dyed a vibrant purple.

"I love your hair," Mercury said.

"Thank you," she replied. "I am so honoured that you let me come here."

Mercury smiled. "I'm glad that you could come. In my opinion, you deserve to be here."

"I really don't … but as long as you think I do."

"I really do."

Mercury actually harboured suspicion that Zafeiri might not be just human; she could actually be what was referred to as Mortal. Mortals were humans that were somehow born with a magical, Lindrean soul. This could grant them certain magical powers, or, like Alex, a Lindrean lifespan. Mortal was actually a stupid term, because none of them were inherently immortal. She was trying to work out how to tell Zafeiri what she thought. The conversation now was leading straight to it.

A great gust of wind blew through the clearing, gathering everyone's attention to its source: Blaze.

"If I could have everyone's attention for a minute," he said, his voice carrying with the use of magic.

The clearing instantly hushed.

"We are here to celebrate an important moment, not just for the two people we are here for, but the wonderful kingdom we are in," he said, sounding more formal than Mercury had ever heard him. "We are here to celebrate that Princess Mercury has found her soulmate in Austin Perry, meaning that these two will one day be King and Queen.

"'Ordinarily, this would be the opportunity for the two to say vows of sorts, but, and I quote, 'there's nothing we need to say to each other in front of a bunch of people,' so that will not be happening." And the formal air was gone.

She shook her head and laughed softly. Her family sure was weird. Exhibit A: Blaze. Exhibit B: Mel, who was walking over to her, managing just fine in her tall heels in the grass. Her long, black hair, pulled back in a high ponytail, swung around her hips with every step.

"Congratulations, sis," she said, wrapping an arm quickly around Mercury's shoulders in a gesture that was supposed to be a hug. "Aren't you two just the cutest?"

"I don't know, you and Seb are pretty cute," Mercury said, teasingly.

Mel pulled a face. "Yeah, no."

"Oh, sure. You say that now."

"Don't start," Mel said, glaring. "I'm going to find someone who isn't going to annoy me now." She started walking off.

"Like Seb?" Mercury called after her. Mel ignored the comment.

"Who's Seb?" Zafeiri asked, grinning impishly.

"Seb's her on-again, off-again boyfriend," Mercury explained, also grinning wildly.

"Oh, I see," Zafeiri said, nodding.

Mercury decided she was going to tell her. "Zafeiri, I've been thinking about something."

"There you are," Amber yelled from somewhere behind Mercury. She came up beside her. "Right back, my arse."

"Hi, Amber."

"Oh, who's this?"

"Amber, meet Zafeiri. Zafeiri, meet by insanely obnoxious best friend, Amber."

"Hi," Zafeiri said sweetly. "Nice to meet you."

"I like your hair," Amber said, unexpectedly.

"Thank you." Zafeiri smiled, making her eyeliner curl around her eyes.

"Anyway," Amber said. "Moving on. How did you get over here?"

"I walked," Mercury replied.

"Yes, yes. Ha ha. Very funny. It is to laugh."

"Don't you quote Daffy Duck at me."

"I'll quote whatever I want," Amber said. "The point is, you need to get that lovely, white dressed butt of yours back over Austin's way, not standing over here with some fairy chick. She can come over, but quit standing out here like a couple of loners, miss centre-of-attention."

"Oh, I'm not a fairy," Zafeiri began.

Amber looked at her, puzzled. Mercury, however, was happy about the comment. It meant that Amber recognised something in her too.

"I was going to say earlier, before Amber so rudely interrupted, that I think you could be Mortal, Zafeiri. You might not be able to do any magic, but I think there could be something there."

Zafeiri beamed. "You really think so?"

"Definitely."

"Aw, what a lovely moment," Amber said. "Now, let's all move our fabulous arses over that-a-way."

"Yes, ma'am," Mercury said, turning and following her. Zafeiri came too.

Amber and all their friends had found a spot to sit in the grass, in the open but somewhat secluded from everyone else.

"Guys, this is Zafeiri," Mercury introduced.

"Hi," Zafeiri said, raising her hand in a small wave and smiling brightly.

Mercury's friends responded with a chorus of hi's and heys.

They sat down.

"So, you're a fairy?" Jem asked.

"Uh, no," she said, glancing at Mercury. "Mortal."

"Like Alex!" Flash said loudly. Mercury couldn't help but notice that her hair was undone.

Alex raised his hand across the circle. "That would be me."

Amber huffed. "My boyfriend, the non-magical one."

Alex raised an eyebrow at her. She did it right back.

"So," she went on, "who's ready for ballroom dancing later?"

That garnered mixed responses.

Seb looked calm, as always. Alex seemed a little worried. But Austin and Jem looked confident. Amber also looked confident. Flash not the least bit worried (but she never seemed worried about anything). And Mel was nowhere to be found.

"You'll all be fine," Mercury assured them. "Now, how about a topic that doesn't make you all look like startled fish?"

Zafeiri laughed. "There's going to be dancing?" she asked.

"Tonight."

"Sounds like it'll be fun. I only wish I had someone to dance with."

"Someone will want to dance with you," Mercury said.

"Some random?"

"Hey, it's someone to dance with."

"If you're sure."

The day stretched on. The sun stayed out. Only when it was finally blocked by the trees did the celebrations move back to the castle. Time for the second part of the festivities, the formal part.

Mercury changed dresses from the simple, white one she had been wearing to a golden and silver one that was high around her knees, but trailed along the floor behind her.

She stood beside Austin at the entrance to the ballroom, looking down at her feet, desperately trying not to pick at the threads of her dress.

"What are you so worried about?" Austin asked.

She didn't answer at first. She didn't know. She was just nervous, those old feelings she thought she had thrown away resurfacing inside her, making her stomach twist and her hands shake.

"I don't know," she whispered, because it was all that she could manage.

She took a deep breath, feeling it shake, hearing it shake, as she drew it in.

"Nothing," she said, forcing her voice to be louder.

She looked up at him and managed a smile. He smiled back and took her hand, looping their arms together, then gestured to the door. "Shall we?"

She nodded.

He pushed the door open and she took a deep breath then they stepped through together.

People. So many people.

Act confident. Just act.

She forced herself to smile as everybody turned to look at them.

They're looking at Austin, not you. You're not alone.

Fabian, standing at the base of the steps leading down, introduced them to the hall of people, and the smile on her face became real. Fabian looked nice in a suit, too.

"Presenting Princess Mercury Winter, and Mr Austin Perry."

They descended the stairs, her heels clacking against the marble. She could feel how tight her hand was on Austin's arm, and she tried to relax. Nobody was watching them anymore, they had gone back to their conversations. She could relax. Everything was fine.

"Care to dance?" Austin asked when they reached the bottom of the steps, and started walking across the ballroom.

"Of course," she replied, smiling at him.

The ballroom was easily the biggest room in the castle, a hall, really. It sported three large chandeliers, twisting silver and gold, accented with diamond and amethyst, hanging from the ceiling. There was an upper level, a balcony running the full perimeter of the hall, looking out over the floor. And the floor of the ballroom was marble, with tables and chairs sitting around the outside.

Some people were dancing, but only a few. Most were seated around the room, just watching the dancers or chatting away. Funnily enough, Mercury saw Zafeiri dancing. She danced well, and she looked like she was enjoying herself.

The crowd parted for them, and the few people already out there instinctively made room for them.

As Mercury focused on dancing, she could suddenly hear the sound of strings that filled the room from the corner in which the small orchestra sat. Honestly, Mercury was still awestruck by the grandeur of the event. She never imagined something like this being held for her.

Austin danced well. It was just another thing she loved about him, how he could dance. She loved how they danced together too. How it was just so easy, so natural.

His eyes were bright as they twirled around the floor. Their fingers easily wound together, and his hand felt perfect on her back. She couldn't help but think how much it felt like a fairy tale. But this wasn't just a story or a dream she would wake up from.

The music ended. The remnants of string echoed around until silence fell, as if the ballroom was holding its breath for the final note.

Absolute silence for a whole seven seconds, and then the music started again. Faster.

Mercury could have danced all night, except she was starting to get hot and needed something to drink.

She walked to the end of the ballroom, to the giant glass doors that opened onto the forest, and looked out into the darkness, watching the flickering shadows on the trees.

She opened one of the doors and stepped out, leaving it open behind her.

The air was cool against her skin, immediately drawing away the heat threatening to burn her up.

Are you alright?

The words weren't really there. They came in the form of a feeling, whispering against her skin. A whisper meant only for her, that only she would understand.

She nodded.

Water? the air asked in its whisper.

She nodded again.

Tiny droplets materialised out of the air against her arms and face and legs.

Much better.

She turned and walked back through the door, making sure it closed behind her.

Music filled her ears again, but it was once again coming to an end. The musicians were taking a break this time.

Conversation quickly filled the space of the music.

As she scanned the hall for any sign of her friends, she felt claws gently on her shoulders, and she turned her head to be licked by a cat. A black cat with glowing green eyes.

"Why exactly?" she asked Austin the cat.

Her question was answered by the flapping of wings overhead, and then a falcon landed on her other shoulder. The cat hissed.

"Why?" she asked Amber the falcon.

The falcon titled its head at her.

She sighed. 'You two are horrible.'

The falcon fluttered back and then it transformed into Amber in a beautiful dark blue ball gown, complete with gloves.

Austin, however, remained a cat.

Amber shrugged. "Why not? You know you love us."

"Do I?"

Cat Austin licked her cheek.

"I'll get you one day, cat," Amber said.

Mercury sighed. They were using telepathy.

"Here's a thought," she said. She picked up Austin from her shoulder and held him in her hands for a second. "You two argue over your weird grudges." She put him on Amber's shoulder. "And I'll go off and find some more normal people to be friends with."

"I don't want your cat," Amber said, taking him off her shoulder. "He's yours."

Mercury pretended she didn't hear and walked off.

She had only taken maybe ten steps when Austin was at her side. Human again.

She gave him a look. "So, what was the point of it this time?"

"Hmm? Oh, nothing. We were arguing about whether I was better, or she was better as a bird. I said I could catch her, so she turned into a falcon."

"I noticed. Is it settled now?"

"Not even close." He smiled.

Mercury had given up trying to work out their grudge ages ago. Although Amber and Austin were great friends, as a Shapeshifter and Night Walker, they had this unspoken rivalry about which one of them was better in terms of magic. It also didn't help that Austin was a cat and Amber preferred to shift into different types of birds.

<hr />

The night progressed well.

Mercury and Austin danced more. And she saw Amber and Alex dancing, Jem and Flash, and, most surprisingly, Mel and Seb.

Zafeiri was also frequently on the floor, twirling around like she owned the place. Mercury hadn't really been focused on *who* she was dancing with; she had just been glad she was. However, she happened to spot her partner as she watched from her seat over by the side, sipping from a glass of water.

Tyrel.

The water started to heat up.

Calm.

There were going to be words between them later. Possibly harsh. Probably harsh.

She took another sip of water.

"Who's that Tyrel's dancing with?" Lithium asked from beside her.

"Zafeiri." Even though she tried to stay calm, the name came out through gritted teeth.

Lithium laughed. "I take it that's not good."

"I think I'd prefer him with about anyone else on the planet. He could even be dancing with Amber. But not her."

They were coming off. Mercury went to stand up, but Lithium stopped her.

"Fire is easily started but not so easily put out," she said cryptically. "Don't be over the top, and don't say something you'll regret."

"I'll be fine," Mercury said. "I never regret what I say to him."

She stood up and started walking over to Tyrel, who was talking with Zafeiri.

She reached them. "A word, please," she said to him.

He glanced at Zafeiri, who raised an eyebrow at Mercury. "Whatever you say, Princess."

It was astounding how much she wanted to punch him whenever he spoke.

She walked. He followed.

They stepped outside, the door closing behind them, and she turned to face him.

"Is there a good reason you were with Zafeiri?" she asked.

"It's not to spite you, if that's what you're thinking," he said, raising his head. It only made him look short.

She used to be shorter than him, but now she was taller. It was quite funny, actually.

"I highly doubt that," she said.

"You doubt everything I say," he replied.

"Only because you give me reason to."

"Well, I'm not. It's just dancing, Merc."

"Do not call me Merc." She didn't think she'd ever heard herself sound as angry as she did with those words. Tyrel noticed.

Mercury had always been picky about nicknames. Amber had always been the only one who could call her a nickname, since they had been friends all through their childhood. And she and Austin were the only ones who could call her Merc. Jem said it sometimes, but for some reason, it still made her a little uncomfortable when he did.

"Whatever you say."

She glared at him. "Just be sure of what you're doing."

She only then noticed that they were standing in the trees, not right next to the door. And she only noticed because she sensed movement in the forest around them.

Tyrel tensed, sensing it too.

She glanced around, but it was hard to see into the dimly lit trees around them, so she relied on the elements to feed her information.

Whispering against her skin, *There's lots of them.*

A feeling in her body from her feet, coming up from the earth: *Humanoid. Most of them.*

And then there was the ever-present ramblings of fire in the back of her head, excited by the situation. *Burning? Do you need light? What do you need?* Its voice wasn't understandable, but she knew what it meant.

An incredible feeling of calm fell over her. It was funny how it happened at times like this. She grabbed Tyrel's hand and pulled him over to her, backing up against a tree, where she pulled them into the shadows, disguising them. It was just in time, too, because a figure appeared from the bushes, walking straight past them. He stopped in front of them and looked around.

Red eyes. He had red eyes.

That told Mercury all she needed to know about him.

He was a Vampire. He had the red eyes that only the Vampire Protector, basically a personal bodyguard, like Ignis was to Mercury. Whoever he was, he was supposed to protect Skylar one day. She didn't know why he would need to be here.

He kept walking and was followed by more people.

Vampire, Werewolf, Siren, Sorcerer, Fairy, Witch.

She recognised one of them in the dim light.

Raven Duskrose.

So, Marisa was coming.

"Trying to hide, are we, Mercury?"

Revenge's voice was right in her ear, and she froze.

The shadows dropped away, not by her doing, though. Tempest was nearby.

"Come along, little Princess," Revenge whispered.

Hands grabbed her arms, and she saw Revenge for the second before she was hit from behind.

25

Phoenix was ready.

She was meeting Shadow today.

And she was going to get to show off what she'd been able to do.

They were meeting in a hall that was hired out.

Shadow arrived, looking unusually flustered.

'Our lesson today is unfortunately, postponed," she said.

"What? Why?"

"Mercury was supposed to be teaching you something today, but she hasn't been answering."

"Oh. So is that it?"

"For now."

"I have something I want to ask you, though," Phoenix said.

"Go on."

"It's about something my parents said. About Lindreans being responsible for human life ... or something like that. They didn't seem too sure themselves. Is it true?"

Shadow nodded. "It is indeed.

"The story goes that the first beings to exist on Lindreas—gods, if you will—became tired of only having each other for company and so tried to use magic to create more beings like them, as they had been created from the magic of the planet. They were successful in creating another being, but unsuccessful in giving it magic.

"These first humans, without magic, could not survive on the planet and began dying, so the gods started looking for somewhere that they could send their creations—which they had now become attached to—so they wouldn't die.

"The goddess of magic, Jinx, was the first to discover a way to travel between dimensions. She found this one that we are in now and saw how alike it was to their own. So she opened a doorway, and the humans were sent away to live on Earth.

"This is why there are different religions all across the world and the ancient religions were different to what exists now. Because those first humans remembered the gods that created them and began worshipping them in the civilisations they created here. But as time went on, their interpretations of the origins of the religions became warped into what exists today."

"That's … wow." Phoenix breathed, her thoughts stunned into silence.

Shadow only nodded her head.

"Thanks for answering my question," Phoenix said, turning to leave, a billion more questions beginning to float around her mind. As she headed for the door, her phone began ringing. She didn't recognise the number but answered anyway.

"Hello?"

"Phoenix?"

"Uh, yes. Who is this?"

Shadow was watching, her head tilted. Curious.

"It's Jem," the person on the phone said.

"How did you get my number?" she asked.

"It's in Mercury's phone," he said.

"Are you with her?"

"No."

"Why do you have her phone?"

"She's missing," Jem said. "We don't know where she's gone."

"Missing?"

"Mercury is missing?" Shadow asked.

Phoenix nodded quickly.

"Have you seen her?" Jem asked, sounding hopeful.

"I haven't. Sorry."

"That's alright," he said and then added, "we might be needing your help."

"Wait. Really?"

"Yeah."

"Where should I meet you?"

"Can you get to Lindreas?"

"Skylar can."

"Meet me at the castle. Skylar will know, don't worry."

"I'm coming. I'll have to get her, though," she said.

"Great," Jem replied. "Just don't get Shadow involved."

Phoenix glanced sideways at Shadow, but her eyes shot straight back to looking ahead.

"See you soon, Phoenix," he said, then hung up.

Phoenix started walking, putting her phone in her pocket as she did, hoping to get away as fast as possible so she didn't have to tell Shadow the details of her conversation.

"Where are you going?" Shadow asked. "Is Mercury alright?"

"She *was* missing," Phoenix said, stopping and turning around. "She's alright now, though. And I'm going home since we aren't doing anything today."

She turned on her heel and kept walking. Out the door. Down the footpath. And Shadow didn't call after her.

<hr />

Mercury was awake, but she hadn't opened her eyes yet.

She still sat slumped in her chair, pretending to be unconscious while she let the elements tell her about her surroundings.

It was a stone room. Old. Mossy. And there wasn't much light. Better than a train, at least. Why was she always getting kidnapped?

People had been in and out of the room. It was empty at the moment, though.

She opened her eyes, and the old, mossy stone room greeted her, barely lit with its tiny windows high up on the walls.

Her hands were cuffed.

The handcuffs were a mix of metals that would take forever to rearrange. Tempest could do something, at least.

Metal was a strange element. Simply because it was regarded as one element, but there were many metals, and each one reacted differently with magic. It was kind of like metals all existed on a different frequency. Each one required a different touch of magic to get it to do what was wanted.

So to break out of handcuffs, each one had to be arranged so they weren't mixed together but existed separately within the mould of the cuffs. And then they could be broken apart. But only then.

As they were, if she tried to simply break them, some would break, but some would become stronger, and some wouldn't react. It was basically a science experiment.

Arranging metals took some time, especially when they were as mixed together as now. Mercury started on arranging them. She didn't have anything better to do.

"She's awake." Voices outside. She vaguely recognised them.

"Now, Mel, why do you think I would let you go in?" a female voice asked her, contempt flowing from her tone.

That was Revenge. Definitely Revenge.

"Let me," a male voice said. And then the door opened. But it closed again.

Well …

"What about that other girl we picked up?" Mel asked suddenly.

"Her?" Revenge asked. "What about her?"

"What are we doing with her?" the male asked. He spoke coldly, almost as if he was both disappointed and angry with everyone. Or maybe he was just upset with Revenge.

"That's Olivia and Martin's job," Revenge said. "Mercury is ours."

The old wooden door began to creak open again.

"Let go of me!"

There was a shout. Female. Whoever it was, they were most definitely not happy.

Sarietta?

"Sounds like they're having some trouble," the male remarked. He was probably smirking.

"Why don't you go check it out, then?" Revenge said. Most probably smirking too. "Mel?"

"Sure," Mel said and then she walked off, her footsteps echoing up the corridor. The distinct sound of high heels.

Finally, the door opened again, and Revenge walked in, dressed all in white—white pants, white shirt, white jacket—followed by a boy. The vampire boy with the red eyes.

"Mercury, how wonderful to see you," Revenge greeted, her dark eyes gleaming, black hair in stark contrast to her white outfit. "This is Jack."

Jack bowed his head.

"Hi, Jack; how's Mel?" Mercury asked.

"How does it feel to be betrayed by your sister?" he replied.

Mercury answered his question with one of her own. "Do all Vampires make a habit of betraying their kingdom? Because we have a room full of them here."

Jack frowned but was silent.

"I'm sorry, Mercury, but you must know what we're here for," Revenge said lazily, as she strolled around the chair Mercury was seated on, draping her arm over the back of it, then coming all the way around and gently stepping back over to Jack.

"Is this the part where you torture me?" she asked, doing her best to sound cheery and push down the memories rising to the surface. A shiver went through her body. She wanted to look at her arms. "Because I'm afraid it won't be happening."

"She makes jokes to hide her fear," Revenge said to Jack.

"How nice of you to notice," Mercury said, smiling.

Jack looked between the two of them. "Can we get this over with? The games are really unnecessary." His voice never lost the coldness it held. Every word was like a spear of ice shooting from his mouth.

"Of course," Revenge said, stepping forward again.

Her fangs started to grow as she approached.

Mercury might have panicked, except she was done arranging her handcuffs, and so pulled her arms apart, snapping the cuffs in two with a thought. As she sprung from the chair, the two halves melted down her arms and formed daggers in her hands.

One of them plunged into Revenge's shoulder. The other, she threw at Jack, but he dodged at the last second, and so it hit the wall and clattered to the ground.

She didn't bother to retrieve it and, instead, rushed for the door.

She slammed it behind her, locked it, and then placed her hand against the door, creating a connection between her and the lock and asked it to break all its inner workings so it couldn't be unlocked.

Then she started sprinting away. Midstep, fire consumed her body, burning away her glittering, gold dress and replacing it with her black and blue outfit, complete with her sword, which she had recently named Krystyna.

Around the corner, round the next. Dead end.

Shit.

There were footsteps heading towards her. They were loud, pounding the ground. Someone running.

The person turned the corner and stopped just before they colliding with Mercury.

"Mercury?" the girl asked, her brown hair swinging against her shoulders.

"Sarietta?"

Yes. Sarietta Penchant in jeans, floral shirt, and denim jacket.

They hugged.

"What the hell are you doing here?" Mercury asked.

Instead of answering, they both quietened. There were more footsteps approaching.

They passed.

"Questions later," Mercury decided. "First, let's get out of here."

"Agreed," Sarietta said.

They walked cautiously back to the end of the hallway and looked both ways.

There was no one in sight.

They stepped out.

"Do you know the way out?" Sarietta asked.

"Nope," Mercury said.

"Me neither," Sarietta replied.

"Looks like we've got a fun predicament on our hands."

"Oh yeah, fun," Sarietta said, deadpan.

"I say we go this way." Mercury started walking.

"Why that way?" Sarietta asked as she followed.

"Because I came from the other direction."

<hr/>

Phoenix stumbled and dropped to her knees, her head spinning.

Skylar stood beside her, slightly bent over. "That still feels weird," she mumbled.

"It will always feel a little weird," Jem said, walking over to them. He had a sword at his hip in an intricately patterned black and gold scabbard.

Phoenix looked up and noticed their surroundings. They were in front of a huge, stone castle with glittering spires. There was a wrought iron gate ahead, guarding the entrance to said castle.

"It's never good to do that too much, by the way," he said. "It can weaken your magic if you do it too often."

Phoenix stood up, and Skylar only nodded.

"So what happened to Mercury?" Phoenix asked.

"Last night, she went outside to talk with someone, Tyrel, and he came back, but she didn't," Jem explained. "He said there were other people out there with them, but he didn't recognise any of them."

"What do you think happened?" Phoenix asked.

"Marisa," Jem said. "Who else would only take Mercury?"

"What are we going to do?" Skylar asked.

"Look for her," Jem said simply. "Because of you, Skylar, we know roughly where Marisa is hiding. So we're going to go looking."

"I-I-I don't really remember the way," Skylar stammered. "And the Dark Forest …"

"It's alright," Jem said. "I don't really know the way, either. But we'll be meeting some people who do."

"Isn't it going to take a while to get there?" Skylar asked.

"That's why we're leaving early," said Jem.

"Early? Oh …" Phoenix trailed off.

It was indeed early. The sun was barely in the sky, cutting down through the trees because it hadn't even reached the top of them yet. On Earth, it had been midday.

"Why is it so early?" Phoenix asked.

"On top of dimension hopping, you've just travelled halfway around the world," Jem said.

"What?"

"Where we are standing right now is Canada on Earth."

"But … it's not cold …?"

"Although the two planets are the same size, same position in space and solar system, their surfaces and even climates are vastly different, because they spin on different axes," Jem explained.

"Canada," Skylar echoed.

"We should get going now," he said.

"Alright, sure. Let's go," Phoenix replied, shaking off that newest revelation.

Jem led the way in the opposite direction of the castle, leaving it behind them in the trees. There were a few houses around, and they usually had long, winding paths leading to them. It wasn't long before the trees dropped away, and they were walking through wide, open fields. Although there were always a few straggly trees around, or some off in the distance.

The road they walked on changed from dirt to cobblestone infrequently and there weren't many other roads that branched off it. Phoenix's legs started to get sore, so she was more than happy when Jem announced they would stop for lunch. They took one of the branches off the main road and walked into a town, stopping at what could only be described as a pub.

The town was small and the buildings were old. Old but pleasant, each made of different, vibrantly coloured stones, lending the town a certain liveliness. Not many people seemed to live in the town, but there were enough walking the streets.

Midway through their lunch, two guys came in the door and walked over to their table.

Jem swallowed "This is Raely Bishop and Flynn Read," he introduced. "People who actually know the way. Our guides, you could say." He smiled. "That rhyme was unintended."

Raely and Flynn raised their hands in greeting and said small hi's. Raely had a nice smile.

The two were of a similar height, though Raely was perceptibly taller. They both had light, brown hair, and Raely's also had flecks of blond. His face was slightly pockmarked, whereas Flynn's was clear. Flynn had blue eyes. Raely's were just a tad darker.

Raely was wearing purple jeans, and Flynn wore a shirt to match, and a blue jacket over it. Raely wore a grey shirt with images in white on it and a flannel shirt over it, not unlike Skylar's. Flynn had on dark green jeans, similar in style to Raely's.

She also noticed the weapons they carried. Raely had a long staff, made of a curious, purple wood. It was curled at one end, bending around in a spiral, and the other end looked like it might be hollow, or hold something in it. Flynn had a bow across his back, made of a dark wood, with swirling images carved down it. He didn't have many arrows in his quiver, but under his jacket, Phoenix saw the tip of a wicked-looking knife. And a whip sat at his belt, a deep black colour with gold flecks on the handle.

They stood at the edge of the table but didn't sit down.

"I don't want to ruin your lunch," Raely said. He had the hint of a English accent. "But we should probably get going if we want to get to the Dark Forest before nightfall."

Flynn nodded his head in agreement.

As they finished their food, Phoenix decided that Raely and Flynn were definitely older than them. Maybe twenty, or close to it.

Jem stood up first, slinking easily out of the booth. Phoenix, trapped in the corner, followed Skylar out.

They left the pub, departed the tiny town, and headed back to the main road.

Their footsteps were soft on the stones, producing only the smallest of sounds.

They snuck around corners and slunk down corridors, trying to be as quiet as possible, and above all, trying not to be seen. Mercury felt that looking around could have been very helpful, but with only herself and Sarietta, was sure it would get them captured again.

So far, they had avoided every sound they'd heard. They had found stairs leading down and taken them, hoping they weren't heading into the basement. There were windows, a good sign.

It seemed almost too easy when Mercury and Sarietta opened a door, and on the other side was sunlight.

Sunlight cutting through the trees. Tall trees, though not as tall as the Dark Forest.

They stood in what Mercury would have called a small, overgrown courtyard, and a set of stone steps led away through the trees.

"We made it," Sarietta exclaimed, though she kept her voice quiet, barely above a whisper. Her nose piercing glinted in the shafts of sunlight.

The elements didn't warn her of any danger, so Mercury rushed to the steps and ran down, leading the way, with Sarietta right on her heels. They followed the steps down, went underneath a crumbling arch, and finally reached the bottom, which led straight into the Dark Forest. Anything was better than being trapped in Marisa's castle.

"I believe I asked you a question earlier," Mercury said, grinning.

"What the hell I'm doing here?" Sarietta asked. "Oh, you know, just casually escaping from prison."

"So, you finally killed him, then?" No hesitation in her reply question.

"Uh huh." She nodded. "One moment we're kissing, the next, BAM! Knife in the chest."

"Brutal."

She shrugged as if it was no big deal. "He deserved it."

"Oh, I know he did," Mercury said. "If you hadn't done it, I probably would have. More detail is needed in this story, though." Then it hit her. "Wait, you escaped from Blackline Prison?"

Sarietta nodded her head, looking both extremely happy with herself and incredibly sheepish.

"Why were you there?"

"It was a misunderstanding," Sarietta explained. "They thought Lucas was really super important or whatever."

"Who did? Because there are a few select people who can send someone there, and most of them are dead."

"Some Vampire guy. Why on earth he had anything to do with it …"

"I'll be looking into it."

"Go ahead. Though it's not really a big deal."

"How'd you get the knife?" Mercury asked, nodding her head to the weapon strapped on Sarietta's leg.

"Stole it off a guard."

"What will we do with you?" Mercury asked, shaking her head but smiling.

"He won't be needing it," she said.

"You didn't kill him, did you?"

"No. But he shouldn't be walking for a while. Or he wasn't." She shook her head, frowning. "I have no idea how long it's been."

Mercury shook her head, but smiled nonetheless. "If I have to start throwing you in dungeons, we're going to have some problems."

"Relax," Sarietta said. "I won't be killing anyone else."

"Are you sure?"

"Positive."

"Great. Because I would really hate to have to send you back there."

Sarietta smiled. "I promise not to get in any more trouble than I'm already in.'

Flynn was leading the way now.

He strode out in front with Raely at his side, the two of them having their own private conversation. About … something. Phoenix wasn't sure what.

She had decided something, though. They were both attractive. And definitely twenty-something.

"I see that look, Phoenix," Skylar said, leaning over to her. "You seem to be missing something, though."

"What? And what look?"

"You're staring," Skylar answered, simply.

"I was not," Phoenix said, indignantly.

"You were," Skylar insisted.

"Was not. So what am I missing?"

Skylar glanced at Raely and Flynn. "They're totally gay."

Phoenix wanted to reply with how ridiculous she thought that was but stopped. She looked back at them and realised that Skylar was probably right; it was entirely possible.

"How do you know?" she asked instead.

"Hot guys," Skylar said. "Do you see the way they're walking?"

They *were* walking awfully close together. "Okay, I see your point."

"And how about their conversation? Not that I've been listening," Skylar said cheekily, "but they just sound like a couple. Their actions too."

"Okay, okay. Do you think it's possible, though?"

"You mean with the whole soulmate thing? I don't know."

It wasn't long until they reached the Dark Forest. After Raely and

Flynn had joined, the trip seemed to go by even faster. On the way, they passed through a town called Duchcast, where everybody was friendly.

They stood on the outskirts now, Raely and Flynn walking up and down the tree line, stopping and peering in every few steps.

Phoenix couldn't help but notice how dark it looked within the trees. And it wasn't just because the sun was beginning to set.

As the two wandered off, Jem turned to face Phoenix and her sister, a serious expression transforming his soft features. "I want both of you to stick close to me," he said. "The Dark Forest is a dangerous place, inhabited with all sorts of monsters that you can't fight with magic."

"They're immune?" Skylar asked.

"We're not sure, but no magic can be used in the forest except by powerful Witches, and it may leave you feeling a little drained."

"You mean magic just doesn't work?" Phoenix asked.

"Yep. It's believed that the Dark Forest is the original source of magic on the planet; where the first people, our gods, were born from.

"Whether that is true or not, you must be careful. The forest is a strange place, that nobody truly understands, but there are a few rules to follow that will keep you reasonably safe.

"Never check behind you. You will feel like you are being watched, but don't try to spot the culprit. It encourages dark spirits to follow you; they will play games with you if you let them. They may even try to entice you by calling your name, like it's brought to you on a breeze, but the air is still in the forest.

"Flynn and Raely are finding the best path. No matter how many times you go through the forest, different things lurk on different paths. They will choose a path for us that doesn't give them a sense of unease or foreboding. That can be hard to find."

Phoenix and Skylar both nodded vigorously, and Phoenix felt chills up her spine.

"Neither of you are carrying weapons, are you?" Jem asked. They shook their heads. "Good. If you take a blade into the Dark Forest, it must be named, otherwise it will turn against you when you try to use it, as the legend goes.'

Raely and Flynn had made their way back over, and Flynn waited for

Jem to finish before saying, "We've decided the best place to start is over that way." He pointed off to his left, his back to the trees.

Jem nodded. "Let's get going, then."

Phoenix looked up at the sky as they headed into the forest. She couldn't see the sun anymore, and the light was beginning to fade. There were stars and the moon.

No, wait, there were two moons hanging in the sky above them.

"Um, why are there two moons?" Phoenix asked as the trees consumed them, and all she saw were leaves high over her head.

"Hmm? Oh, right." Jem turned to her as they walked, following Flynn and Raely. "Caedus and Arian are the two moons. They have different cycles, and these cycles dictate the rise and fall in the power of Vampires and Werewolves; Caedus for Vampires, and Arian for Werewolves."

"Which one was full?" Skylar asked, a hint of worry in her voice.

"Arian," Jem said with a smile, clearly sensing her worry. "If Caedus was full, we'd all know about it."

"Right," Phoenix mumbled.

On they walked.

Her feet were beginning to get sore. Her legs were alright, though. So that was something, at least.

She really wasn't a fan of walking.

A flash of movement in front of them halted her.

She waited a moment and then took careful steps forwards, scanning around her.

Someone stepped out from the trees right in front of her. Or maybe it wasn't a person.

It didn't matter, because she was already flipping them to the ground and kneeling on thei chest.

There was just enough light that she could see their face.

"Flynn?" Mercury asked, surprised.

"Uh, hi," he said, looking up at her.

"Oh, my God, I'm so sorry," she said quickly, leaning back, releasing pressure off his chest.

"Good to see you too."

She smiled. "What happened to the spandex?"

"It's getting washed," he quipped, smiling at her.

"Let's hope it doesn't get shrunk like last time," she said in a jokingly suggestive voice, then stood up.

"Hi, Flynn," Sarietta said, walking over and sheathing her knife.

"Hi," he said, still lying on the ground.

That was when Raely appeared from the trees. When he saw Flynn, he laughed. Loudly. "What are you doing?"

"Being attacked," Flynn said.

"Sorry," Mercury said softly.

Raely looked at her and then back at Flynn.

"Well, when you're done feeling sorry for yourself, we're going to be leaving."

Flynn sat up.

"Who is it?" a voice asked from somewhere behind Raely. "Did you find her?"

Jem stood in the trees, looking in on them. He stopped where he was, observing for a moment.

"Jem!" Mercury shrieked and ran to him, wrapping him up in a hug. "What the hell are you doing out here? Those two, I expect, but you?"

"What do you think?" he asked in reply, hugging her back.

"You know you don't have to come looking for me," she said, releasing him.

"You know that I'm going to, though," he replied.

"What are little brothers for?" she asked, teasingly.

He sighed. "Seven days."

"Seven days that make me older than you."

It was then that she noticed Skylar and Phoenix just behind Jem, standing around awkwardly, like they weren't sure what to do with themselves.

"You brought them?"

Jem glanced back and shrugged. "Maybe not the best decision, but nothing bad happened."

"Apart from being in the Dark Forest. Nothing bad at all."

Jem laughed. "Okay, okay. Not a good decision. Yes, I see that now."

"Um … guys? I hate to interrupt this lovely moment and all, but shouldn't we be moving? You know, getting somewhere safe?" Sarietta asked. She had her knife out again. Something wasn't right.

Mercury wished that she could have consulted the elements, but magic didn't work in the Dark Forest. That's what she hated about it. She had, however, made the wise decision of melting down the rings and necklaces she wore into the pistols they were supposed to be before entering. They now sat holstered on her thighs. She reached for one of them. It slipped into her hand easily, and she held it out, watching all around her.

There was a deep growl somewhere off to her right, and she flicked around. But the first was quickly followed by another, and another; a series of growls all in quick succession, surrounding them.

26

Phoenix stood beside Skylar in the little clearing, watching Mercury and Jem, Raely and Flynn, and the other girl slowly forming a circle, coming in together as they concentrated on the space all around them.

She had heard the growls, and they had chilled her. Something was out there, and she didn't want to find out what it was.

She wanted to transform. She wanted to transform so badly, but she felt that drain on her magic, almost like something blocking it, just as Jem had said.

More growls echoed among the trees, and Phoenix backed up, eyes flitting around.

Mercury looked over at her and Skylar, now with both her pistols in hand, then back out.

"Get behind us," she instructed, moving out to give them a gap into the circle.

Phoenix and Skylar scurried in. It was just in time too. Because it was at that moment that the creatures finally arrived.

The darkness seemed to shrink away from them, growing into big, long shadows that became solid and extended upwards. Eyes in the form of glowing, yellow orbs appeared near the top of them, and the shadows detached from each other as they continued to grow. Then they dropped back down to the ground when they were almost the height of the trees, limbs forming in the seconds it took the shadows to bend over to the ground.

Their bodies compacted, becoming thick instead of long.

They were tall, even on four legs.

They started to solidify around the edges, the wisps of shadows trailing

off them turning into hard lines that were neither fur nor skin, but just …
there. The lines disappeared after a second, though, becoming wispy
shadow once again.

They didn't seem to have any substance, and yet there they stood on
feet that still trailed off at the end. They weren't round or clawed; they just
were. There was no muscle, yet Phoenix was sure that if one tried to hit
her, it would knock her to the ground.

The yellow eyes glowed brighter, and they seemed to be the one thing
of actual substance inside the mass of solid shadow, even if they were only
hovering lights.

"What are they?" Skylar whispered.

Mercury, standing in front of Phoenix, tilted her head back to look at
the creatures that now stood before them. Her hands dropped to her sides.

"Screw it," she said. "Everybody run!"

Phoenix didn't need to be told twice. She sprinted off into the trees
right behind Flynn, running for their lives.

At first, it seemed like they might be alright. But then there was a
deafening roar, and the ground shook as the creatures came in pursuit. If
one thing was for sure, they would never outrun these monsters.

Phoenix glanced back and only saw a great darkness behind them,
somehow darker than even the forest had been. Floating within it, however,
were yellow dots. Phoenix could see Mercury at the very back, running
hard.

The horrible feeling came over her that she was going to trip. It seemed
inevitable.

No. Not. Going. To. Trip.

How long would they have to run for, though?

Her feet and legs were already sore from walking all the way here, and
now they were running.

She glanced back again and saw the things of shadow simply melt
around obstacles in their path. And they were getting closer, easily gaining.
Why wouldn't they? They didn't have to dodge around …

Tree!

Phoenix stumbled and just managed to avoid getting impaled on a tree
branch sticking out at her. She swung her whole body wide around the tree
and then she was running again.

"This way!" Jem called, out in front.

He turned right, around a big cluster of trees and bushes, and they all stampeded after him.

The darkness was growing around them again, somehow more comfortable than the light. The light meant the creatures were close. Darkness meant they were safe.

They stopped, panting for breath.

"Where's Mercury?" Jem asked, looking around.

The leaves above them began to shake, something moving form tree to tree above them.

Light flooded around them as the shadow things drew close again, drawing the darkness away.

Phoenix didn't think she could start running again. Her lungs ached, and her throat was dry, every breath dragging through it and stinging.

Mercury flipped out of the trees above them, landing in a crouch, sword out. She sprung up, swinging her sword, and it passed straight through the neck of one of the creatures as they approached.

The part of shadow that made its head detached from the rest and floated in the air for a moment, then morphed back into the shadows. But the creature simply grew a new one from its shadowy mass.

It wasn't an instant growth, however, and while it was happening, Mercury drew one of her pistols and shot through it, where its eyes hovered in a quivering mass of nothing.

The shot was loud, much, much louder than the stupid little gun Rachel had brought to school. It was deafeningly loud. A booming cannon compared to Rachel's pissy little toy.

The head stopped growing. The shadows shuddered and then started to disperse.

Mercury relaxed as they did, her shoulders dropping. "Huh. It worked."

She smiled back at them, and Phoenix felt herself relaxing.

It was short-lived. Because now the other ones had caught up.

Mercury fired another shot, aiming for the next one's eye, but it easily morphed around the bullet and was unharmed.

"Only works when they're already injured. Got it," Mercury said, then turned around and started running again.

Phoenix watched as, in one swift movement, she holstered her weapons and then jumped towards the closest tree, her hands closing around a branch, then flipping herself up and climbing farther into leaves.

What Phoenix wouldn't give to have been able to do that at that moment. But no. She had to run. Running it was. She forced herself on, praying to some unknown entity that it would be over soon. The creatures were so close that Phoenix was sure if they could breathe, she would have been able to feel their breath on her neck.

Mercury dropped out of the trees again, sword flashing in the dim light, and separated another head from the shadow mass. She landed and spun as she drew her pistol again and shot it in its glowing eye.

The shadows dispersed once again.

"Need some help?" the other girl, whose name Phoenix didn't know, called back to Mercury.

"Help would be lovely," Mercury answered.

The girl nodded, spun, drew a knife strapped to her leg, and threw it expertly. It flew, spinning end on end, and sliced straight through the next shadow creature, tearing apart its body. Mercury then shot it, and the shadows dissipated, making the area around them dark once again.

There were just two more left. Just two more. It was almost over.

Phoenix was pretty sure she'd never been more scared in her life, but at the same time, it was just so exhilarating, being here, being a part of what was happening.

"Skylar," Mercury called.

Skylar looked back. So did Phoenix. It was a force of habit for her to look when her sister's name was called. To look out for her.

"Take this." Mercury threw one of her guns forward, and Skylar dropped back and snatched it out of the air easily, looking surprised with herself. Phoenix could see as she ran that her sister's legs may have been moving, but her mind was now on other things.

Skylar spun and started running backwards, just in time for Mercury's next trick.

She stopped, spun, unsheathed her sword from across her back, and dropped to the ground, sword swinging up as the creatures passed over the top of her.

As soon as it happened, Skylar raised the pistol in her hands, both of them firmly gripping it, and fired two shots, both of them hitting the last creatures. So Mercury *had* been teaching her some things.

The shadows disbanded, spreading out, bringing back the darkness of the night, almost overwhelming the little gang, who now stopped, breathing hard.

Mercury didn't stand from where she had dropped to the ground; instead, she sat up and spun around to face them all, crossing her legs. There were leaves in her hair.

Phoenix sat down, despite not wanting to. White shorts had not been a good idea.

The rest sat down, forming a circle.

"What were those things?" Phoenix asked, looking down at the dead leaves scattered around her, playing her hands through them. She flicked one over as she waited for an answer and …

"Whoa!"

A huge spider jumped out at her.

Phoenix tried to stand up but slipped in the leaves and fell back.

Gunshot. From Mercury.

The spider was dead.

Phoenix moved back into the circle. Slowly.

"I don't know what they were," Raely answered. "Never seen anything like them."

So apparently, Mercury shooting spiders wasn't something to be alarmed about.

"They were a witch's creation, no doubt," Mercury said. "Marisa even. But maybe not. Any Witch could have made something like that."

"Why would they want to?" Skylar asked.

"Witches do things like that," Mercury replied. "But I really wish they wouldn't."

There was silence for a while.

"Anybody up for taking watch while we sleep?" Flynn asked.

All eyes shot to him.

"Fine, fine. I'll do it," he groaned, getting up and retrieving his bow from across his back. "You all better thank me tomorrow."

"Thank you," they chorused.

Flynn studied the trees around them and chose the best one to climb into. He settled on a low branch, bow in hand, arrow at the ready. "Sleep well," he called down.

Phoenix lay her head back slowly, shifting around in the dead leaves and hoping there weren't any more spiders.

27

Phoenix woke the next morning and stared up at the leaves for a moment, wondering where she was.

Right. Dark Forest. Evil things. Spiders.

The thought of spiders made her bolt up, flicking dead leaves and fallen branches away to make sure there was none on her.

Jem was standing nearby, sword in hand, and he smiled upon seeing her awake.

"Good morning," he said.

She mumbled something that might have been "Good morning."

Mercury groaned and rolled in the leaves, her hands coming up to shield her face. "What's the time?"

Jem checked his watch. "Seven thirty."

"Too early," she mumbled, but sat up anyway.

Phoenix then realised that Skylar and Raely were nowhere to be seen, and in fact, Flynn was now the only one still sleeping.

"Where's Skylar?" Phoenix asked.

"She and Raely were awake early," Jem said. "They were too restless to wait around, so they went on ahead."

Betrayal. Betrayal of the highest kind. "Oh."

"Don't feel too bad about her leaving," Jem said kindly. "Caedus is almost full. It's completely normal that she'd be feeling restless like that. She needs something on her mind. And Raely knows the way well, so she'll be safe."

Phoenix nodded but didn't reply.

Mercury was now waking Flynn.

"Flyyynn," she said, leaning over him. She nudged him. "Flynn!"

He sat bolt upright and smacked his head into hers.

"Son of a …" Mercury fell back, hands to her forehead.

Flynn laughed diffidently, grinning.

Mercury glared at him. "Don't laugh."

Now the girl, Sarietta, was laughing.

"Sorry," he said.

"Remind me never to try to wake you up again."

She stood up, rubbing her head, and Flynn stood up too.

"Shall we get moving?" Jem asked, watching the scene, smirking.

"Wipe that grin off your face," Mercury said, giving him a look but smiling nonetheless.

Flynn led the way back through the forest, and they were out of it before midday. When they reached Duchcast, everyone they passed moved out of their way, clearing a path for them.

"What's going on?" Phoenix whispered.

People bowed their heads as they passed, and Mercury bowed back to them. Jem did also.

"It's called being royalty," Flynn whispered back.

They stopped for brunch in Duchcast, eating with a lovely woman called Viridis Leaf. She had the best strawberries Phoenix had ever tasted.

They arrived back at Elpidas that afternoon, just before the sun began to set. On the way, they had left Raely and Flynn back where they had met, and had eaten there again, too. Flynn, upon leaving, turned into an owl and flown away over Raely's head.

Phoenix was ready to collapse. All she wanted to do was go home and get into bed.

She and Skylar said goodbye to their companions, and then Skylar teleported them back home. Phoenix needed to learn how to do that.

She opened the front door, and they walked inside. Phoenix didn't even care about dinner; all she wanted was to sleep in her own bed.

Her foot was on the first step when her mother called her.

"What is it?" she called back, frozen on the stairs.

"Remember that show you two auditioned for?" her mum asked, coming into the corridor, where Skylar appeared in a doorway.

Phoenix nodded, vaguely remembering something a couple of weeks ago in amongst all the crazy her life had become.

"Well, they called back," she said, her voice gaining excitement. "They want you on the show."

"Really?" Skylar asked, moving into the hallway from where she had been leaning against the doorframe. "That's great! Phoenix, how great is this?"

Phoenix was too tired to care.

She blinked, shook her head, and said, "It's really cool. I'm tired."

And then she headed up the stairs, leaving them behind.

Mercury stood by the gate and watched Skylar and Phoenix disappear. Now there was just Sarietta left.

"Where shall Miss Penchant be going now that she's free?" Mercury asked.

"Home," Sarietta said. "I am going home."

Home for Sarietta was Alium, the capital city of Varietas. She was a Shapeshifter, after all.

"It's been so long," she continued. "I just want to go home. Sleep in my bed. My real bed. Wear my old clothes. Just live there again." She sighed, reminiscing. "It'll be so nice."

"Do you want to use the portal?" Mercury asked, gesturing into the courtyard.

A portal was something that every kingdom had. It worked in a similar way to teleporting between dimensions, except it was between places in Lindreas, specifically the capitals. And because it was done through an object, rather than one's own magic, it didn't have any effect on the body, unlike dimensional teleportation.

"No, it's alright. I'd rather make the trip."

"If you're sure."

"I am," Sarietta said, and started heading away. "Goodbye," she called back, shifting into a bird. A large albatross.

Oh. So she was travelling like that.

Mercury headed into the castle. Through the giant entry hallway. Up the stairs. So many stairs. She reached the top.

Lauren Trickey

"Merc!"

She turned as Austin hurried up the stairs behind her.

God, Austin.

She was so relieved to see him, and he hugged her as he reached the top of the stairs. She laughed, wrapping her arms around him, sinking into him and almost giving up on her own legs.

"Have fun, did we?"

"Oh, you know it," she said. "Fighting strange monsters is my idea of fun."

"'Oh, and here I was thinking that it was shooting things."

"Well, see, that's involved in fighting weird monsters."

"Ah. Oh, yes. Of course it is. Silly me."

They started walking down the corridor.

"And what have you been doing all on your lonesome?" she asked.

"You really wanna know?" he asked. "Mainly just trying to catch Amber."

She stopped. "She's still here?"

"They all are," Austin said. "I'd love to say it's because they're worried about you, but I'm pretty sure it's just because they enjoy staying in a castle. Well, except for Mel."

"Yeah. Mel," Mercury said drily, heading back to the stairs. 'And here I thought I was going to get to sleep. But there are people here."

She found them in the ballroom. Playing a game. She cleared her throat at the top of the stairs.

Amber, the peregrine falcon, swooped down and landed on a table. Flash, the other bird of prey, did too. Alex stood quickly, dropping what was in his hands.

She glared at them all for a moment then broke into a smile.

"I don't know what the hell you think you're doing in here," she said, racing down the stairs. "But I'm willing to forget it as long as you didn't break anything."

Alex shook his head. Flash shifted back, giggling.

"Nothing was broken," she said.

Amber chose that moment to shift back as well.

"They're dirty rotten liars, Mercury," she said. "They broke eeeverrrything."

"Good to see you, too," Mercury replied.

28

The first day of filming went by in a breeze.

Phoenix wouldn't lie; it felt amazing to be back in front of the camera, acting again. With Skylar at her side. How they were meant to be.

Just wait until Rachel and her stupid friends—like Aelana—saw this. God, they'd be jealous. Not that they wouldn't be jealous of magic, if they knew about it. But they couldn't know about that.

Phoenix couldn't wait to hear what they had to say back at school.

Phoenix spoke her lines perfectly. Only because she had spent all her time memorising them as soon as they'd been given the script. Skylar messed up a few times. Only because she was nervous.

They returned home just after dark to find Shadow on their front lawn.

"Ready to go?" she asked.

"Not really," Phoenix wanted to say. She sighed.

"Sure," she said instead.

Back at the Powerhouse Museum. Back among all the weird objects. In the dark. Phoenix was sick of being in the dark, where she couldn't see.

She sat down on the chair as Shadow instructed, ever alert of what was happening around her, of the bowl settling on her head.

Jade always felt weird watching whoever sat in the death-chair, as it had so nicely been named. Now she felt weird knowing that she was going to be last. Lucky last. It probably wasn't lucky.

She went through the portal first, emerging on the other side in a bright city, almost the exact opposite of the last one. Funny, how these things worked. Twins with worlds so different from each other's.

The buildings here glistened, casting rainbows out into the world from the sunlight that shone on them. Skyscrapers reached up to the clouds that floated lazily in the sky. Of all the places they had been, this was the most modern.

Aelana, Ash, and Skylar followed Jade as she wandered, letting her lead the way. Heavens knew why they thought she knew what to do.

It hadn't been five minutes when she heard the rush of water. Around the bend, there before them was a massive waterfall, flowing from under the ground and falling into a giant cavern. Masses of water ran from under the city, pouring over the edge and down into nothingness. It wasn't sewage, though; it was fresh, clean water, rushing from all directions to create a circular waterfall.

Jade walked warily towards the edge, keeping a few steps away. With no railing to stop her from falling, she wasn't going to risk it. She peered down, into what might very well have been a bottomless pit, and then stepped away and turned to the others. But they were staring past her.

She turned back around and saw it. The ruby-studded bracelet levitating in the centre of the massive, rocky hole.

"How do we get it?" Aelana asked, but Jade was thinking.

"If I grow a branch out," she said, talking to herself more than anything, "then someone could walk along it. Probably Skylar, since she's the smallest."

They were watching her as she paced, thinking out her ideas.

"That sounds fine to me," Ash said, taking a step back. "I'm perfectly fine with doing nothing this time around."

"Oh, you won't be doing nothing," Jade said quickly. "No, you and Aelana have to watch out for the Shadow Lurkers." She stopped pacing. "Sound good?"

They nodded. Ash conjured a dagger in each hand. She gave one to Aelana. "Let's do this."

Jade spun back around to face the bracelet and the gaping hole. She looked down at the ground where the water was flowing from beneath her feet, and a branch started to grow, as if from a tree. It extended forwards towards the middle of the hole, maintaining a reasonable thickness all the way out. It stopped its growth just past the bracelet.

She turned to Skylar, who was now standing beside her.

Skylar looked out at the branch and then stepped onto it. She held her hands out by her sides for balance, taking one slow, careful step at a time. Every time it looked like she was about to fall off, she easily adjusted herself.

"Don't look down," Jade heard her whispering to herself.

She didn't look down. She kept her eyes ahead, locked on the bracelet.

When she reached it, her right arm came forward, and she plucked it from the air where it floated.

Skylar turned around and gave Jade a weak smile.

So far, so good.

"How's it looking?" she asked Ash and Aelana, but still watching Skylar.

"There is absolutely nothing," Ash answered.

"Ditto," Aelana called from where she stood on the far side of the waterfall.

Jade glanced around quickly, to confirm.

Skylar was making her way back now, halfway across.

It's going to be alright. We're going to make it.

Skylar's feet touched down on the pavement, and Jade breathed a sigh of relief.

"I did it," Skylar said triumphantly.

Still no sign of any Shadow Lurkers.

"Great, let's get out of this place," Ash said, walking back over.

Aelana joined them, and they headed back to the portal.

Despite how well it seemed to be turning out, Jade had a bad feeling. And her suspicions were confirmed when they reached the portal. Blocked by a horde – what else was there to call a group of undead – of Shadow Lurkers.

They were stopped in their tracks, facing down the horde.

"Well, shit," Ash said, rather bluntly.

They stood frozen for all of three seconds, and then a spear was thrown from the midst of the horde. Aelana ducked away quickly, getting well away from it.

The Shadow Lurkers started moving forwards.

"Now looks like a good time to run," Ash said.

So, they ran. Back through the wide boulevards of the city and breaking off onto smaller and smaller streets. It wasn't long before they had been split up.

Jade found herself in a dead-end street, cornered by one single Shadow Lurker, who backed her up towards a water fountain. He had a bow on his back. All she had to was get it off him.

Okay. Okay.

He was drawing.

Oh, crap.

She ducked the first arrow, dodged the second, then took a few quick steps towards him, and grabbed his bow with both her hands.

He growled at her. Actually growled.

She snapped right back, baring her teeth. Then she yanked the bow from his hand and swiftly drew an arrow from his quiver and shot him with, taking a few steps back before firing.

She retrieved the arrow and the quiver off his back. Now it was time to find the others.

Ash was found fighting off three of the Shadow Lurkers with a quarterstaff, waving it around easily and keeping them away from her.

Jade shot the three of them in the backs of their stupid little heads and then rushed over, collecting her arrows. None of them broken.

Aelana was just down the street from Ash. Claws on her hands, wolfish fangs bared. They retracted once the danger was gone.

"Did you see where Skylar went?" Jade asked.

Ash shook her head, but Aelana nodded. "Down that way."

Jade followed where she gestured, turning the corner. What had first felt like a beautiful, bright city, was now turning into a maze of mirrors that Jade wasn't having fun navigating. She distantly heard hissing and growling, and followed it, until she found herself face-to-face with Skylar.

"Whoa!" Skylar fell back but managed to catch herself before tripping over.

Jade couldn't help but notice that the city was beginning to darken. The sun was disappearing, and the stars grew brighter above them.

"We need to get back to the portal," Skylar said, now leading the way. A trickle of blood dripped down her arm.

They easily navigated the streets, meeting up with Ash and Aelana again on the way. Then they stopped just up the street from the portal.

There were Shadow Lurkers still there, guarding.

Jade raised her bow and drew an arrow. She walked from one side of the street to the other until she found the best shot.

She fired.

And three of them dropped dead, skewered on the one arrow.

The others noticed her and started rushing towards her, but now that she had a bow in her hands, she was basically unstoppable.

She rid them of their Shadow Lurker problem easily, and there stood the portal, ready for them to return.

29

Jade was always careful when she returned home after her adventures out with Shadow. She had become exceptional at climbing up to her bedroom window and sliding in without making a sound. However, this time, as she closed the window behind her, there was a light cough, and then her lamp flicked on.

"Where have you been, Jade?" her sister Zalisha asked, a hint of amusement in her high-pitched voice.

Jade had never been good at lying to either of her sisters, especially Zalisha.

She turned around to see Zalisha sitting in her desk chair, light angled to play shadows across her face, and her wickedly excited smile. Her blonde hair was tied tightly up in a high ponytail, revealing her delicately pointed, long ears.

"Out."

"Where?"

"With Nick and Willow, where else?" Jade said, trying to brush it off.

"You're never just out," Zalisha replied. "Otherwise, I'd have to say that those two were becoming a bad influence on you. Then I'd have to tell Ivy. Maybe even Mum."

Jade froze. "I'm too tired for this, Zalisha. Can't I just go to sleep?"

"Tell me where you've been, and I'll let you sleep. I promise I won't tell. As long as it's a great story."

"You promise?" Jade asked. "Not Ivy, not Mum, not anyone?"

"I pinkie promise," Zalisha said, smiling and holding out her hand, finger extended.

Jade reached forward and wrapped her own little finger around her sister's, holding for a few seconds. "Alright, I'll tell you. And if Mum or Ivy confronts me about any of it, I'm breaking your pinkie."

"That's what a pinkie promise means, doesn't it?"

So, Jade told her about everything that had happened since the 'accident'. She was slow to mention Shadow, and Zalisha was shocked when she finally said the name, but didn't come at her with anything like "You were told never to speak to her" or "What were you thinking?" She just listened patiently to Jade's story, and Jade was so grateful for it.

"So that's what you've been up to," Zalisha said when she was done, grinning slyly. "I knew there was something."

"Or someone," she added.

Jade sighed. "Of course, you knew."

"Nothing gets past me." Zalisha smiled, but then her expression turned serious, a slight frown creasing her light features. "Are you going to continue?"

"You're not going to stop me?" Jade asked.

Zalisha paused to think this over for a moment. "Can you get it? The arrow?"

Jade nodded. "I don't see why not. We've come this far."

Zalisha paused again. "Then I won't stop you, and I won't tell Mum or Ivy.

"We need that arrow back, Jade. You know it just as well as I do. As much as I know I should be persuading you away from Shadow; if you can get it back, I don't see the hurt in getting her help for just a little longer."

Jade smiled. One of her rare, true smiles. "Thanks. I'll get it; don't worry."

30

Jade had never thought about it until now, but Ash was graduating. Ash was finished year twelve; meanwhile, Jade was only in year nine. Such a difference in age that Jade had never contemplated. They were the same height, so it had never occurred to her until she sat there in the school hall, watching Ash on stage, receive bits and pieces for her graduation.

The holidays had to come to an end eventually, and they had. With little word from Shadow in the first few weeks back at school.

And there definitely wouldn't be anything from her for the next week, since the hall was being used for various activities, including the year twelve graduation. Jade had always been one to worry about those sorts of things, but right now, she was just looking forward to spending the afternoon with her friends. There was swimming in her future.

***

The air was hot, the sand hotter, but their bodies were cool, covered in water that dripped off them onto that hot sand, and their towels. Jade, Nick, and Willow watched the gentle waves running up the shore to greet them.

"Have you finished that assignment yet?" Nick asked.

"Which assignment?" Willow replied, looking up from her feet to meet Nick's eyes.

"The English one," he said, his face just as horrified as Willow's.

"Oh." She smiled, and Nick smiled back, relieved.

"What about you, Jade?" he asked.

"Of course, I've done it," she replied. "Why is that even a question?"

But she was scanning her mind now for the missing assignment. Had she done it? She couldn't have missed it; she never forgot to do schoolwork, but … no, she must have. She would go home after this and check. And if she hadn't done it, by some mysterious twist of fate, then she would, because she would have to. Nick only ever asked that question when the assignment was due the next day of school.

"Just making sure," he said simply. "You never know when you might forget."

Sand kicked up behind them, feet marching their way across the sand.

"Jade!" It was unmistakably Zalisha.

Jade turned and watched her sister as she stopped at the edge of the towels. The elegant curves of her face were twisted with worry.

"You have to come home," Zalisha said. "Like, right now."

"What's wrong?"

"You'll see; just come with me now. Ivy wants to see you."

Ivy. Ivy, Zalisha and Jade's older sister, wanted to see them. When Zalisha said that, it was never good.

"What happened?"

"You'll find out when you get up and come with me."

"Alright, alright." Jade stood, shook out her towel, and then wrapped it around her, drying off quickly. She then pulled on her skirt and singlet—black even in the hot weather—and trudged off after her older sister.

"Bye," she called back to Willow and Nick. "See you later."

Jade dumped her towel over her desk chair as she entered her room. Well, she almost did, except Ivy was sitting in it.

Zalisha stood by the door nervously then finally came in as Jade crossed to her bed and sat down there, leaving her towel on the floor instead. Neither of them spoke, just waiting for their elder sister.

She sat in Jade's desk chair like she owned it, like she owned the room and everything in it. Nothing belonged to Jade but the clothes on her back, and under her sister's gaze, even that was doubtful. She looked to Zalisha, and Zalisha flinched. Her hair was tied up, revealing her long, delicately pointed ears, wisps of pink and purple hair curling around them.

"Why have you been talking to Shadow?" she asked, her voice cool and commanding.

Defiant or regretful? The decision could make or break this conversation, make or break Jade.

"I was tired of hiding, and she offered a solution," she said softly, solemnly.

"It never occurred to you that there was a reason we were told to stay away from her?"

"Of course it did!" Ivy narrowed her eyes, and Jade regretted raising her voice, even so slightly. "But I didn't see another option. If I had raised my concern to you or Mum, you both would have shut me down."

Ivy spun in the chair, swinging it side to side as she thought. She narrowed her eyes once again, this time at an invisible mark on the wall. Her ears pricked back and forth as the chair gently came to a stop again, this time facing Zalisha. "How long did you know?"

Zalisha stood straighter, eyes opening wide. "Not even a week, I swear."

Ivy considered this, effortlessly moving her seat back around to face Jade. A smile broke upon her face. "You are so lucky that I'm fed up with this too," she said. The smile faded as she said, "We need that arrow back, Jade. These aren't the best conditions, but do what you have to. We're all relying on you."

"I promise," Jade said. "I promise I'll do my best. I promise I'll look out for myself. I promise I'll get it back."

31

It was heavy in her hand. Cold too.

The metal of the trigger guard bit into her finger, and Jade started to wonder why she was doing this, why she was there. There was no need for this. Why did she need to learn how to fire a gun? She could use a bow; she had magic. But Shadow was adamant that she learn, and Mercury wasn't around to make any arguments.

It turned out Shadow was available for lessons, and in that mysterious way of hers, she had freed the hall for the occasion.

"Now all you have to do is pull the trigger," she said calmly.

Jade didn't want to. She could go her whole life without needing to pull the trigger of the gun in her hands or any other.

But she did.

It was a mini explosion in her hands; she felt that she should have gone flying back, but all she did was almost punch herself in the face. It wouldn't have been unlikely for her to squeal at the God awful bang that came from it, except that Jade didn't squeal.

She dropped the gun and took a few steps back, turning to see Shadow, rather impressed.

"Well done," she said warmly. "Perfect shot."

Jade didn't bother to look at the target. "Won't someone have heard that?"

"Not at all. Now, you're ready."

"Ready for?"

"Ready for your turn. This is it, Jade. The end is finally in sight."

She faintly heard the final bell for the day ringing, but she was far too focused on Shadow's words to bother with it. This was it. The end. Her turn. To get back the arrow. To help her family, and not just that, but her kingdom too.

They arrived at the Powerhouse Museum, all five of them and Shadow. Driving in peak hour traffic as they had, it took far longer than before, and it was darker than Jade had been expecting.

They entered just as before, with Shadow gliding in like she owned the place, no alarms, no sirens. Just silence. Eerie, longing silence.

They hadn't reached Shadow's contraption, the death-chair yet, but Shadow stopped. She was gazing around intently, nose sniffing in an animalistic way. She turned back to them, around again, and retrieved her phone.

Something was wrong.

32

Marisa heard the door open but didn't turn around. She watched the world outside her castle through some of the only windows that had glass in them. Glass that she had put there.

"Marisa," Revenge began, timidly.

She didn't answer.

Revenge had been stupid. Cocky and stupid. They'd had Mercury right here, but she'd escaped. That's what happened when you were cocky.

"What do you want?" she asked, spinning around. She knew the anger in her eyes that Revenge shied away from.

"They're almost finished," she said. "And we don't have a way of stopping them."

"We can stop them at any time," Marisa said, turning back to the windows. She saw the flash of surprise on Revenge's face. "You remember Poison, the fairy girl?"

"Yes."

"Turns out she's good for something."

"What's that?"

"She's been watching the Evans household closely, following the Song girls when necessary."

"And?"

"She knows where they are. They are with Shadow, as we speak."

"When are we leaving?"

Marisa turned around again. "You are not going, my dear."

"I promise I won't mess up this time," Revenge began to say.

"No. Olivia and Martin will go. With Rogue and Zach ready to back them up."

"You think that Mercury will be there again." A statement, not a question.

"I'm certain that if she's not, Shadow will call her at the first sign of trouble."

"You do remember that Mercury is afraid of Vampires?" A way of getting her to agree to let Revenge go.

"Then Fate can join them as well."

33

Mercury arrived, dressed as she always was. She hopped off her bike, left her helmet on the seat, and let herself in the way Shadow had instructed.

It was dark inside. Murky, gloomy, eerie dark.

She could feel, faintly, at the edge of her senses, people. Not Shadow or the others. But someone else. A group of someone elses.

Vampire.

Night Walker.

Siren.

Werewolf.

Sorcerer. Not doing a good job of hiding their presence.

And a Fairy. Lurking somewhere.

She approached Shadow, wary of those others lying in wait, and didn't even have time to open her mouth before their ambush.

They emerged from the murky, gloomy darkness, magic at the ready. As usual, Shadow stood back and watched as Mercury jumped into the fray.

She released a flashing light from her hand as a set of clawed hands came towards her face, ducking under them to see Rogue the cat chase off after the light. She spun as her head bopped back up, vines quickly growing from the floor to wrap up Fate and Zach, the clawed duo.

A flick of the wrist, and the darkness rolled out like a wave, knocking Olivia off her feet as she reached for Mercury's shoulder. And then there was Martin.

She unslung Krystyna, metal clips that connected to the back of her jacket melting into the blade, as she swung it forward to chop at the onslaught of greenery from Martin. How he loved to use Earth magic. Roots to trip her, leaves swept up in a breeze to blind her. Yet it didn't work.

Martin quickly gave up his strategy and instead ran up close to her. She swung for his head, but he knocked the blade away and grabbed her wrist.

"Let's go for an adventure," he said.

The world flashed around them, and they were standing in a jungle.

"Sneaky," she said and swung her sword up. Except it wasn't in her hands. Martin smiled.

Like he could trick her that easily. She knew exactly where they were, and so instead of bothering with him, she took a few steps back, turned on her heel, and ran forward to dive off the waterfall. She spread her arms wide in a swan dive, before bringing them forwards and plunging into the water.

It was cold, but she didn't dwell on it, surfacing and swimming for the river bank. After pulling herself out, she turned and waved up to Martin, who stood at the edge of the waterfall on the drier rocks, then ran off into the trees.

She was careful not to slip on the moss as she ran, watching her feet closely. This path had been the site of more than one great trip from her, resulting in skinned hands, arms, knees, the works.

She checked her watched reading it carefully.

She now had five minutes before she could use magic again. And at least fifteen minutes before she could go back. Waiting twenty minutes would have been better, but she didn't have the luxury of time right now. Otherwise, she risked depleting her magic in the short term and shortening her life span in the long term. Either fifteen minutes passed, or she reached Elpidas, and with her running skills, it was pretty obvious to her which one would come first.

<hr />

Olivia was now holding Mercury's sword: carvings down the blade, liquid bubbles dripping down from the hilt, and snowflakes drifting up from the other end, meeting in the middle. Mercury and winter for Mercury Winter. Jade had noticed them before, and it had taken her awhile to realise what they meant.

"I've been waiting for you girls," she said.

With Mercury's sword in hand, she turned and cut straight down, releasing Zach and Fate from their earthy prison. That disembodied flashing light whizzed past with the little black cat—no more than a kitten, really—chasing after. They passed Olivia's feet, and she kicked the cat; after a few seconds, it turned into a girl, a girl in camo cargo pants and a tight shirt. She shook her head, lying on the floor, then sprang to her feet.

The Vampire and the Werewolf were coming towards them, clawed hands shining.

"Girls, get behind me," Shadow said, stepping in front of them.

Jade backed up, almost tripping over Ash.

Olivia raised a delicate eyebrow at Shadow, and after a moment, Shadow collapsed on the ground, unconscious. Olivia smiled at them.

"Um …," said Phoenix.

"Weapons! Get your weapons! Fresh from the Siren!" Ash called loudly and started conjuring things. A sword for Aelana, daggers for Skylar, a staff for herself, and a bow, arrows and all, for Jade. Phoenix glowed brightly beside them for but a second, then she shrank instantaneously before their eyes and became a hovering light.

Jade took the bow, nocked an arrow, and aimed at Olivia. A snarl came from Fate on her right.

"Well," Olivia said, amused. "Don't you think you're just the big heroes now."

34

"It's not working," Revenge said to Marisa, now on the phone with Poison Lily, the little fairy spy.

Marisa wasn't happy; that much was obvious. She was trying hard not to show it, though.

"Martin rid them of the biggest problem," Marisa said. "They can pull through." She only sounded like she was trying to convince herself.

"At least send Tempest," Revenge begged.

"Tempest is nothing without you, and you know it," Marisa replied.

Revenge ignored the comment.

"I'm only giving them one more chance to redeem themselves," Marisa continued. "But they have that chance."

35

Mercury stepped through the portal, and when her feet touched back down on that soft carpet, the sounds of clashing blades erupted around her. Well, blades against claws, to be accurate.

Her sword was lying on the ground just a few metres away, beside Olivia, who had an arrow in her leg and was gritting her teeth trying to pull it out. If she had touched the sword, she was so dead.

Mercury retrieved Krystyna and glared down at Olivia. There was no point in bothering with her, really. She wasn't going to cause any trouble, since she certainly wasn't going to pull the arrow out of her leg.

Shadow was just sitting up, dazed. She stood, slowly, eyes scanning around her and finally settling on Mercury. As she made her way over, aching slow, Mercury took the opportunity to assess the fight.

They were certainly holding their own, though Skylar had a trail of blood down her arm, squaring off against Fate. They both moved faster than anyone around them, hissing, clawing at each other, Skylar with small daggers in her hands. Crude weapons, but effective nonetheless, as evidenced by the tiny slash above Fate's eyebrow.

Ash had backed Zach into a corner and was holding him there, while Phoenix flitted around the Night Walker girl with bursts of fire.

Jade staggered over as Shadow reached her, tripping through the fighting and slinging the bow over her shoulder.

"We have to do it now," Shadow said, guiding Jade to the chair.

"I'll go in," Mercury offered, following them over.

"No, I need you here," Shadow replied.

"There's one of me and three of them. Plus you," Mercury argued. "I'll go. You're better off with them here."

Shadow didn't seem to see a point of pressing it, so Mercury made her way to the portal, watching as images swirled into existence through it.

Mercury stepped through, her body tingling as she did.

She was in a forest. The appropriately named Riverglen Forest, as it surrounded the city of Riverglen. It was a nice, sunny day. But that didn't mean much. Mercury could sense them in amongst the trees, watching her, studying her.

She started walking.

Mercury only knew what Shadow had told her after she'd made her. But that was that Jade hadn't seen even a hint of her object, the beautiful golden arrow, tipped with diamond. It could take hours to find. Days, even.

She didn't have hours. She didn't have days. She had to find it now.

She also knew that there was a tiger around here somewhere, probably just waiting for the perfect moment to strike. Or maybe it was guarding the arrow. Now that was possible. Time to find the tiger. That was, of course, easier said than done. And these Shadow Lurkers were apparently rather sneaky.

She would admit that the forest was beautiful. Bright, sunlit, and so very green. So much nicer than the Dark Forest. It was pleasant to walk through.

Well, it would have been pleasant, if she wasn't constantly aware of the things lurking in the shadows, around her. Shadow Lurkers, doing what they did best. They were nothing more than glorified zombies, though, and they didn't scare Mercury all that much. They could, however, pose a problem in a big enough group, just like zombies.

Still, they were only a problem if they actually chose to show themselves. Which didn't seem to be happening right …

An arrow came rocketing out from among the bushes.

Mercury twisted to the side and almost impaled herself on a dagger, thrown from the other side of the path. So close. Too close.

The Shadow Lurkers didn't show their faces, though, and Mercury was left standing alone on the path. Yes, Riverglen Forest had a path leading through it. Again, so much nicer than the Dark Forest.

She watched the trees, making sure they didn't have any more plans, then was off again. They didn't bother her for what felt like ages, but in fact, it was only five minutes. Mercury reached the pool of clear water Jade had drunk from and looked around.

"Tiger?" she called out softly.

Rustling in the bushes.

She spun.

Just a rabbit.

Jade had been here, but there was definitely no sign of the arrow. Mercury continued on.

This was beginning to get boring. No glowing, no tiger, no Shadow Lurker horde after her. Hmm. It was then that there was movement in the trees above her, and the tiger dropped down, light on its huge paws. It roared at her, showing its enormous teeth.

She took a step back.

Fear gripped her in the face of the striped animal, but then she saw it. The glowing, golden arrow sticking out of the tiger's back leg.

"Oh, Lord." Mercury groaned inwardly.

The tiger started stalking towards her; she backed up again, straight into the pointed tip of a spear. She spun as the tiger leapt and ducked just in time, throwing herself into a roll out of the way.

The tiger took down the spear-toting Shadow Lurker woman. Then twirled around, eyes on Mercury again.

More Shadow Lurkers seeped out of the trees.

Just great. Everything at once. That's what she got for declaring this outing boring but a minute ago.

The tiger seemed overwhelmed, spinning back and forth, eyes racking over all the newcomers.

Mercury, however, was in her element now.

As the tiger spun around and around, she ran forward, pulled her legs up, flipped over the top of it and her foot came down into the face of a broad-shouldered man on the other side. When she landed, she bent her legs, dropped to the ground, and swept away a couple more of them with her leg.

The tiger came at her, figuring her as the biggest threat, but she flipped backwards and then jumped over it again, rolling when she landed on the other side.

She came up, dodged the swing of a sword, spun, and kicked, knocking the wielder off her feet.

Somebody tried to stab at her from behind with a dagger, but she swept her body to the side, her hand coming up and grabbing their arm. She twisted, and he tried to scratch at her with his other hand. She swatted the hand away, then spun her whole body around, still holding his arm tightly. The dagger was released as he tried desperately to pull his arm away. She let go and then kicked backwards, and he was on the ground too.

The tiger had gone for attacking other Shadow Lurkers, which she was grateful for. But there were too many of them for just Mercury and the tiger to deal with. Well, not if she used magic.

She let loose her control over the fire constantly nipping at the back of her mind, when she froze, a horrible feeling bubbling up in the pit of her stomach. No fire started to stop the Shadow Lurkers from what they were doing. She could only watch in frozen horror as one of them—a woman with beautiful, glittering grey eyes and the blondest hair—stepped forward and ripped the arrow from the tiger's leg. The tiger howled, roared, and then dropped to the ground, moaning. But there was no blood from its wound, because it wasn't real. It came with the world around her, and that wasn't real, either.

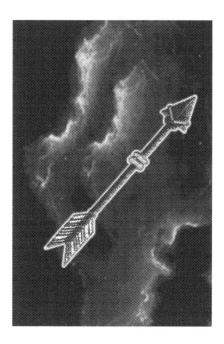

The woman Shadow Lurker met Mercury's eyes as she did it, and it was like staring into a reflection. She couldn't will herself to move as the Shadow Lurkers ran off down the path, with the arrow in their possession.

For a long moment, she didn't even want to move. Those eyes stuck in her mind, flashing back at her, and it was then that she finally stepped out of the daze. She needed answers, and the only way to get them was to find the Shadow Lurkers, specifically that blonde one. She needed to know something very, very important.

Her legs were shaking furiously, she realised, as she started walking. And so were her hands. She started to run, to throw off her shock, and because she couldn't risk losing them. They had the arrow, and they had knowledge that she so desperately desired.

Now that they had their prize, the Shadow Lurkers weren't bothering to be stealthy through the trees. They ran fast, cheering their triumph, making them easy to follow. They were fast, though, a lot faster than Mercury, and she definitely couldn't keep up.

They were, however, easy to track, with the help of magic.

This way.

The Earth called her around bends, through bushes, and over a stream. It took her too long to realise that they were heading away from the city, not towards it. And what was away from the city in the direction they were moving? The Gaols.

Mercury raced down the path, now knowing where she was going and not needing any more help.

There are traps ahead, the air whispered.

She ducked the swings of blades from tree branches, leapt the spike pit, and flipped through the poison darts, all without breaking her stride.

Stupid Elves and their stupid traps.

She reached the other side of all the traps, and now nothing stood between her and her goal but tall, stone walls.

Mercury stood at the bottom of The Gaols, inspecting the wall of the stone tower, finding the best possible way up. She wasn't stupid. She wasn't going to rush ahead because she was blinded by what she desperately wanted. And she certainly wasn't going to go in the front door. Way too obvious. No, she was going to scale the curved outside wall that was at least a hundred metres high. Ignoring her fear of heights, it was a perfect plan. Now, it may have seemed like a bad idea, but she was confident in her ability, and so the fear disappeared. Almost.

She started climbing, her fingers gripping tightly onto the stones she could get them on. The Gaols were old, but the Elves looked after them well, so cracks and slipping stones that could be used to climb were harder to come across. This was what she was good at, though. And if she ever needed to, she could use magic to force stones from their place. She didn't have to do that much.

The stones were cold and dry, which made climbing them so much easier. Her fingers didn't slip from them, and she hoisted herself farther and farther up the wall with a mix of skill and utter determination. And, of course, she didn't look down. Just up and at her hands.

Halfway up, and she heard voices, speaking in another language. Lasinre. It was the language of Sorcerers, but her knowledge of it was still low. She had only just started learning, and so most of the words were through one ear and straight out the other.

She climbed closer slowly, the voices coming from a window just above her and over to the right.

This was it. Her fingers hooked over the window sill, just enough to hang from, but not too much as to be obvious to whoever was inside. Her feet shifted restlessly on the stones, trying to find the best position to support her.

Footsteps inside moved away from the window. A door opened. And closed again.

Mercury waited a second, checking for any more sounds of movement before swinging herself up and into the room. The window was big enough for a fancy trick, so she pushed herself off and into a handstand on the sill, before flipping over and landing inside the room.

It was definitely a cell. One of the nicer ones, since the walls were made from stone, and it had a proper door, even though the wood was rotting. The details of the room weren't important to Mercury, though, because sitting there, right in front of her, was the arrow.

She walked carefully forwards on the balls of her feet, hands by her sides, eyes flicking around. But there was no one else there, nowhere to hide, and so the arrow was hers for the taking, sitting on a table in the middle of the cell. There was something beside the arrow. Papers. Mercury glanced at them but couldn't read any of it.

Her hand closed around it. Right hand, just in case she should need to do anything with her dominant left hand. She turned to go, and the door opened behind her. She spun, reaching for a dagger from her boot, but stopped dead when she saw who it was.

The blonde woman with the grey eyes.

Like looking in a mirror.

"Who are you?" Mercury asked.

The woman smiled cruelly and didn't answer at first. She held her hand out and spoke, but in Lasinre once again, and Mercury couldn't understand any of it.

The woman started walking towards her, and Mercury clutched the arrow to her chest. She continued speaking, and Mercury tried desperately to remember the sounds she was making so that later, she would know what the woman was saying. She walked closer and closer, taking light steps in black boots.

She was dressed in black leather, as well. Tight fitting, and wearing boots all too similar to Mercury's own.

"Who are you?" Mercury asked again, trying to feign fear and worry in her voice. She was pretty sure she sounded convincing.

The woman continued to circle the room with her cruel smile, and when she stepped close enough, Mercury's hand flashed out, grabbed her wrist, and twisted.

The woman dropped to her knees and looked up at Mercury in surprise. She didn't even try to struggle, just stared. As if she couldn't believe that someone could catch her like that or have the strength or technique to bring her to her knees so easily.

"I asked you a question," Mercury said, glaring down at her.

The woman looked as if she wasn't going to speak, but then her eyes softened, and two words left her mouth: "Emerald Wolfsong."

Mercury tightened her grip and twisted further, close to breaking. The woman didn't show any sign of pain.

"And?"

The woman spoke again, still in Lasinre. There was only one sentence that Mercury understood from her ramblings. The very last one: "Please take care of Isobel; she needs you." Or something along those lines. Fabian had taught her enough to at least understand that.

Mercury released her and took a step back. The woman stayed on her knees. As her hand slipped through Mercury's, she felt something drop into her palm. Mercury looked down at it for only a second.

The object was small. Thin and black, with buttons along one side and what looked like speakers. A voice recorder. She slipped it into the pocket of her pants.

She pulled a dagger from her boot and held it out in front of her as she backed up to the window. The woman just watched her go, a surprising look of triumph in her eyes, and also shameful defeat hiding just behind it.

She reached the window, turned, put the dagger back, and swung herself out.

Falling. With an empty void of nothingness in her centre. It was exhilarating and terrifying. She wanted to scream but also to laugh.

When she was barely a few metres above the ground, she let the air take her in, becoming part of it, and floated gently down the rest of the way. Her feet touched the ground, and now all that was left was to find the portal and get back.

◆━◆━◆━◆━◆

Jade sat in the chair, watching the others fight, Shadow flashing around, switching between cat and human. She was dimly aware of the portal off to her left but couldn't look at it.

Olivia had disappeared a few minutes ago. One moment, she was there, the next, Martin appeared beside her, and then they were both gone.

Ash was clearly the best fighter among them. She moved fluidly, whipping around, spinning, and switching from staff to daggers and back again.

Aelana, on the other hand, looked like she didn't know what she was doing and didn't want to be there, but she was trying her hardest, despite the fear in her eyes.

The portal glowed brightly, and then Mercury came into view. She ran straight over to Jade, clutching a golden arrow with a diamond tip in her hand. Jade threw herself from the chair and came to meet her. Mercury held the arrow out, and Jade took it.

"Time to end it," Mercury said. "Fire away."

Jade picked up the bow from where she had left it on the ground and nocked the gleaming arrow.

The Night Walker was jumping around the place, shifting back and forth, just as Shadow was. She had to go first.

Jade let the arrow fly, but Rogue had noticed, and so just before it hit her, she simply disappeared. The arrow didn't stop, though. Instead, it turned around, changing paths and targeting the Werewolf boy, instead. He tried to leap out of the way but wasn't fast enough, and the arrow hit him in the back, barely missing his spine.

The Vampire girl dropped down beside him, then looked up and growled at Jade. She put her hands around him, and then they were gone too.

And that was it. No one left to fight, nothing left to do. The arrow sat on the ground where the Werewolf had been.

Jade picked it up.

It was over. They had … won.

36

Revenge stayed well out of Marisa's way as soon as she heard the news. It was partly because she didn't want to be around her while she was angry, and partly because she knew she would end up saying something along the lines of "I told you so," and that would just prove to make Marisa angrier, and would make her start targeting Revenge.

She tried to stay away as long as possible, but in the end, Marisa came to her.

"Do not start thinking that this is the end," she said.

Revenge didn't say anything, just let her speak.

"I still have other plans. The Perish girl, for instance. And we both know that sweet Mercury Winter has not found her precious wand yet."

Revenge smiled. "Oh, yes. I know."

She had been going to suggest both those options to Marisa, actually, after the anger died down.

"It is going to be harder to achieve our goals, but there are still ways we can go about it."

"You always have a way," Revenge replied.

Just as Marisa was leaving, she turned back around. "Oh, and I want you to keep an eye on Mr Danger," she said.

"Jack? Why?"

"It is just a feeling. But you must watch him all the same."

"Of course."

EPILOGUE

Mercury placed her sword in its scabbard on the special shelf in her wardrobe, followed by her daggers.

She took off her jacket and pants and white tank top, and dressed in something more comfortable: a loose shirt and shorts.

Her hair was undone next.

She pulled the band from the end of the plait and ran her hands through it, untangling it, and leaving the walk-in wardrobe.

Emerald Wolfsong.

The name was engraved in her brain, along with the words she had spoken.

There were a million things she had to do, and yet at the moment, all she wanted was food. A nice meal for one of her last nights in her castle before she traded it for the familiar environment of Earth and school.

Because school had already started again, and she definitely needed to get back to it.

She headed down the gold, sweeping staircases, the smell of cooking food drifting up to her. Bacon, there was definitely bacon.

She walked into the dining room to see her family already seated: Austin, Jem, and Mel, Blaze and Lithium and their children, James and Lena, and Fabian and Ignis too.

She sat down with them and ate.

As dinner came to an end, Mercury looked up at Blaze. A question was burning on the tip of her tongue, and she had to ask it.

"Blaze," she said, "who's Emerald Wolfsong?"

Blaze spat out his drink and turned to her after a moment. Mel dropped her fork, a piece of crispy bacon hanging off the end, and Lithium's eyes widened.

Nobody spoke for a long time. Blaze seemed incapable of speech.

"Mercury, I think that's a conversation for another time," Lithium said slowly, her eyes comforting.

"No, it's alright, Lith," Blaze said, his voice uncharacteristically soft.

James and Lena, only ten and seven years old, looked on in confusion, James opening and closing his mouth like he had his own question to ask.

Blaze took a deep breath and closed his eyes. When he opened them, he was looking her in the eye.

"Our mother," Blaze said, much louder. "Emerald Wolfsong is our mother."

Lauren Trickey

Printed in the United States
By Bookmasters